EUGENIA PRICE'S
THE BELOVED INVADER

"That ever-rarer creation, the good, old-fashioned romantic novel . . . The plot traces the pattern of love—happy, requited and lost—in an idyllic southern setting . . . This romantic story, with its ambitious theme, and its confident answers, is one that will engage and comfort many people."

—*Chicago Tribune*

"A novel of the quality and character we hardly hoped to see ever again. Sustained integrity of fine writing and a story that is fiction but also authentic biography . . . A love story that runs the gamut of human emotions."

—*Christian Herald*

The Beloved Invader

Eugenia Price

BANTAM BOOKS
TORONTO · NEW YORK · LONDON

THE BELOVED INVADER

*A Bantam Book / published by arrangement with
J. B. Lippincott Company*

PRINTING HISTORY

*Lippincott edition published August 1965
8 printings through August 1973
Bantam edition / June 1977
2nd printing .... November 1978*

ISBN 0-553-12712-8

Published simultaneously in the United States and Canada

PRINTED IN THE UNITED STATES OF AMERICA

To
Joyce Blackburn,
the friend with whom
I found the Island

The Beloved
Invader

I

Chapter One

When he swung into the saddle on the borrowed mare at daybreak on a December morning in the year 1879, young Anson Dodge could think of nothing except that he hated his father.

The New York streets had been rutted with ice when his mother and Ellen had seen him off for the south a few days ago. Now, as he galloped coatless across the southern end of St. Simons Island, through the red gold of the lingering Georgia autumn, the city seemed unreal. As unreal as that Anson Greene Phelps Dodge, Sr., could be his father.

"You haven't been with him since you were thirteen, son," Rebecca Dodge had said, sitting between Anson and Ellen in the carriage because they wanted her there. "Six years bring a lot of change—more than a young man of nineteen realizes. He'll be a stranger to you."

Waiting for the ferryboat that would take him across the Hudson to the train, his mother had tried once more.

"Your father will be his usual charming self. He'll act as though six years' absence from us is nothing at all."

Anson covered her gloved hands with his. "None of what you're saying is penetrating in any way except to remind me that I love you desperately, Queen Victoria!"

"I'm neither old enough nor plump enough to remind you of Queen Victoria, and I should resent that."

"But she doesn't." Ellen laughed. "After all, you said it, my love. And that makes it gospel truth."

"Not a bit of it." The older woman tapped Ellen's muff with the back of her hand. "You're going to marry this son of mine, Ellen, and you'll discover even he will make mistakes!"

They laughed, a little too gaily, and jumped at a warning toot from the ferryboat. He kissed his mother, as always aware of her cologne and the scent of her furs and her reassuring shoulders. She patted his arm once firmly, and he knew she would say no more about his visit to his father. When he turned to Ellen, her arms were open to him; Ellen, slender and almost as tall as he, a long, black ostrich plume plunging from her green velvet hat to touch the place on her throat he loved. "Please hurry back to me." And then he had run to the ferry just before the icy gangplank was hauled up.

Now, he was galloping the mare down the narrow shell road away from the big St. Simons Mills, where Anson Dodge, Sr., managed the family's lumber interests on the Island, trying to decide why it had seemed so important to see his father again before he married Ellen.

"We all think highly of your father here on St. Simons Island," Horace Gould, the young bookkeeper at the Mills, had told him yesterday when he met Anson's boat from the mainland. "I don't know what we'd have done for a livin' here without the Mills. After the War, I went three years with no work."

Young Anson switched the mare lightly for more speed. He should have known his dark, handsome father would charm the Island folk. "I hope you'll ride up the Island to see old Christ Church at Frederica, Mr. Dodge," Horace had said. "Your father seems so interested in our having a new church here at the Mills."

Too angry this morning to ask his father for a horse, Anson had agreed to ride Horace's mare, Bessie, and was grateful that Horace was there to see him off. Anson, Sr., was there too, smiling, making his infuriating, fatherly speeches. "I know you'll have a wonderful day, son. I imagine Horace has told you about Fort

Frederica and the dilapidated old church. When you see that church, you'll realize why we need a new one down here at the Mills." Anson Greene Phelps Dodge, Sr., one arm around Horace Gould's slight shoulders, waved vigorously as his son rode off down the road, leaving young Anson no alternative but to wave back.

The road from the Mills turned north, away from the sea, toward the ghost town of Frederica and Christ Church. Almost without realizing it, he began to slow Bessie to a trot. He had ridden about three miles, he guessed, into a silence made by birds and wind and trees.

With his mother, he had walked through cathedrals in Europe and experienced something of what he experienced now, but he had felt small and unrelated to the cathedrals, in awe of their grandeur, half afraid of their shadows. The impact of this moment alone on Frederica Road pushed out the walls of his soul, but he was not in awe of what he saw. He was at one with it. No one was watching. He didn't need to act mature or traveled or educated. He could be himself. Not the son of a wealthy stranger for whom he had been named; not the grandson of a famous New York merchant prince; not even the beloved son of his beloved mother. He could be himself.

Anson turned in the saddle, looking slowly from tree to tree along the wooded walls of this bright, deep place he had found. He saw the trees untouched except by birds and raccoons and rain and wind and the light: the way they began in God's mind, tree beside tree, dense, standing together at random and at home. A furry raccoon padded out from the palmetto thicket. "Hello!" Anson called. The coon glanced at him casually, then went back into the color and the wonder. Back into the pine trees, oak trees, gum trees, cedar trees, nut trees-butternut, he supposed, as yellow now as butter and lighting the woods all around him.

He marveled at the light. As magnificent as these trees were, they would be like any other trees without the Island light. Dismounting, he hitched the mare to the silvery stump of a dead oak tree and ran to stand in the heart of one long, sharp shadow that slashed the white shell road, half expecting to feel it. He felt the warm morning sun instead, right in the heart of the shadow, and, delighting to discover that this was not shade but true shadow, walked to the edge of the woods a few feet from the narrow road. For a moment he stood with his hands thrust self-consciously into his pockets, his head to one side, pretending to examine something in particular. Then he remembered no one was watching. Like a jubilant child, he leaped the ditch and threw both arms around a big live oak tree.

Smiling at himself, he swung back into the saddle and moved slowly up Frederica Road again. That had been a silly thing to do, hugging a tree, but he didn't care. It was all right if he hugged a tree, all right with him, all right with the Island, all right with God.

He had just glimpsed the crooked wooden cross through the high, spreading branches of the churchyard oaks when a flock of red-winged blackbirds stretched a hundred sudden wings and shot away into the bright, dark woods. He reined the horse and thought of Ellen.

"Ellen," he whispered, "Ellen, look at that brave little church!"

Deftly, quickly, as though he were keeping an appointment, he looped the reins through the rusty hitching ring in the trunk of a tall tree and walked into the stubbly expanse of churchyard.

The square, small building looked as though it had been brutally shaken. "That was our church," Horace Gould had told him, "and we were mightly proud of it. It was built in 1820, back when St. Simons Island was prosperous and most everybody happy. I remember when I was a boy how we kept it painted and the yard mowed and swept. The Yankees shot out the windows with rifles. Crushed the belfry with a cannon charge. Used our altar for a meat block, carvin' up the cattle they stole from us. You ought to see that altar, Mr. Dodge. It'd break your heart."

His cap in his hand, Anson walked reverently up the overgrown path toward the church. The front door was locked, the windows were boarded over. He cupped his hands around his eyes and peered through a crack, longing suddenly for a glimpse of the splintered altar. The crack was too small, the shadows too deep. I'm glad they've protected it, at least, he thought, and turned toward the tall oaks, which seemed to him the only undamaged reminder of the shape of things on St. Simons before the War, their heavy, twisted arms still holding the solid values of the proud, simple Island people who had worshipped there.

Anson had sympathized with Horace Gould's uncomplaining grief over the shattered church. Now that he was faced with the sight of the desecration, he felt sympathy sharpen into a sense of personal loss and outrage. He walked north toward the cemetery crumbling under the high pines and myrtle trees and holly. There he found the graves of the people who had loved this Island and this church . . . Gould, Cater, Postell, Wylly, Stevens, Taylor, Couper, Hamilton, Armstrong, King, Bass, Hazzard. He didn't smile at the flowery phrases carved on the stone markers, as he had when he explored old graveyards in England or Virginia. He made no attempt to recreate flesh and blood people from the unfamiliar names on their tombstones, deciding this one was a virtuous man, this one a wicked old reprobate, this woman a nagging sister-in-law to that patient widower, this one the town bore. Instead of wandering idly from grave to grave, he hurried around the collapsing iron fences, up and down the paths between the plots, as though he had a personal interest in finding them all.

A fading bunch of caladium leaves in a tin can stood on a Stevens grave; the Taylor, King, Postell, Stevens, Bass and Gould plots showed recent care. Were these the only people who had come back to St. Simons after the War? Were the other plantation houses standing empty, perhaps charred and silent, up and down the tangle of island woods and marshes? Where did Horace Gould live? Anson knew about the Hamilton plantation at Gascoigne Bluff where the Mills now stood. His father and his grandfather had bought that tract of land in 1866.

He stood still. His father . . . where had the hatred gone? What was filling up the place where it had been just this morning when he left the Mills? The foreign Mills! Out of place, awkward, blustering into the poverty and gentility of this Island to supply work and food and clothing for the people who had no choice but to be grateful. Anson hated the idea of slavery; now he also hated the humiliation that came to St. Simons when his father brought his charm and his money and his Mills and the offer of a new church for the defeated white folk and the Negroes who were afraid to leave the Island or their former owners.

"Dear God," he cried, "do You care as much about this place as I think You do? What am I doing here feeling as I feel now?" He leaned hard against the weathered side of the clapboard church. "What have you done with my hatred, Lord? Where is it? I demanded to know where it is! I don't know myself without it. I didn't come here to lose my heart to an almost desolated rebel island. I came here to lose my— my—" He pushed both fists against his eyes. "I came here to lose my—*fear* that I may be like my father!"

He had said aloud to God in this quiet place what he had never before been able to admit even to himself. Anson knew his father to be a brilliant scoundrel whom most people loved, but who loved no one. A philanthropic poseur, imitating his own father, William E. Dodge, who was an authentic man of God. He knew him to have pretended to hold Union sympathies with his northern friends, while he negotiated subversively with Napoleon III to double cross the Union. He knew him to be restless, always on the move from one part of the growing Dodge empire to another, making speeches at board meetings about the ideals and principles held sacred by every member of the Dodge family,—but himself. Young Anson looked like his father, possessed his attractive, impatient personality, despised his arrogance.

Having confessed to himself and to God what he feared most, he felt a clarity that matched the Island light invade his mind. His relief at having faced the truth was so invigorating, he was able to start sorting out his own confusion. Youth seemed to be his big obstacle. He had not lived long enough to try himself; and yet his love for Ellen had driven him to see his es-

tranged father once more in an attempt to discover himself quickly, before they were married; before he risked
doing to Ellen what his father had done to his mother.
If his motives were clear and unmixed like his grandfather's, he would feel free to marry her. If he were
such a man as his father, he could not.

In the uncluttered silence of the churchyard, he
felt almost at peace with himself; not worthy of Ellen,
no man could be, but almost at peace with himself—
unrelated, for the first time, to his father.

Kneeling to read the inscription on a Wylly marker
shaped like a broken marble column, he said, "Mr.
Wylly, saint or scoundrel—I hereby bury my fear beside you. You see, Mr. Wylly, my fear is *dead*." He
tried to laugh, and wished for Ellen. Ellen in a ceme-
tary? Ellen would bring life into this gentle, neglected
peace. No, she would merely join the life that was here,
unmistakably, in the midst of the ruin and the desecration. The War had spread death across St. Simons, yet
he realized resurrection at this moment as he had never
realized it before.

Anson took a deep breath of the piney air and
stood up. The Island light broke in slim shafts across
the worn, crumbling stones; although a man could weep
here and bring his grief, he would somehow always be
safe from total despair. Watching a yellow-throat swing
from a festoon of moss, he asked himself if a young
man of nineteen could know he belonged to a place as
he felt he belonged to this small, meagerly populated
strip of land. Would Ellen share his dizzying, mounting
desire to be a part of St. Simons? Not of the life around
the big, noisy Mills. To him, *this* was the heart of St.
Simons: Frederica and Christ Church.

Anson watched an ancient buckboard rattle into
sight from around the curve in the shell road to the
north, pulled by two bony horses, carrying a man and a
woman on its narrow board seat. He ran down the path
and waved.

"Good morning!" he called.

"Whoa—whoa, boys." The man was as bony as the
horses. "What a' ya doin' here, boy? This is private
property."

"A church is private property?" Anson was smiling. "Good morning, Ma'am."

He bowed to the thick woman huddled inside her shawl, who neither smiled nor acknowledged his greeting.

"Is the weather always so clear and beautiful on your Island?"

"Nope," the man replied. "We get rain, same as other places. You from down at the Mills, are ya?"

"Well, in a way I am. My father is in charge there now. I'm Anson Dodge."

"Hm. Thought you was a Dodge."

Anson laughed. "Does it show that much?"

"Sticks out all over. Reckon you're up here sight-seein'. Won't take long. Nothin' much left to see. Giddap!" He snapped the reins over the horses' rumps and looked straight ahead as the buckboard groaned into a slow start.

"No, wait—could you spare just a few minutes?"

"Whoa—whoa, boys. Reckon so."

"I'd be ever so grateful. I—I'm terribly interested in this place, Mr.—?"

"Bass's my name. P. D. Bass. What is it ya want, young fella?"

"Well, I don't exactly know what it is I want. I would like to know something more about this church. Are there any plans to rebuild it in the future?"

The woman jerked her chin up and spoke for the first time, still looking straight down the road. "Only rebuildin' done on this Island'll be done by Yankee money fer a long time to come."

"I see," Anson said carefully. "But this is such a lovely spot, don't you want it rebuilt? Wasn't it your church?"

"Yep, but it ain't our church no more. We ain't 'Piscopal no more."

P. D.'s wife nodded, agreeing with him. Encouraged by her nod, P. D. grew more helpful. "You wanta talk to old man Gould down the road."

"Gould? I know Mr. Horace Gould, the book-keeper at the Mills."

"That's Horace A. You want his old man, Horace

Bunch. He kin tell ya all about this church. Only meet-in's they hold now are in his parlor. That your hoss hitched there at the tree?"

"Yes, I borrowed it from Horace Gould to ride up here today. He's been very kind."

"Thought that was a Gould hoss. Fatter'n most hosses you'll see around here."

"Could you tell me where I'll find Mr. Horace Bunch Gould?"

"Yep. Black Banks, his place's called. You passed it comin' up Frederica Road. Jist ride back down three mile an' turn in at the first cleared road on yer left. Giddap!"

The old buckboard creaked into motion, and nei-ther passenger showed any sign of hearing when Anson called his thanks after them.

Anna Deborah Gould, a big turpentine jug in her hand, waved to the slim Negro woman standing in the door of her cabin and walked across the wide lawn of Black Banks plantation. As she neared the big house, a horse and rider rounded the curve in the narrow, sun-streaked Black Banks road, and her serious face bright-ened. Anyone would be welcome! More than a month had passed since a visitor had made the trip up Freder-ica Road to Black Banks; there had been only her brothers, Horace and James, coming home at night from the Mills. Anna recognized Bessie, trotting toward her, but the rider was someone she had never seen be-fore, and she felt trapped, about to meet a stranger in the blue cotton dress she had worn all morning making soap with Ca.

"Good morning," the stranger called.

"Morning," Anna shouted back, hiding the turpen-tine jug behind her. With her free hand, she brushed at her brown hair, remembering the tussle she had with Nancy's sick baby when she swabbed his sore throat with the fiery liquid.

"Is this Black Banks, where the Goulds live?" An-son dismounted, bowing to Anna.

"Yes." Her voice didn't sound like her voice at all, and she blushed as she set the jug on the ground, deciding he had seen it anyway. "Yes, this is Black Banks." She had never had conversation alone with a strange gentleman like this. Except at the Mills, there were almost no young men on St. Simons Island.

"Is Mr. Gould at home?"

"Which Mr. Gould did you want to see, sir?"

"Mr. Horace Bunch Gould. I already know his son."

Anna smiled. "I see you're riding his mare. I guess it's my father you came to see."

"Look here, forgive me, please. I should have introduced myself. My name's Anson Dodge. My father is in charge of the Mills here. I'm just down from New York."

Anna caught her breath. "I'm Anna Gould, and I'm honored to meet you, Mr. Dodge. My father is over at fishing ground for a catch of trout, but he should be home soon. In time for dinner—oh, will you take dinner with us, Mr. Dodge?"

"Trout?" Anson asked easily.

"Yes, if Papa's lucky." She grabbed up the big jug, wondering if her beautiful sister, Lizzie, would have just left it on the ground, pretending it wasn't there. But Anna said, "This is turpentine, we cure everything with it." And over her shoulder, as she hurried toward the house, she called, "Hitch your horse at the big oak, Mr. Dodge. I'll go inside and welcome you properly at the front door—up that flight of steps there."

Once safely out of his sight around the corner of the house, Anna ran across the back yard and burst into the kitchen on the ground floor, shouting, "Ca! Ca! Never mind finishing the soap balls now. . . . Make some tea—no, make some coffee—no, make both tea and coffee. We've got a visitor—Mr. Dodge, young Mr. Anson Dodge is here!"

Ca's merry brown face appeared from behind the big soap kettle. "Mistah Somebody mus' be here, Miss Anna. Ain't nothin' jogged you up like this since Ca can remember."

"Did you get it straight, Ca? Make both tea and coffee!"

"I got it straight, all right, but what about you?"

"Why, I'm going up to let him in at the front door."

"Totin' that turpentine jug?"

Anna banged the jug down on the wooden sideboard and dashed out the kitchen door and up the back steps two at a time. She raced the length of the piazza and only slowed to what she hoped was a sedate, ladylike walk once she was through the entrance to the living room and on her way to the big front door. As she reached for the knob, she remembered her hair! Too late now, he wouldn't notice her anyway, she supposed, and he must not be kept waiting.

She smoothed her long skirt hastily and flung open the heavy door. Anson was waiting for her.

"Welcome to Black Banks, Mr. Dodge!"

Chapter Two

He looks like every picture I've ever seen of Robert E. Lee, Anson thought, as Horace Bunch Gould led the way up the wide wooden stairs from the dining room to the sparsely furnished parlor on the first floor of the rambling tabby house; tabby, his host had explained, was a durable mixture of burnt shells, lime and sand, used by the Guale Indians who had once inhabited the Island.

Dinner had been simple: fresh-caught trout fried in corn meal, mustard greens and piles of grits, but Anna and her mother, Deborah, served it graciously, and, in spite of the fact that the Goulds were outwardly unlike his mother and Ellen, they made Anson feel at home, as he had felt on Frederica Road that morning. He had never known simple, provincial people like these. His mother wore English-made gowns and carried herself like a queen, but she would like soft-spoken Deborah Gould, and he knew Deborah Gould would like his mother.

Anson had scarcely noticed when Anna cleared the table and hurried from the room. But when he entered the parlor upstairs with Horace Bunch, she was there ahead of them, building up the fire against the coming chill of the short winter afternoon. The two men surprised her in the unladylike act of lifting a heavy oak back log from the wood piled generously beside the hearth.

"Let me help you, Miss Anna!"

One of Anson's hands touched hers as he took the log and heaved it all the way to the back of the sturdy andirons. They laughed, and Anna began nervously piling on shorter pieces of oak until her father chuckled, "Hold on there, young lady, you'll roast us alive!"

"I don't blame her for being reckless with wood like this, sir. We'd pay a fortune for it up north. Here, Miss Anna, let me have some of the fun."

"You can poke the fat pine under, Mr. Dodge."

"Fat pine? Is that what you call it?"

"Just smell it," Anna said, holding out a jagged piece of pine, brown-streaked and sticky with resin. Anson felt its surprising weight and then inhaled vigorously, pressing the pungent wood against his nose, until Anna laughed again.

"What a pity to cut down a tree like that!" Anson turned to Mr. Gould, still holding the wood in his hands. Then he smiled at Anna, sniffed the pine again, and pushed the big splinter under the pile of logs. They all watched, Anna and her father as expectant as Anson, until the embers left over from the early morning fire exploded the pine and sent the blaze roaring up the Black Banks chimney.

"I never get used to our pine," Anna said.

"Can anyone ever take anything for granted on this Island?" Anson looked from one to the other of his new friends, and then he grinned. "Except maybe Mr. P. D. Bass and his wife?"

"Oh, P. D.'s a good man in his way, son." Anson was beginning to look forward to Horace Gould's chuckle. "Funny thing you met P. D. and Emma right off. On the other hand, it's just as well. They're part of our Island. I've always felt I needed P. D. and his wife to keep me cut down to size. The Lord doesn't waste a thing, if we give Him a chance. Like these trees we're burnin' up in our fire now. You mentioned it's a pity to cut them down, but they're not wasted."

Anson thought a moment. "Even the ashes are good for your garden, is that what you mean, sir?"

"That and the pleasure we're all three deriving from this good fire."

Anna was listening intently.

"Is this why you're not bitter about the War, Mr. Gould? I expected bitterness down here."

"Bitterness only poisons the place it settles." Horace Gould spoke quietly. "And I reckon I'd hate for my family to have to live with a poisoned old man. It's a waste of time to carry a grudge. As I see it, bitterness is downright selfish."

"Selfish, sir?"

"Selfish. Didn't you feel like his buckboard had run over you after you met up with P. D. this morning at the church?"

Anson smiled a little. "I guess I did."

"You're new here. P. D.'s bitterness caused him to forget his manners. Don't you figure he was selfish to foist his bitterness off onto you when you didn't start the War?"

Anna broke in flatly. "You talk like a Northerner, Mr. Dodge, and educated to boot. That just set fire to P. D. Bass."

Horace Gould laughed. "My daughter faces facts, Mr. Dodge. And I'm proud of it."

Anson bowed when Anna excused herself and left the two men alone. The older man settled himself in a shabby highbacked chair and gestured toward the one handsome chair in the room. As Anson sat down in the tapestry-covered platform rocker, he rubbed the delicately turned mahogany of its arms; its smooth patina pleased his eyes and his fingers.

"That's one of the few pieces we were able to hold onto after the War was all over," Mr. Gould said simply. "We call it the Black Banks chair because it was part of our home before we had to evacuate the Island. That chair, and the drop-leaf table over in the corner, and that big divan all took the trip to the mainland with us, on a flatboat, and back after it was over."

"What happened to the rest of your furnishings, sir?"

"Well, the Yankees lived here awhile, you know. When I finally got back alone in 1866, the house was stripped. They even found the silver we buried. The rest of what we managed to get out lies somewhere at the bottom of Buttermilk Sound. One of our flatboats sank just a few hundred yards offshore."

Every word seemed important to Anson. "I beg your pardon, if I shouldn't be asking this, but would you tell me about it—about the War and your family and—and what they did to your church at Frederica?"

"Would you like to roast some chestnuts while we talk?"

"If you'll show me how. They're favorites of mine, but I'm afraid my only experience with them has been to buy them already roasted from a vendor on a street corner. I made myself sick in Rome once, sneaking away from Mother to gorge myself on roasted chestnuts."

"Been to Italy, eh?"

"Yes, sir. My mother is fond of traveling." Anson hoped he hadn't put a barrier between them; in the warmth of that relaxed moment, he had forgotten that only the rich could go abroad.

"Don't frown, son. I'm not a bit envious that you can travel. America needs men who understand the world on the other side of the water." Horace Gould reached behind his chair and brought out a bowl of chestnuts. "These are my big indulgence. Now and then they get a few baskets in down at the Store at the Mills, and my son James brings me a bag. Here, just throw a handful in front of those embers, and stir 'em a little with the poker now and then."

Anson tossed the chestnuts near the shallow bank of red embers and watched them begin to swell in the intense heat.

"Could you get me inside the old church at Frederica, Mr. Gould?"

"Yes, son, I can take you in. I've got the one key, I guess. I'm the only living vestryman left on St. Simons. The church isn't much to see now."

"The altar is still there, isn't it?"

"Yes. Just about the way they left it. Oh, Reverend Brown from St. Mark's over in Brunswick tried to get up enough money to fix things a little after the War. He was a good man. But it seemed like the heart was gone out of the people. The people were mostly all

gone, to tell you the truth. Right now there are only five
communicant families left on the Island. That isn't
enough to do much. The church endowment was lost
when the Savannah Bank failed. After two or three
years, Reverend Brown gave up too. Everything stopped
but our services here at Black Banks. We've managed to
keep them going every Sunday. Sometimes there's only
Goulds here, and Mack Postell—old faithful—but we
have the Prayers anyway. And God is always with us."
Horace Gould peered into the fire. "I believe those
chestnuts are ready now. Just scrape 'em out on the
hearth to cool a little."

Anson began rolling the roasted nuts onto the
stone hearth. "Did everyone evacuate the island, Mr.
Gould?"

"Had to. Confederate orders. My father's lighthouse made too good a light for the Yankees to aim at."

"Was your father the lighthouse keeper?"

"For a while, until he bought his own land at St.
Clair, adjoining Black Banks here. But Father came to
the Island in the first place back before the War of
1812 to build the lighthouse for the Federal Government."

"It's a really magnificent tower. I admired it coming over on the boat yesterday."

"Well, that's not the one my father built. His was
intentionally destroyed by a Confederate bombardment
right after we all left the Island. I've always been thankful I was gone. Thankful Father had died. It would
have broken his heart to see that tower come down. The
Government built the new one three years ago, but the
description and a photograph of my father's tower are
still up in Washington. I keep promising myself I'll get a
copy of that photograph. As a boy, I was pretty proud
of the Gould lighthouse. Still am."

"Sir, were you in favor of seceding from the Union?"

"No, I was not." Mr. Gould spoke quickly. "Some
here were hot for it, naturally. But I've always been
proud of George Washington and Tom Jefferson and
John Adams and Ben Franklin. Those men laid the
foundations of *my* country for a united organism of

states. I believe in what they did. I believe in America. I hoped to the very last for another way to settle things. So did your Grandfather Dodge, a Northerner. He negotiated actively with both Northern and Southern states right up to the end."

Anson looked surprised. "You knew my grandfather was a member of President Lincoln's Peace Conference?"

"Yes, I knew it. I've been an admirer of William E. Dodge for as long as I can remember. Saved every copy of his speeches I could find. Before and after the War. I was in no position to make myself heard, but your grandfather was, and he tried right down to the first shot that was fired. I understood the causes for the War—at least some of them—but no matter how our economic principles differed, no matter how we differed politically, no trouble is ever great enough to make it plausible for men to go against what the Lord God Himself said, and He said, 'A house divided against itself cannot stand.' "

"Did you see action, Mr. Gould?"

"Yes, some. I was forty-eight, too old for the Regulars, when the war came, but finally a State Militia was formed under Major G. T. Smith for over-aged men, and they accepted me in that." He chuckled. "They called our regiment The Babies, but we fought hard just the same. Maybe harder, to prove ourselves."

"Where were you?"

"In the trouble at Savannah and Atlanta."

Were you wounded?"

"Oh, yes, I was wounded. But I think you'd better get Mrs. Gould to tell you about that. It was harder on her than it was on me."

"May I throw on another log, sir?"

"Help yourself. But don't ever ask that again in this house. We want you to feel at home with us."

Anson selected the biggest log, promising himself he would leave when it had burned.

He said, "If I'm imposing on you, forgive me, but who found the little church first? I mean—after the War, who discovered what they had done to it? Was it the Reverend Brown?"

"No, no—I happened to be the first one back. I rode first here to Black Banks, and even though I couldn't get inside, because some carpetbaggers had felt free to give my home to a little family of Negroes, I at least knew it was still standing, and figured in time I'd get my legal rights to it again. As it turned out, I had to borrow money from a cousin up north and buy it back. But that day I was so thankful to see the old place still in one piece, I just lit out ridin' up Frederica Road as hard as I could go."

"To the church?"

"To the church, to give thanks to God for Black Banks. To ask His help in getting it back again. But since I had to pass right by St. Clair, I decided I'd ride out there to make sure it was still standing too. St. Clair was my father's plantation, you know. He built one of the most beautiful houses on the Island there for my mother: bigger, more elaborate than our place here. I loved that house because I was such a happy little boy growing up there. I knew Mary, my sister, who had to be forced to leave the old house, would be anxious to know if it was all right, so I rode on out there before I went to the church. Rode hard, a bad storm was blowin' up."

"What did you find?"

"Only the first-floor walls still standing." The older man's eyes filled with tears, but his voice was steady. "They had built such a fire out of St. Clair that even Mary's roses had been mostly burned to the ground. She must have had several hundred varieties of roses. People came from all around to see 'em and get slips off of 'em."

"And—and then you rode to the church."

The old man took a deep breath, and one constricted dry sob shattered his poise; just one, involuntary, unashamed. "Yes, then I rode back to Frederica Road and on up to the church."

"Please! Please tell me what you found."

"I heard the bad news before I saw it. Heard the old doors banging in the wind. Knew it had to be those doors, there was no one at Frederica at all, they had told me at the Government office at the Pier when I rowed back that first day. The Taylors and the Stevenses and the Basses hadn't returned yet. Old Man Cole tried to hide at Frederica for a while; used to wave his blanket every sundown so the Taylors and the Stevenses would know their homes were still standing. They found refuge on the mainland across at Thornhill. But they had told me Old Man Cole waved his blanket one Thursday evening over a year before, and then never waved it again. I knew he was gone. Nobody there to be poundin' on anything. It had to be our church doors banging in the wind. It was."

"Did you go inside?"

"Rode right up to the door on my horse. Seemed like I couldn't wait to get it over with, storm or no storm. I tried to prepare myself for the worst. Tried to reason with myself: now, maybe the only damage is what the weather has done, with the doors open; maybe they didn't even go inside the church. I remembered how proud we all were of our church floors. Varnished floors, as glossy and smooth as a good table. I stood there a minute half afraid to go inside, thinking things like how well our hinges had held up with the doors bangin' that way. The windows had been broken out. Not by the wind, I knew. They had been shot out, everyone. I looked up at the pretty little steeple, and it had been shot, too. Cannon fire had blown away one side of it, but the Cross was still there." His voice broke to a whisper. "But you know, after being so anxious to see inside, I suddenly couldn't go in."

"I can understand that."

"Still, I knew the Lord was there with me, so I knelt down on the front steps and asked Him to give me the courage I didn't have on my own. Pretty soon the wind died a little and the doors stopped banging, and I walked on in. At first, I couldn't see much, it was so dark. The sky was rolling outside with big, black clouds. I stumbled, and a family of mice raced past me out of a nest of old paper and blankets. Then my eyes got used to the shadows, and I began to see it all. They had bivouacked in our little church. Some of the pews were turned up to make bunks, others had been chopped up for firewood. All those woods around the church, mind you, but those fellows chopped up our pews to burn. The floor was weathered and part of it was burned out; all of it was littered with paper and empty cartridges and refuse and filth of every kind. The pulpit was turned over, and beside it I found our pulpit Bible the Postells had bought, with part of its back burned off and its pages torn loose and blowing around in the wind. And"—the old man's chin trembled, and his eyes brimmed with tears he made no effort to hide—"and then I saw the altar. Our fine, sacred little altar where we had met the Lord so often in the Holy Communion. It had never been a fancy altar, but it was ours, and it was the very best we could manage, being such a small congregation. As I stood there all I could think of was a vile, pagan orgy before an altar to a heathen god." Horace Gould straightened his shoulders. "They had used our altar as a meat block on which to cut up the cattle they had stolen from us after we were gone. Almost a year had passed since they left St. Simons, but the debris, the dried entrails, the hacked-off hoofs and tails and heads of our cattle were strewn about our altar, and its once smooth polished surface was splintered from the axe blows of a band of men gone insane in the house of God!" His head dropped heavily. "I ran outside and was sick."

A dog barked somewhere in the bright afternoon sunshine, and after a long moment Anson managed to whisper, "Mr. Gould, does it help at all that I'm living through this with you—today?"

Horace Gould tried to smile. He leaned forward and patted Anson's knee. "Thank you, son. I believe you are. But it's all right now."

"No, it is not all right. It's all wrong. Evil and wrong."

"The time's too late for anger now. Anger tore our country apart in the first place. Anger, and people hating other people just like themselves, without trying to understand what they felt about things."

Anson jumped to his feet. "Don't you see, though, I haven't felt any anger about the War until today. I was born the year it broke out, but all this time it's just been something my grandfather talked about and prayed about and something I studied in history books. In fact, because I admire my grandfather so much, I suppose my sympathies were with the North."

"Your grandfather didn't hate us, son."

"No—no, he didn't. But—my father was a Southern sympathizer, and that was enough to make a Yankee out of me!"

Horace Gould kept silent, knowing his young guest had not meant to say that much about his father. The big clock in the corner ticked loudly; Anson realized he hadn't noticed it before this moment which swung heavily between them. They had felt comfortable together. Now neither man could think of anything he could permit himself to say aloud. Anson poked the fire again. Horace Gould stroked his forelock. Finally, the older man said, "Sympathies of the kind your father had don't matter now. No one needs sympathy any more."

"You do, sir. Your family needs it, the South needs it."

"No, you're wrong there. Compassion, yes. But not sympathy in the way we used that word during the War—not taking sides. The North needs our compassion and we need theirs. But most of all, we need faith in the United States of America. The kind of faith Thomas Jefferson had when he wrote to John Adams, just before his death, and said that evil could destroy us, but it could never disjoin us. It didn't. We're still together, Mr. Dodge."

Anson sat down. "That's right, of course. But people are rich again in the North, sir. Women in New York City pay twenty-five hundred dollars for a single gown to wear to a ball. People ride around over seven new miles of carriage roads through Central Park in brass-trimmed phaetons, roomy barouches, or elegant closed broughams, any one of which costs more than enough to feed your family for a year. The magazines and newspapers shout that the Civil War is still a burning memory in all our minds, but it burns only according to how many thousands of people turn out at Madame Demorest's fall fashion opening because General Grant and General Sherman are there!"

Anson was on his feet, pacing back and forth from

the big west window to the fireplace, gesturing as emphatically as he talked.

"I attended the Centennial Exposition at Philadelphia three years ago in 1876. A powerful fourteen-hundred-horsepower Corliss engine drove all the mechanized exhibits. There were telegraphic wonders, typewriters, telephones. But mostly there was fashion! I was only sixteen, but I could tell there was more interest in what Mrs. Frank Leslie was wearing than in whether or not the women of the South had enough to keep them warm in winter. Oh, now and then some lady of fashion deigns to mention the women of Dixie. Someone wonders superciliously on a porch at Saratoga where all those 'darling' Southern women are. 'Wouldn't you think,' they say, 'they would get over their peeve and summer again at Saratoga like before the War? They always added so much charm, those fragile Southern ladies in their crinolines and their fetching coiffures!' "

Horace Gould chuckled softly, enjoying Anson's imitation, but the boy went right on.

"They wonder why Anna Gould and her sisters aren't there, but they don't really care."

"They're just talking, son. Talking without thinking first. They know why our women aren't there."

"Yes. They know crinolines are out of style now!"

"Are they? That's too bad, isn't it?"

Anson looked down at his hand. "My family—the Dodge family—rides through Central Park in an enormous barouche."

"And do you really believe your people don't care about us down here? What about your grandfather, and your father spending his time at the Mills?"

"My grandfather is an authentic Christian man, I know that."

"Then don't blame him for being rich. He's worked for his money. Your Grandfather Dodge came from a plain family like mine, son."

The young man's face brightened. "Yes, he did. He worked his way up, but how did you know that?"

"I told you I've admired him for years. He's one of

the Americans I admire most. He cares about us down here."

"But I'm sure many of your people feel about the Mills the way I know P. D. Bass feels. I wish my grandfather could show his caring without making money in the process."

Horace Gould was silent for so long that Anson stared. His host was smiling broadly. "I'm so downright comfortable with you, son, I keep forgetting how young you are. Keep your ideals, but don't let them keep you away from reality. How could your grandfather do more than he is doing without giving away the very source of his ability to do all he does for mankind? I happen to know that he's one of our true philanthropists. He does give away thousands of dollars to missions, to the Young Men's Christian Associations, to libraries, schools, churches—none of that makes him a profit. But if he gave it all away and stopped trying to make any more, he'd be as helpless as I am in no time. He'd lose his wide influence for good. People would pay no more attention to his opinion than they do to mine."

Once again Anson sat down in the Black Banks rocker, leaned his head back, and closed his eyes. Horace Gould looked at the young face closely, took note of the regular, extraordinarily handsome features, saw the shadow of some kind of suffering already there, tried to imagine how Anson would look a few years from now, with a little age on him. This is an unusual boy, he thought. I wonder if his father know it. He looks like his father, has his mannerisms, but he's not like him. If he finds himself, though, he could be a great deal like his grandfather.

Finally Anson spoke. "I'm sorry I preached a sermon, sir."

"I'm glad. It helped me get to know you better."

Anson toyed with the thick gold watch chain looped across his vest. "If I'm to make it back to the Mills before dark, I'll have to leave now. I—I've promised to spend the evening with my father. But may I come back?"

Horace Gould smiled. "P. D. Bass is through with

Episcopalians now, but he gave you the right information. Evening Prayers of Christ Church Frederica are said here every Sunday afternoon, right in this room, and we'd be honored to have you join us."

"Thank you. I was hoping you'd say that."

Horace Gould rose from his chair and put his arm around Anson's shoulders. "You come back and see us any time you get a chance, how's that? And give our regards to your father."

Anson frowned. "Sir, how well do you know my father?"

"Not too well. I doubt if anyone here knows him well."

"I doubt it, too."

"But we're grateful to him, and don't forget, now—you're always more than welcome at Black Banks."

"That's what Miss Anna said—'Welcome To Black Banks.' "

"You'll find my daughter and I agree on most things. Come again, as soon as you can."

Chapter Three

That evening, young Horace Gould and Anson sat together on the top step of the white clapboard Mills office. The red sun was dropping into the marsh behind them, and the towering live oaks they faced flowed with color, their trunks crimson, their waving moss pink. Anson watched the trees and wondered what it would be like to have lived here all his life, to have had a father like Horace Bunch Gould. He would have to see his own father tonight for their first real talk, but he put it off, telling himself he'd fare better if he sat here a while longer, letting the trees gather him into their silent certainty. And then he thought of the church at Frederica, and the protecting oaks standing guard there at the end of one more day.

"Before I saw your church, Horace, I always felt I'd hate being peaceful. Now I realize I've never tried peace before."

Horace Gould was quiet like his father, but too young yet to have his strength, Anson thought. Maybe I came here to find his father instead of mine. But that wasn't true: he was able now to admit to himself that he longed, for the first time since he was six years old, to find the man for whom he was named. There had been the happy years of growing up with his mother: years of travel, private tutoring, ponies and then horses of his own, fine carriages, a beautiful home, a room full of books. But no father, except on special occasions, sometimes years apart. Divorce would have been against the teaching of the church and so, of course, was unthinkable. He and his mother had been left with no way out, and no hope. But he was hoping again, as he sat on the wooden step beside his new friend, postponing the appointment with his father in spite of his hope. He watched the color turn pale blue on the moss and suddenly wondered if St. Simons Island had changed A. G. P. D., Sr., in the four years he had lived here through sunsets like this, under the guardian oak trees, beside the quiet river and the marsh.

The Mill whistle blew, the big saws grew quiet, and the millhands straggled by, going home, each of them greeting Horace; and Anson wished he knew them too. He said good evening to them anyway. The people from the office stopped to chat on the porch before they walked toward their homes, and he tried to enter in, to be neighborly, but small talk had always been difficult for him.

When they were all gone, Anson fell to studying his father's house, Rose Cottage, sprawled luxuriously among the other pleasant houses built for the families of the men with responsible positions at the Mills. Rose Cottage was larger and more handsome than even the Hamilton plantation house, still standing near the river in its grove of oaks and cedars, and had taken its name from the spacious rose gardens and pomegranate hedges behind its elegant white fence. His father must be at Rose Cottage now, he thought. What did he do there alone, in the big house? Was it possible that his father *had* changed?

As Anson studied the Gothic lines of Rose Cottage, admiring its wrought iron work and its ornate lightning rods, a man and woman came out its front door, crossed the piazza, and walked toward them over the wide lawn.

"Well, look who's comin'," Horace said. "Evenin', Miz Bass—P. D."

P. D. Bass and Emma marched by, barely nodding. When Anson said good evening too, P. D. turned slightly, slowing a step behind his wife, still bundled in her coat and heavy shawl. "Too bad yer father's leavin' jist when you got here, Mr. Dodge."

Anson stood up. "What did you say, sir?"

"Let 'em go on past," Horace whispered.

But P. D. stopped now to be sure Anson heard him. "I say it's too bad yer paw's leavin' jist when you got here to spend Christmas with him."

Emma Bass nudged her husband with her elbow and stopped too, still looking straight ahead but listening intently.

"We jist left yer father. Been here aimin' to try to trade him for some lumber we need to mend our fence at Frederica. Says we have to wait now fer yer uncle, Norman Dodge, to trade with us. Says he's leavin' to-night. Got a telegram from up north today." P. D. squinted, studying Anson's face. "You act s'prised, Mr. Dodge."

"No, nobody's surprised, P. D.," Horace said quickly. "Most likely Mr. Dodge Sr.'s got business up north. But he'll be back before long."

Looking disappointed, the Basses continued on their way toward the Wright and Gowen store where they always hitched their buckboard on their rare trips to the Mills.

Anson's face was white. "You knew this, Horace?"

"Not till just now, I didn't know it. But you don't ever want P. D. and Emma to find out you don't know all they're talkin' about—or thinkin'. I haven't seen your father since you rode off this mornin'."

"They're coming back, Horace. You do the talking."

"Somethin' else on your mind, P. D.?" Horace called.

"Mr. Dodge didn't tell us he was comin' back to the Island at all." Emma spoke with her head in the air, looking beyond them.

"Said he was leavin' fer good," P. D. added.

"Well, that may be," Horace remarked calmly. "Mr. Dodge is a busy man. He's got a lot of other interests besides this one mill operation, you know."

"We could tell you was s'prised at the news about yer father, Mr. Dodge." Emma almost looked at Anson this time.

After the Basses marched off again, Anson made

no effort to hide his shock. "Don't telegrams come through your office? Who sent my father a telegram?"

"Nobody. He didn't get any."

"A long distance telephone call, maybe? Don't you have a telephone here now?"

"Yes, got one last year, but calls come through my office too. He didn't get any calls. No letters either. The mail boat didn't make it over from Brunswick today for some reason."

Anson's voice was grim. "I thought so."

"You don't want to put too much stock in what P. D. and Emma say, Mr. Dodge. They don't exactly lie, but they specialize in stretchin' the truth."

"I'm much obliged for the use of Bessie today," Anson said, and walked abruptly toward Rose Cottage.

He went straight to his father's room on the second floor and entered without knocking.

Anson, Sr., sorted a neat stack of freshly ironed shirts, examined them for missing buttons, and then laid them carefully in a drawer of his steamer trunk before he turned to see who had entered his room.

"Well, son, so you finally returned to St. Simons Mills! I couldn't imagine what you'd found to amuse you all day in this God-forsaken little parcel of sand and scrub palms. Sit down, sit down, if you can find a place. Try this chair by the window, where you can behold our glorious sunset over our glorious marsh."

Anson made no move toward the chair, nor did he listen to his father's vigorous talk. He was feeling his heart break again as he had felt it break just before that other Christmas. He had been six years old. "We'll all be together this Christmas for certain, Anson," his mother had assured him. "Your father is going to stay with us all through the holidays, and he has big plans for the two of you. He's going to take you sleighing for as long as you want on Christmas afternoon!"

Anson had never known again the kind of suspense and anticipation of that week when his father had come home every night laughing and paying full attention to his son, stamping his feet inside the big front door, brushing the fresh fallen snow from his black hair and the velvet lapels of his greatcoat, declaring himself to be Kris Kringle's righthand man. "We'll not only go sleighing, son, you and I are going to trim our Christmas tree together—not even your mother will be in on it," he would say, and Anson would have to be shushed because he laughed too loudly and sometimes yelled and raced through the house to keep from bursting with excitement.

Even his mother, who had not yet lost hope for a miracle in their little family, seemed caught up in the new and secretive plans for Christmas. "I'll stay out of the house altogether, while you trim the tree, dear," she promised, "if that's what you and your father want."

"Men always get more things done without a woman around," young Anson had said, quoting, she supposed, and swaggered off to find his father. "We're going to fix a stocking for you, though, if you're good, Daddy says."

Anson's father hadn't spent Christmas with them since the boy had been old enough to love it as a special time for plans and surprises. He was beside himself with joy, hugging his father's hard thighs, pounding them almost frantically at times, until his father shouted, "Cut down on it, son!" and his mother worried that he would make himself sick.

At last it was Christmas Eve, and as soon as his mother kissed him and left for church, Anson had run, skidding and skating along the polished upstairs hall, to his father's room and burst in, forgetting to knock.

"Where's the tree, Daddy? Where's our tree? It's time now, isn't it? It's Christmas Eve, it's Christmas Eve!"

"Cut down on it, son. Can't you see I'm busy?"

And without another word, Anson, Sr., had finished packing his alligator bag and snapped it shut.

His mother had never again assured him of anything concerning his father. His mind had accepted the facts, but his heart had learned nothing in the thirteen years between that Christmas and this one, and he felt it break again.

For a long painful moment, the sudden Island sun blinded him as it shot in off the river, and he was aware only of a shadowy stranger moving briskly about the strange room.

"I'd hoped you would get back before sundown, Anson. I had my heart set on giving you a personally conducted tour of our splendid operation here. Of course, I know you're more interested in books and beautiful phrases than lumber, but the fact remains that you are a Dodge, and Dodges and lumber go together, my boy."

Anson was no longer blinded by the low hanging sun. He was blinded by his own rage.

"Yes, sir"—his father went on—"Dodges and lumber go together like ham and eggs. Or, down heah in Dixie ah should say they goes togethah lik' hayum an' grits."

Anson stood in the middle of the room, his fists thrust deep into his pockets.

"Well, now, tell me, son, how did you like our little ol' Island? Did you ride up to Frederica? Didn't the Yankees make mincemeat out of that church?" Anson, Sr., was smoothing six pairs of fine worsted trousers, preparatory to hanging them across the wooden bar of the big trunk. "I'd like your Grandfather Dodge to see the church at Frederica. He'd write a check in a minute for a new one at the Mills. You see, we plan to have as much of the Island's economy as possible centered right here. And no matter what anyone says, churches are a part of an economy. In a remote place like St. Simons, they're the center of social life too. As matters stand now, old man Gould and his son keep the Island's social life divided by holding sketchy little services of some sort in Black Banks parlor every Sunday. Some of our people here at the Mills are so religious they drive all the way out there to attend. A very unhealthy situation. You may have passed Black Banks today. Now, where the devil did I put those shirt studs?"

"When did you decide to leave, sir?"

"Ah, here they are. What?"

"I said, when did you decided to leave St. Simons Island?"

"Oh, I guess that telegram hadn't come yet when you left this morning, had it?"

"No, it hadn't."

"Well, I received a wire about noon from New York, urging me to leave at once for our mill operation in Pennsylvania. Labor trouble. Just the kind of thing I like to get into and untangle." He glanced briefly at Anson. "Too bad it had to come just before Christmas like this. But business is business, and I've a marvelous idea for your holidays."

At least he said he was sorry this time, Anson thought, wishing he could laugh. His father was no longer afraid he would scream and beg and cling to his legs all the way down the stairs, prying at his fingers around the handle of the same ugly alligator bag that now stood packed and locked by the door.

When Anson showed no interest in his marvelous idea for the holidays, his father turned to face him, all smiles, his left eyebrow raised in the way that always preceded the exaggerated impish wink Anson hated. "You can wire your mother and Ellen and have them take the next train south! You can all have a beautiful Christmas together. With Ellen home in New York City from abroad, I fail to see how you can live without her anyway. What kind of lover are you?"

The wink. Anson gritted his teeth.

"Better still, call them up. Horace can make connections for you with our line in Brunswick, and you'll be hearing your mother's voice in a matter of minutes. I tell you it's made an enormous difference to have the telephone service. Before that I felt like Robinson Crusoe, except for your grandfather's Western Union and the outrageous social life forced upon me. These Southerners will wear a man down with entertainment."

"Are you leaving tonight?"

"On the *Ruby*, at six o'clock. That is, if she makes it on time, which is almost never. My valises are already down at Steamboat Landing, except for that one. My trunks follow later."

"You're not coming back, are you?"

"Who knows? But Warren Fuller is an excellent mill superintendent, and your Uncle Norman will love this place. You see"—he made a sweeping gesture around the master bedroom—"I've already built a family house for him. This rose garden is the talk of Glynn County. Norman's the community type. He loves the noble Dodge role and plays it to the hilt. These provincial folk will *revere* Norman, and he'll thrive on it."

"My Uncle Norman has helped create what you call 'the noble Dodge role'—the worthy part of it!" Anson snapped. He didn't know his uncle well, but he had to hit back.

His father laughed. "I've always said you should have been good old Norman's son. Or, better still, with your religious bent, you should have been your *Reverend* Uncle Stuart's son."

His father turned to face him, his left eyebrow cocked again for the wink.

"Of course," A. G. P. D., Sr., went on, "if you had been Stuart's son, then you would be Ellen's brother, and your big romance would be too naughty for even the Dodge name to cover. Anyone known it's stretching the old name to the limit to cover the fact that you two are first cousins."

Anson took a step toward him.

"Naturally, I'd be proud to have a brilliant beauty like Ellen for a daughter. But, like you, my boy, I admit I'd much rather have her in a more *intime* relationship!"

His father winked, and Anson struck him solidly on the jaw. He toppled against the wash stand, and the heavy ironstone pitcher shattered the mirror behind it.

The older man slowly kicked the fragments of glass under the big dresser and smiled crookedly. "Why don't we stop pretending?"

Anson stared at him.

"Give up, son. I'm just *not* a family man." He examined the small cut on his face in the broken mirror. "No one can say I haven't provided materially for you and your mother—you're a rich man right now—but since Rebecca and I don't get along together, why try?"

Anson had never heard his parents argue. For as long as he could remember, he had been chilled by the cold formality growing up in the space that existed between them. He wished again that he could laugh at the ridiculous, old-fashioned determination to keep up appearances all these years, but he had been too wounded by it. It was why he had to be sure about himself before he could marry Ellen.

"Isn't it sensible to give up and stop pretending?" At least on this point, his father had changed.

"You can stay. I'll leave."

"Not at all. I've been wanting to get way from this place for over a year. The people here are not like the typical seedy mill inhabitants. They're really quite civilized and cultured in a middle-class way. There's nothing I can do to avoid social life with them, and they bore me. They bore me with their goodness, their morality, their everlasting piety. They bore me the way your mother bores me."

Anson clenched both fists and then let them fall at his side. His mother had delighted him every minute of his life. "The way my mother *bores* you?"

"Exactly. I didn't send for you, you came to me, and since you did, you should know the facts. My mind is made up. I'm leaving *now*. That is, as soon as I patch my face a bit." He wiped the trickle of blood from his cheek, as casually as a man who has cut himself shaving. "I plan to locate permanently in Canada at our operation there, as soon as possible. You'll hear from me from time to time, when necessary."

A. G. P. D., Sr., extended his hand. Anson made no move toward it.

"All right, have it your way. But I hope we have things straight. Frankly, I'm quite relieved. I've grown to despise the strain of pretending. I'm indispensable now to the Dodge empire, so there's no more need for it. My esteemed father will simply have to accustom himself to my lack of Dodge conformity."

Anson saw the whole picture. His father had been playing politics with Grandfather Dodge until his career was firmly established. The Dodge holdings had grown so large that Grandfather could not operate without him. The hollow pretense that he was a husband and a father had worn out its usefulness.

Anson bolted from the room and ran outside into the still faintly colored evening, sick with the realization that he would probably never see his father again.

He was still walking, away from the Big Mill, past the cypress mill at the south end of the Dodge property, past the row of shacks where the Negro millhands lived, and into the woods along the marsh, when he heard the *Ruby* whistle her departure.

That long-ago Christmas Eve, he had tumbled after his father down the wide staircase, screaming and pleading and clutching his narrow trouser legs, all the way to the front door. When his father had looked down and laughed at him, he had let go and crumpled inside the heavy door, as it closed firmly from the outside.

Now, he crumpled beside the darkening marsh, more in despair than a small boy can be, more in need of finding himself in this new blinding finality than he had needed his mother to find him that other night. The tall, stiff marsh grass dwarfed him, as he sat on the damp ground, the way the big door had dwarfed him. Even the copper sky looked angry that the sun had left it, and Anson felt afraid again. Not of the darkening marsh and river and woods around him; he would find his way back to Rose Cottage, he supposed. He was afraid of himself. His father had struck at him in his cruel, civilized way, and he had struck back like a stevedore. It made him afraid and ashamed that the new identity which he believed he had found in the churchyard, only that morning, should be so quickly gone.

"He made me do it!" He spoke in a sharp whisper, to the marsh, to the river, to the sky or the woods or any part of St. Simons Island that might pay attention to him again.

He thought of the Goulds and longed to feel worthy of them now, in spite of what he had just done. The light was almost gone from the sky, except for one brown-gold streak along the horizon where the *Ruby* puffed toward the mainland.

"My father forced me to strike him. He wanted me to do something to make me despise *myself*. He has always done this to Mother and to me. We are never in the right with him. He keeps on putting us in the wrong, time after time, to ease his own conscience over us. To leave himself free of us."

A wind had sprung up, cold, rattling through the winter marsh, but Anson sat huddled beside the stiff grass, too stunned to notice the chill. And then he began to think more clearly. His father had not put them in the wrong this time. He had put them *out of his life*. This time, A. G. P. D., Sr., had been honest, at least. He felt no further responsibility for his wife and son, and he admitted it. They had gone on secretly expecting more of this man than he had given them a right to expect. They had gone on resisting the fact that he was as unlike his father and his brothers as a man could be. Now at last it was coming clear to Anson. His father was gone, as he had never been gone before. A slow, painful acceptance pushed out the old rebellion, and Anson stood up, aware of shame because he had descended to violence, aware of loneliness, aware of the dark coming now so fast he could no longer make out the flat curve of the Frederica River except against the brightening glow of the slab pile burning above the Big Mill.

A live oak towered beside him. He stepped back, not touching it, but looking all the way to the top of its wide, heavy branches, wanting it to draw him back to the Island and the peace he had known that morning. "I need you," he said aloud to the tree. "I need you to help me to be real."

Slowly, he followed through the twisting pattern of the big branches, up, up, and there he met the sky and the first burning star; the brown glow gone and the clear black blue come, and with it the beginning of clarity for Anson Dodge.

The strong southwest wind carried the sound of the *Ruby's* thin whistle across the five salt creeks that separated St. Simons Island from the mainland. The little steamboat was landing in Brunswick. He thought of his father, leaving the boat with a spring in his step, free now of the people at the Mills, free of his son, free of his wife. "My father is false. But God is not false, and *I do not need to be*. I am A. G. P. D.'s son, but I am God's son, too." He reached out then and touched the big tree, then turned and walked, exhausted, in the direction of the Mills and Rose Cottage.

As he groped his way along the dark narrow road past the millhands' shacks, Horace Gould came toward him with a lantern.

"Guess I walked the wrong way," Horace said, as though nothing unusual had happened. "Been up at the other end pokin' through the woods lookin' for you. . . . I was just afraid you might get lost," Horace went on. "These woods can be pretty black when there's no moon."

"Thanks, Horace. I'm causing you a lot of inconvenience."

"I'm honored if I can be of any kind of help to you, Mr. Dodge."

"I wish you'd call me 'Anson.' "

"All right, Anson. I'd like to."

The two young men took a short-cut through a field.

"The light helps, Horace."

"Yes. That's true. Light helps."

Anson laughed a little. "That's a sermon."

"Yeah?" Horace was pleased. "Say, did my father tell you we have Christ Church services at Black Banks every Sunday?"

"He certainly did. I'm coming this Sunday."

"Oh, good!" After a moment, Horace said, "Your father wrote out a telegram to your mother before he left, telling her to bring someone named Ellen to spend Christmas with you."

Anson was relieved that he felt no sting this time. He saw his father in a new light now, and "light helps."

"I didn't send it, though. I thought I'd wait to see how you felt about it."

"Thanks. I'm glad you waited. I want to rewrite that telegram and sign it myself. On second thought, maybe I'll call them tomorrow—or tonight!"

Anson set the pace now, his exhaustion forgotten, and they walked faster.

"Will they come on such short notice, Anson?"

"Mother and Ellen? Yes, they'll come. They're the two people on earth about whom I can be certain.

They're stopping at the same hotel for the holidays, too. Can you help me make my connection with New York tonight?"

"If we hurry. Central closes down in Brunswick at eight P.M."

"All right, I'll race you."

Horace almost caught up with Anson as he sprinted across the unfamiliar field and bounded laughing up the porch steps of the Mill office.

"What's the matter, Horace? Come on, man. We've got to call my girl!"

Chapter Four

Ellen and Rebecca Dodge hurried arm in arm down the long red-and-green-carpeted hotel corridor. Ellen's hands shook as she unlocked the door of their suite, and then she could control her excitement no longer.

"He called us—he called us, and we're going to him!" she shouted, waltzing Anson's mother round and round the big sitting room, singing the *Blue Danube* at the top of her voice. After a few turns, Rebecca sang with her, and they finished with a flourish, as Ellen released her aunt into a big velvet chair and hurled herself dramatically toward the high windows overlooking winter-bound New York, crying, "New York, are you listening? He called us! We're going to St. Simons Island, Georgia, to spend Christmas with my wonderful love. Do you hear me, New York? In just five days I'll be where I can look at him again, and listen to his gorgeous theories, and touch his face. Listen, world, *we're going to him!*"

Rebecca Dodge smoothed her hair, laughing. "Surely the whole city came to a sudden halt with that announcement."

"No"—Ellen sighed—"it moves right along in its petty pace, unaware that the universe has just been turned upside down. Oh, Rebecca—I'm going to see him!"

"You're still shouting, Ellen."

"And I mean to continue to shout." She swooped around the room again, the long, full skirt of her woolen walking suit whirling. "I mean to shout and sing and dance until I learn to *live* with this great truth."

"Great truth, my dear?"

Ellen stopped, her hands on her hips. "The great truth of how much I love your son. Oh, *why* was my father a Presbyterian minister? I should have learned ballet in order to be adequate to this moment."

She circled the room once more, her arms above her head.

"You're doing all right, child." Rebecca laughed, then frowned. "I wonder what he's doing tonight, right now, down there all alone on that Island."

Ellen stopped dancing. "Did Anson tell you why his father left so abruptly?"

"You know better than to ask a question like that, my dear girl. No one knows *why* his father does anything. I only hope he didn't hurt Anson too much. I thought our boy sounded fine, though, didn't you? As though he were—well, in control of things?"

"He will always be in control of things, that man!"

Rebecca wanted to smile, but she didn't, and Ellen knelt by her chair, intense and caring.

"Should I feel selfish? Tell me how to be with you in all my joy over your son, when his father is—the way he is with you."

Rebecca embraced her. "You know better than anyone on earth how to be with me, Ellen. Even at seventeen. Better than Anson knows, sometimes, because you're a woman. And very advanced for seventeen."

"Thank you for loving me."

"Oh, my dear, don't thank me for something I couldn't possibly help."

"But most women in your position would resent the woman her son wanted to marry."

"Most women? I don't know about that. But I do know my one joy now is in you and Anson, in my dreams for your life together."

"Why can't my parents feel that way about us? What makes you so intelligent and farseeing?"

Rebecca laughed. "Never compare us, Ellen. That is unfair. They are good parents; your father's work at the college in Syria has simply kept them away from you too much during your school years. Anyway, it isn't easy being your father and mother."

"Why?"

"Because you're not a run-of-the-mill daughter. You're an artist—a writer. And a good one."

"Am I?" Ellen got up." Am I a good writer, Rebecca?"

"Anson and I think you're so good we both mean to do everything we can to see that nothing stops you from finding out how good you can become. Your talent has special meaning for us both. But it does make you rather complicated."

"My mother and particularly my father think my writing is a young girl's whim."

She is even more beautiful when she is being solemn, Rebecca thought, but she said, "It takes a certain kind of peculiar person to understand an artist. Perhaps Anson and I are peculiar."

Ellen brightened. "But isn't it marvelous we have each other to be peculiar with?" She wrinkled her nose. "What a literary sentence that was! But I do thank you for loving me and believing in me. And I thank Anson, too. Honestly, I'd much rather be spending Christmas with you two than with my own family, dear as they are. That's lucky, isn't it, since they're in Syria anyway?" Ellen lifted her big photograph of Anson, in its silver frame, from the window still and held it at arm's length admiringly. "Isn't he amazing, Rebecca? How many men want to encourage their wives' abilities? Almost none. If they're rich, they want a crushable violet to pamper. If they're poor, they demand a drudge."

"Ellen, always remember your Grandfather Dodge when you make a sweeping statement like that. He not only still loves your grandmother like a young lover, he reveres her as a human being. I'm still angry with you and Anson for slipping off to be alone last year on their golden wedding anniversary."

Ellen's eye twinkled. "That was my fault. Your son wanted to be conventional."

"I doubt that."

"Oh, but he did. Anyway, we only stayed an hour

down by the Hudson. And it turned out to be the most important hour in history."

"I know. You fell in love, during that hour, and started everyone worrying about you both right in the midst of the festivities."

"Everyone but you."

Rebecca smiled. "Yes. Everyone but me. I'm an incurable romantic, but so are your grandparents."

"Will they ever understand how Anson and I love each other, Rebecca? Will they ever begin to take us seriously?"

"I'm afraid they take you very seriously, my dear. That's scarcely the point of their anxiety."

Ellen stood holding Anson's photograph against her breast. "But Rebecca, Anson and I met as strangers that day at Tarrytown. We hadn't seen each other since I was two and Anson four! I'd been at school abroad. We're not like first cousins at all. How can they be so stuffy?"

"Now and then you ask a very young question, Ellen, and it never fails to surprise me. I'm genuinely sorry you and Anson didn't hear your Grandfather Dodge tell us about his marriage to your grandmother and their life together for all those fifty beautiful years. According to their viewpoint, they are not stuffy to object to your marriage with Anson."

"Then what are they?"

"Principled, I imagine. Moulded by their backgrounds, yes. But stuffy? No."

"Oh, I know they're both old darlings. And I keep clinging to the hope that eventually they'll understand how we love each other—how tragic it would be for us not to be together. After all, Rebecca, your principles are just as high as theirs. Why are you on our side?"

Rebecca sighed. "I don't know."

"Does it worry you that you are?"

"Indeed not."

"Then why does it bother you that we didn't hear Grandfather make his dear, flowery speech that day? We've both read it since. Daddy has faithfully recorded it in the archives."

"I want you to have seen the way your grandfather looked standing there in the drawing room of their country place, his spare figure erect, his hair and side whiskers almost white, his voice so gentle." Rebecca leaned her head back on the big chair and smiled, repeating her father-in-law's words from memory: " 'Our marriage took place on the twenty-fourth of June, 1828. And as we had never had any other attachment, ours was one of real affection; and we can truly say today that however strong it was then, these fifty years of married life have only tended to increase it from year to year. It has grown brighter and brighter to the golden day.' Just think of that, Ellen—think of fifty years of growing happiness."

The girl looked at Anson's picture again, and then asked carefully, "What do you think they really feel about their son—who is also your husband?"

"They're loyal to him, but I'm sure he breaks their hearts too."

Ellen replaced the photograph on the window ledge. "Then your heart is broken, isn't it?"

"It was. I think it's only weary and a bit wary now. One must have something tangible to fight or overcome in order to keep trying, to keep feeling. For years, Anson, Sr., has given me nothing to fight about or try for. Only everything to wear me down. I think I'm just tired now when I think of him."

"Do you still love him, Rebecca? Do you still love Anson's father?"

"I don't know."

"Did you ever love him the way I love his son?"

The older woman didn't answer.

"Forgive me for asking. It's just that I want so much to learn to be right with you, to be your friend."

"Ellen, no one else in the family seems to agree with me, but I'm all in favor of becoming your mother-in-law. By ordinary standards, we are not supposed to love each other as we do. But I consider you both my daughter and my friend." Rebecca smiled. "In fact, you must marry my son because I need you so much, just the way you are."

"Wouldn't it be marvelous if Anson and I weren't so young?"

"Then you could just go ahead and get married with or without family approval?"

"Yes, Rebecca, yes!"

"Don't worry, I have a feeling the family will come around to our side in time. Your grandparents understand love." Rebecca Dodge eased herself out of the big chair. "My dear, I must begin to watch my waistline! Now then, if we're to catch that early train tomorrow, two southbound women I know had better start packing."

They hugged each other. "Do you think he's as excited as we are, dear Rebecca?"

"Twice as excited, Ellen. After all, there are two of us!"

Anna Gould set the big tureen of oyster stew in the center of the table, and her younger brother, James, started to ladle it into their bowls.

"Hold on a minute, Jimmie," Horace Bunch said. "We haven't thanked the Lord yet."

"Sorry, Papa—but make it short. I'm starved."

James kept the big ladle in his hand, ready to begin dipping and talking almost before his father said Amen.

"I knew Horace was makin' a mistake to stay at the Mills again tonight. I told him we'd have oyster stew. Mm-m. Does that smell good!"

"Watch your manners, James." His mother smiled, but he knew she meant it. "Did poor Horace have to work late tonight?"

"No, he got through early. But he's with the boss's son, polishin' the apple, I reckon. Junior said he needed someone to talk to tonight, so meek and mild Horace said 'sure.' "

"You needn't accuse Horace of apple polishing just because you'd be doing it if you had a chance." Anna grinned at her talkative brother and handed him the plate of biscuits.

"I've got no reason to butter him up, sister. I'm only keepin' my job at the Mill till the prow of the good ship *Barcelona* heaves into sight. And then your *handsome* brother is off to South America." James popped a fat oyster into his mouth. "My, how I'm goin' to be missed!"

"You *will* be missed, son." Deborah laid her hand on Jimmie's muscular forearm.

"That's what I say. Maybe it's a good thing young Dodge has come on the scene. He'll liven things up. He's quite a bit like me."

"*What?*" Anna choked on a biscuit.

"He is. He's dark and handsome and dashing and witty and intelligent, and two to one he's got a hard head like mine."

"How do you know so much about Mr. Dodge?"

"I met him, didn't I? And I am an excellent judge of men. Women too, for that matter." Jimmie shook his spoon at his sister. "But you mark my word, young Dodge has a mind of his own. He's got poor old Horace jumpin' through hoops right and left. Horace has been right at Junior's heels ever since Senior left the Island."

They all stopped eating and stared at him.

"Mr. Dodge Sr. left the Island?" As she usually did, Deborah looked at her husband to catch his reaction before she said any more.

"What do you mean, his father left the Island?" Anna demanded.

"Just what I said."

"Now, James, this is no joking matter." His father looked stern. "Stop fooling around and tell us what happened."

"He just up and took the *Ruby* last night. No warning to anybody. I could tell even Junior didn't know he was goin'. Course, he didn't let on to me, but I could tell the way old Horace was pussy-footin' around the subject that something was fishy." James talked with his mouth full, relishing his role of reporter even more than the oysters, and he loved oysters. "But, it seems his mother and cousin are comin' down for Christmas with Junior anyway. And man alive, is he excited! Any more biscuits, Anna?" He took the last two.

"Not yet, but Ca has more in the oven. When is Mr. Dodge's mother coming?"

"End of this week. Is this all the plum butter?"

"No, there's more, but can't you stop eating for two minutes and make some sense?"

"I'm makin' sense, sister. What else is there to tell?"

"How do I know what else there is to tell? I'm asking *you*."

"Look, sister, I just met Junior before I rode off for home today. He was even surprised to find out I was another Gould. Acted like I was an outsider, an' him an insider."

"I don't believe that," Anna snapped.

"Young Dodge is from the North, and a big city to boot, son."

"What's that got to do with it, Papa?"

"His ways are different from ours, that's all." Horace Bunch was firm. "When he had dinner with us yesterday, we liked him fine. We all felt he was just like one of us underneath."

"That's right, Mr. Gould, dear," Deborah said. "And we want him to feel at home with us. You be polite to young Mr. Dodge, James."

"Mama, I'm always polite!" Jimmie looked around the table at his family. "What's all the fuss? Course he put on his Sunday self when he was here for dinner. And he's all right. I've got nothing against him. Junior's just a spoiled rich kid, shootin' off his mouth in front of us guys at the Mill, 'cause he's havin' visitors from *Noo* York."

"I expect he is excited his mother's coming. The boy's only nineteen."

"And I'm only twenty, Mama. But I'm twice the man he is."

"In your opinion!" Anna got the plum butter from the sideboard and banged it down on the table beside her brother.

"In my opinion," James agreed, plunging a spoon into the thick, red-amber preserve.

"We've had enough of this talk, children. Was his father called away on business?" Horace Bunch reached for the plum butter too.

"How do I know? That's where the funny part comes in. I asked Horace, and he just clammed up."

"Well, it seems to me it's none of our business," Deborah said. "And we all hope you were nice to him, James."

"Mother, I was charmin'! I always am." Jimmie took two more biscuits as soon as Ca set the hot stack on the table. "Oh, I almost forgot, you're supposed to ride in with Procter Green in the buggy tomorrow, sister."

Anna dropped the spoon in her bowl. "What do you mean I'm supposed to ride in with Procter Green?"

"That's what he said."

"That's what *who* said?"

"This Dodge fellow."

"For what? What am I supposed to do?"

"Give him a hand or something."

"If you don't stop gulping your supper and start making sense, James Gould—I declare, you make me so mad, I could shake you!"

"Why? This fellow just wants you to ride in with Procter tomorrow and help him get Rose Cottage ready for his company from the North. What's so funny about that?"

Anna turned to her father helplessly. "Oh, Papa, make him tell me. Make him stop acting this way."

"What way? What way am I actin'?"

"Like James Gould!"

"Is that bad?" He mussed her hair.

"Stop it!"

"What's eatin' on her, Mama?"

"You handle him, Mr. Gould, dear."

"Don't tease your sister any more now, son. Tell her what she needs to know. What does Mr. Dodge want her to do for him?"

"Search me. What is there to do when you get ready for two rich women to visit?"

"That's what I want to know," Anna flared. "How do I know anything about rich people? And what if I don't want to ride in with Procter Green or anybody else?"

"Quiet down now, Anna, and eat your stew," Deborah said.

"Did Horace tell him I'd come, Jim? Did *you*?"

"This Dodge fellow figures everybody wants to please him, in my opinion. He figured you'd jump at the chance. He's looked in the mirror, don't worry."

"What's Procter supposed to do?"

"Junior wants somebody to groom his father's horses. He's got three beauties, and all the old man cared about horses was a way to get him there. Seems young Dodge is nutty over horses, an' he was carryin' on to have somebody work with 'em. I told him Procter would come."

"Is Procter old enough to go, Mr. Gould, dear?"

"He's thirteen, Deborah. Knows horses, too. I expect his mother would be glad to have the boy earn a little extra money."

"But will she let him go all that way? You know how she fusses over Procter."

"If Anna talks to her, she will. She trusts Anna, like everybody else does. You'll have to handle it, daughter. Better ride over this evenin' before dark."

"Well—I'll talk to Procter's mother, Papa, but what do I know about fixing up a house like Rose Cottage?"

"Don't worry, Junior'll be full of ideas. I'll bet he never runs down."

"What's the matter, don't you like him?"

"What the matter with *you*, sister? Sure I like him. I wouldn't want to cross him, but I liked him. And two to one he'll have all the old maids' hearts in his pocket by next week."

"That's uncalled for, son," Horace Bunch said.

"Yes, it is," Deborah agreed.

Anna's eyes blazed. "What's that got to do with it anyway?"

"Not much, I'd say." James paused a moment, and leaned back in his chair, his teacup in his hand. "Young Dodge is going to marry his cousin, Ellen. And the way he looks when he talks about her, he won't know there *are* any old maids on St. Simons."

Chapter Five

Anna and Procter Green bumped along in the buggy behind old Tom, toward St. Simons Mills, past where the miles of cotton fields had been before the War. Through the cloudy, mist-hung morning, they could see the old furrows still running away toward the marsh. "It sure looks like rain, Miss Anna," Procter Green said, sniffing the damp breeze that blew the always stubborn strands of hair from under Anna's close, dark-blue bonnet.

"That's just my luck, Procter. I haven't been down Frederica Road this winter so far, and the one day I get to come, the sky's hanging down to the tree tops."

Procter smiled, and Anna sneaked a look, thinking that when Procter smiled it was almost like the sun coming out.

"Yeh," the boy sympathized, "I know how you like the red gum trees in the bright sun. You always say you sure do like the red gum trees when they turn color. I'm sure sorry, Miss Anna. Looks like it coulda been a nice day. But I'm havin' the best time, anyway."

"Are you chilly?"

"No, Ma'am. I'm warm. You sure musta knit a lot of wool into this sweater you give me last Christmas." The boy smoothed the thick bright-red sleeve of his sweater. "I sure do like it. I'm keepin' it for good, like today. My mother's only had to wash it once, I'm keepin' it so good."

"You look fine in it, too. You're getting to be a

50

man, Procter. Makes me feel old to see you growing up so fast." The reins lay loosely in Anna's hands; old Tom knew the way, and no one ever had to hold him to keep him from taking the bumps in the road too hard.

"Was I just a baby when you first saw me?"

"You certainly were just a baby." Anna smiled. "Just a little old bawlin' baby about a foot and half long. You were born right at the end of the War, just before we came back to St. Simons Island."

"Did you all have to go to Burneyville to keep the Yankees from shootin' you down?"

Anna laughed. "Well, I don't know that they would have done that, Procter. But all the white people left the Island."

"Didn't any of the black people go to Burneyville?"

"Oh, yes, Ca and her family and Adam Procter went with us. But there were over two thousand colored here, and they couldn't all go."

"The Yankees wasn't mad at the black folks, was they? Why wasn't they, Miss Anna?"

"I guess they weren't actually mad at anyone. It was just war. And you mustn't say 'they wasn't.' Remember I've told you *they* is plural. You must say 'they weren't.'"

"Oh, yes, Ma'am. I forgot. Well, I sure am glad you got to come back, Miss Anna. You're my best friend."

"Thank you, Procter. I'm glad I got to come back." She smiled tenderly at the boy. "I'm glad I'm your best friend, too."

"An' even though my people doesn't—don't belong to the Goulds any more, you and me still sort of belong to each other, don't we?"

"In the very best way there is, Procter. I think a lot of you, I wouldn't be taking you to a fine young man like Mr. Anson Greene Phelps Dodge, Jr."

Procter's eyes widened. "Is that his name? All that? Anson Greene—what?"

". . . Phelps Dodge, Jr. His father is Anson Greene Phelps Dodge, Sr."

"Can white people and colored have the same name? My name's Green like part of his!"

"Oh, yes." Anna laughed. "People can have the same name, all right. But names don't really matter. It's what's inside a person that matters."

"Is Mr. Anson Greene Phelps Dodge, Jr., good inside?"

Anna didn't mind blushing in front of Procter. "I don't know him very well. He only came to our house a few days ago, but my father thinks he may grow up to be a great and good man."

"Does he need to grow up?"

Anna smiled. "I guess everybody does, Procter. But Mr. Dodge is only nineteen."

"You're a lot older than that, aren't you?"

"I declare, it's a good thing we're friends, or I might dump you right out of this buggy for that!"

"Don't you like to be old, Miss Anna?"

"I'm not quite twenty-four. Is that so old?"

"Well, it's sure a lot older than me. Or Mr. Anson Greene Phelps Dodge, Jr."

Anna was quiet a moment. "Yes, I guess it is."

"Miss Anna, are you gonna get paid money too?"

"Procter, I declare, you are talkative today! No, I'm not going to get paid money. I'm just going to help out."

"Are the Goulds rich?"

"Lands, no! Anything but. Nobody's rich on St. Simons Island after the War, Procter. You know that."

"Is Mr. Anson Greene Phelps Dodge, Jr., rich?"

This boy always made Anna smile, but the way he savored Anson's long name was the best yet, she thought. "Yes, Mr. Dodge is rich. All the Dodges are. But if the rest of the family is anything like Mr. Anson Dodge, they're awfully nice people. He's—well, he's different, Procter. Seems older than nineteen, too."

"Is he one of your best friends, like me?"

Anna urged Tom to a brisk trot. "Procter, I declare, how many more questions do you have left?"

"Is it bad to ask questions?"

"Well, no, I reckon not."

"Then do you like Mr. Anson Greene Phelps Dodge, Jr.?"

"Of course, I like him! I'm human, I guess."

"Do all humans like each other?"

Anna turned to the bright-eyed youngster sitting beside her on the buggy seat and shook her finger at him. "Procter Green, you listen to me. If you talk this much to Mr. Dodge, he won't want you to work for him. He needs someone to work, not talk."

"Oh, I'll work, Miss Anna. But as long as we're ridin' along in the buggy, I can't work, so I talk."

"You sure do. Why don't you sing me a song?"

"Does Mr. Anson Greene Phelps Dodge, Jr., like you?"

"To be such a little one, that's the nosiest nose I ever saw! How do I know whether he likes me or not?"

"I know you like *me*."

"But you and I have known each other for thirteen years."

"Will I have to know Mr. Anson Greene Phelps Dodge, Jr., for thirteen years before I know whether he likes me or not? How long is he gonna stay?"

They were inside the Mill settlement now, and Anna said, "Giddup, Tom!"

Sitting on the edge of the buggy seat, Procter looked around, his eyes wider than ever. "Great Jehosophat, I didn't known it was this big down here at the Mills, Miss Anna! Is this a city?"

Anna laughed. "No, it's not a city."

"How big is a city?"

"Oh, big and stretched out, with lots of streets and roads and buildings, I reckon."

"Have you ever been to a big city?"

"No, but my brothers and sisters have."

"Miss Anna! Look at all the big boats with sails on 'em!"

"Isn't that a pretty sight? They're mostly from far off foreign lands too."

"One, two, three, four, five, six, seven—are there that many foreign lands, Miss Anna?"

"Yes, Procter. More than that. Eight, nine, ten, eleven, twelve, thirteen ships docked at the Mills today. Just to make a big show for you, I'll bet."

Procter grinned. "What do they carry in them boats, Miss Anna?"

"*Those* boats, and they just carry rock for ballast on the way here, then carry our lumber back."

"Do they pay money for our lumber?"

"Yes, they do. Lots of money. Look, Procter, do you see what looks like a little island out there in the river?"

"Looks like a pile of rock to me."

"It is. The only rocks on our sandy island, and every one carried in on one of those big ships as ballast."

"What's ballast, Miss Anna?"

"Something heavy to hold the ship down in the water where it belongs. And I think I'd better drop a few rocks in you to hold you down, too."

The boy threw back his head and laughed. "Is that big square house way out there the Mill?"

"Yes, that's the Big Mill. There's another one, down the river there. But that's a cypress mill."

"Do they have to have special mills for every kind of wood, Miss Anna?"

"I reckon, Procter. You'll have to ask my brother, Horace, about that."

"Are we gonna see Mr. Horace too?"

"Not now. I wouldn't want to bother him at the office." Anna sighed. "But I wish I had him to help me introduce you to Mr. Dodge."

"Will that be a big job?"

"For me, it will. I guess I didn't think about that when I said I'd come. Now that we're here, I'm a lot more nervous than you are."

"Oh, I wouldn't worry, Miss Anna. I'm right with you."

Anna stood in the wide paneled hall of Rose Cottage, waiting for Anson to return from the barn, where he and Procter had gone to inspect the horses. She had never seen teacups and pitchers and plates and figurines like the ones she stared at now through the glass doors of a tall china closet. Anna remembered the Gould china, which the Yankees had smashed so that not one cup was left with a handle. She remembered the silver, too, which had been so carefully buried; the hiding place had been found, the silver stolen. She remembered their nice parlor furniture, every piece as handsome as the one remaining Black Banks chair.

She was six years old the cloudy winter day in 1862 when they loaded their most cherished pieces onto one of the two rented flatboats, along with the Negroes and their hogs and pigs. It took three days' hauling in wagons and oxcarts to get it all up Frederica Road to the pier, but finally she and her mother and father and brothers and sisters climbed aboard the second heavily loaded lighter and started across St. Simons Sound toward Brunswick, just a week before the Yankees landed on the Island. Halfway across the Sound, the first lighter turned over and sank under the gray water. Anna watched the furniture vanish from sight, as the hogs and pigs, squealing and scrambling for a foothold on the doomed chairs and tables, drowned before her eyes. Anna had cried bitterly, and her mother had hugged her close, while the Negroes were rescued and hauled, soaked and frightened, onto the boat with them. She had cried over the dear tables and chairs and their piano she was learning to play, but she knew she had wept more for their pigs and hogs. This comforted her somehow, standing alone in Rose Cottage, because she knew furnishings like these would never mean more to her than living creatures. She smiled. Not as much, and that's lucky, because I'll always have more hogs than china!

Anna stepped into the quiet, richly furnished living room spread graciously across the front of the house. Wonderingly, she touched the high, graceful back of a chair upholstered in black satin, with a pattern of gold leaves. She doubted if those high windows had ever been opened to let the marsh breezes into all this order and perfection. Anna loved the marshes, almost as much as she loved the woods, and while everyone else sat on the front piazza at home in the evening, she preferred the back, where the marsh stretched away through the windings of the little Black Banks river to the sea. She admired the beauty around her now, but she was more miserable than impressed. She pictured Anson and his fiancee, Ellen, at home and at ease among the dark mahogany pedestals and inlaid cabinets in the Rose Cottage living room, dustless and shut away from the marsh and the river outside. Ellen, she supposed, would sit gracefully in the green velvet chair, and Anson would lounge, poised and comfortable, on the big divan with its heavy blue fringe and silk tassels.

She scolded herself for being there and wished for the hundredth time she hadn't come. What do I know about planning meals for his mother and Ellen? What do I know about the way rich folks eat? At Black Banks before the evacuation, there had always been plenty of everything. But during the three years in which Deborah Gould huddled with her children around the wobbly old table in the shanty where they had found refuge in Burneyville, more than once she had been forced to explain that they didn't have enough to eat because Papa couldn't provide for them; he was away fighting in the War. "But we've got each other," Deborah would say, in her quiet voice, sipping her "coffee" brewed from parched corn, often eating nothing herself, so there would always be something on each child's plate. And Deborah had managed to keep them all well, a miracle directly traceable to her faith in God and her beloved Doctor's Book.

How Mama would love this room, Anna thought, and hoped Deborah could see it sometime, could enjoy a cup of tea from the china in the big glass closet in the hall. Dear, beautiful Mama. Prettier than any of her daughters; slight and straight, with a sweet mouth and large, black-fringed gray eyes. Anna studied her own face in a gilded, oval mirror. One thing sure, I don't look much like Mama. I look more like my brother James. She smiled, then frowned. Everyone knows James is good looking, including James, but it just looks plain on me! Then she stopped frowning, knowing what her father would say at this point, what he had said over and over during the difficult, lonely, uneventful years after the War, when the other Gould girls had been offered a formal education by relatives in the North—all except Anna. *But you're our Anna,* Papa would say, and it always warmed her and strengthened the already deep bond between father and daughter, because he never felt a need to elaborate. *You're our Anna* gave her identity enough to go on.

She missed her sisters, Angie, Jessie, Lizzie, Jennie, May and Helen, all married or working or in school up north, but it was almost as though they weren't her sisters any more. Life for Anna Gould was waking up every morning to still another day on St. Simons Island, glad with it under the sun, sad with it on rainy, dark days, but always a part of it, as the Island was a part of her. He sisters had left, but she would never leave, even if she could.

Anna and the Island belonged to each other, and she was content with it especially when she and the Island were alone under the piece of bright sky they shared. But here she stood waiting for the rich, overwhelming young man whose penetrating eyes so disturbed her that she had never been able to look at them long enough to discover their color; and she was rebelling. Not that he was going to marry someone named Ellen, but that she was trapped in Rose Cottage, aware of a growing panic at seeing him again, aware of an awkwardness that stiffened her body, aware of her desperate need to be outside with the Island, free of the soft carpets and the velvet and the polished wood.

Her bonnet was choking her; she untied it with a jerk, and stood holding it in her hands, wishing with all her heart she could run to the buggy and head back up Frederica Road where she belonged.

The kitchen door banged.

"Miss Anna? Miss Anna, where are you?"

She had never heard him raise his voice before.

"Here I am, Mr. Dodge."

He charged in, rubbing his hands together briskly, his thick black hair tousled from the rising wind outside. "Say, Procter is magnificent."

"I reckon he plied you with a thousand questions."

"He did. But that's good. There's no other way to learn."

Anna thought he looked much older than nineteen and, even with his hair mussed up, more impressive than anyone she knew except her father.

"In fact," Anson was saying, "Procter has be-witched me to such an extent that I doubt if I'll know whether his work is good or not."

"Oh, Procter'll do good work for you," Anna said earnestly.

"Come now, I'm not all that serious. You'll have to learn when I'm joking."

She felt like running away, but he took her bonnet and laid it on the hall table, and said they had better get busy.

"I'm afraid I don't know what you want me to do, Mr. Dodge. I really want to help you, but I hope you'll remember I'm just a country woman."

He looked at her sharply, as though he needed to decide this for himself. His eyes were dark, she guessed, but she looked away.

"I know you'll be patient with me," she stam-mered.

"No, I won't be. Patience is not one of my virtues. But I'm not expecting to need it with you."

"You'd better start expecting to need it, because you will."

Anson laughed. "Say, I like that. But I don't be-lieve you."

She almost managed a smile, and Anson, dismiss-ing the matter entirely, rubbed his hands together again and said it seemed to him the best place to start was with a confession: he didn't know any more about the house than she did, and suggested they take a tour to-gether. The stairs seemed steep as she climbed in silence to the second floor of Rose Cottage.

"Like this room?" he asked, as they stood in the doorway of a bedroom hung with white-fringed yellow draperies and carpeted with a thick yellow Brussels car-pet so lush with cabbage roses that Anna hesitated to step on it.

"Oh, yes! Yellow's my favorite color."

"This is going to be Ellen's room. I've already de-cided."

He hadn't mentioned Ellen to her before, appar-ently taking for granted Horace had told her everything. He was a mixture of courtesy and bluntness, she thought, and tried to concentrate on what he was saying.

"Ellen likes simplicity, even more than I do. I imagine we'll have quite a time furnishing our own home someday. Today's furnishings seem to be getting more and more elaborate. 'Gracious,' the dealers call it. Ellen calls it 'clutter.' "

They continued their tour, checking the linen supply, making lists, Anson opening closets, rubbing his hand over the highly polished furniture in each room, examining it for dust.

"I must say Sibby keeps this place clean."

"Sibby Jackson's a good cleaner, and a good woman," Anna said.

"Do you know Sibby?"

"Oh, yes, we all know each other on the Island. There wasn't but a handful of us till the Mills, you know."

Anson grew suddenly serious, and his black brows drew together. "I know the Island's economy needs them, but I wish the Mills weren't here. I wish this house weren't here. I wish it were at Frederica—in the woods near the church. Or near Black Banks. Do you know how fortunate you are to live up there, Miss Anna?"

Anna looked straight into his eyes this time. "Yes," she said, "I know."

And then he went back to being vigorous and impressive, and Anna turned her eyes away. "Well, now, if you know Sibby, why don't you go downstairs and tell her what to do about the kitchen? I'll only confuse her, and anyway, I don't think I can wait much longer to see how Procter's doing in the barn."

As soon as he was gone, Anna sighed with relief, gave herself a good talking to about the fact that she should know about kitchens if she knew anything at all, then went downstairs and pitched in with Sibby. And for the next hour the two women worked side by side.

Sibby was too fat to climb, so Anna was on a tall wooden stool, wiping off a high shelf, when she heard

Procter scream and Anson shout, "Miss Anna! Miss Anna! Come here—hurry!"

"Jesus have mercy, Miss Anna! Somepin's happen bad," Sibby moaned, wringing her hands.

Anna jumped to the floor and raced out the back door and across the side yard around the pomegranate hedge to the tabby barn. Procter was lying on the barn floor, sobbing and clutching his leg, rocking back and forth. Anson had ripped the boy's trousers and was holding his own necktie in a tight tourniquet just above two small bloody punctures on the calf of Procter's leg.

"Was it a rattler, Procter? Did you see it?"

"Yes, Ma'am, it was a diamon' back, an' I'm gonna die, Miss Anna, just when I got to workin' for Mr. Anson Greene"—he winced—"Phelps Dodge, Jr."

Anna examined the bite.

"Am I gonna die? Is this like dyin'?"

"Run for the doctor, Mr. Dodge. The last tabby house down the road toward the cypress mill. And hurry!"

Anson ran.

"Don't let me die, Miss Anna!" Procter clung to her.

"You don't want to do anything but lie stock still, now, to keep the blood from circulating any more than it has to."

"But it hurts—that tight thing hurts, worse an' worse."

"I know it does, but I can't turn it loose. It keeps the poison from going to your heart."

The boy lay against her, his eyes rolling, wide and scared. Anna rubbed his forehead and held him with her free hand.

"What the doctor gonna do to me, Miss Anna?"

"He'll fix that snakebite, Procter."

"I'm scared of a doctor. I want you to save my life, Miss Anna."

Procter began to cry again; Anna remembered he had never seen a doctor.

"Hush, hush, I'll be helping him, don't you worry."

But the boy grew frenzied with terror and was

clinging to Anna, choking and screaming, when they heard someone running toward the barn.

"Don't let him kill me, Miss Anna! Don't let the doctor kill me!"

Anson rushed in alone, carrying a bottle of turpentine and a knife. Anna knew Dr. Massey was not coming. "Sibby said he went to Brunswick on the mail boat. Won't be back today at all. She said to bring this."

He held out the knife.

Anna took it from him, her face white and, talking to Procter as hard as she could about being brave, did what she had to do. The boy screamed when the blade cut into his flesh, then caught his breath and held it as Anna placed her mouth over the wound and began to suck. Once, twice, three times she drew the venom into her mouth and spat it out on the barn floor.

She motioned for the turpentine. Procter screamed again when she splashed it into the open wound, and then the boy watched her, horrified, as she rinsed her mouth with the burning liquid.

The next minute Sibby was puffing into the barn loaded down with clean cloths, sheets, blankets, hot water and a box of Epsom salts. "Outa my way, Mist' Dodge." Seeing what Anna had already done, Sibby handed her the water for her mouth. "Don't say a word, Miss Anna, an' don' swallow. Keep spittin', chil'. Keep spittin'."

When Procter's leg had been swathed in hot salt packs, Anna helped Sibby spread a pallet for him on a pile of straw, loosed the tourniquet a little, and nodded to Sibby. For now, at least, they had done all they could do.

"Thank you, Jesus," Sibby breathed, "for Miss Anna Goul'."

"I'll put him to bed in the house tonight," Anson said.

Anna shook her head, and Sibby told him in no uncertain terms that Procter would not be moved at all until tomorrow.

"Who's gonna ride home in the buggy with you, Miss Anna?" Procter asked. "You can't ride up that road all by yourself."

"Don't worry about me. I'm staying right here with you tonight."

The boy lay back on the pallet and in a few minutes grew quiet.

Anna walked slowly to the barn door and stared out at the gray, turbulent afternoon. Dark, thick clouds were piling in from the ocean. The gulls wheeled noisily over the marsh, riding the erratic wind. "I declare, I believe it's going to storm," she said, smiling a little.

But Anson didn't smile. He was studying Anna intently. "I feel as though I've been hit by a locomotive," he said, "and all I did was watch."

She looked down at the barn floor, embarrassed.

"What manner of woman are you, Anna Gould?"

Chapter Six

Rebecca Dodge turned her teacup round and round in its saucer and studied Ellen's face across the table in the train's diner: a truly beautiful face, she thought, no feature incompatible with another. The heavy, brown hair, the straight proud nose, the full mouth, the dark eyes Ellen had learned already to guard naturally as she passed men in public—not noticeably, *naturally;* all her face was beautiful, as though it had been carefully created. But with Ellen, there was more than beauty, there was *life*. To look at her now, as she watched the dusky rows of pine trees slip past in the evening outside the train window, one felt the life within her, a spirit on tiptoe, alert, all interested in what it was destined to discover at any minute: the new thing, the unexpected, and yet, by Ellen, expected, because she was more at home with the potential of her years than anyone Rebecca Dodge had ever met. It will not surprise this child when her years ahead turn out to be glorious, Rebecca thought. She will be ready for them. She is one of the blessed few who will know what to do with joy.

Ellen forgot the landscape, turned back to Rebecca, and smiled. "You seem 'lost in your thoughts,' dear Rebecca, as they say in almost every magazine story."

"I was lost in my thoughts of you, and they interested me. You shouldn't have interrupted."

"Should I ask what you were thinking?"

"No. No girl is ever as humble as she should be at

seventeen. Not even you. So, don't ask. I was merely trying to gather up all the reasons why I believe you to be the kind of woman you are."

"Rebecca, Rebecca, can you believe we'll be in the same state with him tomorrow morning when we wake up?"

"When *you* wake up, my dear. I've never been known to sleep a wink in one of those berths. Oh, I admit they're better than sitting up as we used to do, but I only catnap."

"I tried to stay awake last night to savor every marvelous minute that moves us closer to him, but the clickety-clack of those train wheels always lulls me to sleep. In spite of our berths being so near the stove."

Rebecca reached for the check. "That clickety-clack carries a bumpity-bump with it, and every 'bumpity' bumps me the wrong way. There must be an art in learning to sleep on a railroad car not unlike learning to post on a horse. You've simply mastered it, my dear, and I haven't."

Ellen laughed, and Rebecca laughed with her, as she counted out the money.

"Even if I did learn to master the rhythm of the rails, child, I'd still lie there worrying about how I was going to get dressed the next morning!" Rebecca leaned across the table to whisper, "My dear, do you sleep in your corsets? Or do you punish yourself by having to struggle back into them in that lurching, cramped little dressing room of a morning?"

"I take them off! I'd much rather struggle for a few minutes in the morning when I'm fresh, than to feel like a jack-in-the-box with the lid closed all night. Take them off tonight—you'll sleep much better."

"Hm. Perhaps. But with my figure it's more than a few minutes' struggle the next morning. Anyway, I imagine I joggle less when I'm corseted. And, what if there's a train wreck or a robbery? I'm ready in that event, and look at you."

Ellen wrinkled her nose. "Train robberies only happen in the wild west on the frontier, dear Rebecca. And this train has a mission—it's not going to be wrecked."

Rebecca laid her money on the waiter's check, then poured hot tea into each of their cups. Ellen went back to watching the rows of pine trees, black now in the coming darkness, and Rebecca envied her her dreams. Being with Ellen made her remember when Anson's father filled her world. It seemed she had always been going to him, or waiting for him to come home; until more recent years, when even the waiting had come to an end.

"Do you wish your Anson were going to be there, Rebecca?"

The older woman set down her cup. "That is simply not fair, reading a woman's mind like that! I forbid it from now on."

Ellen smiled at her. "You're not very forbidding, even when you try to be. But forgive me, if I shouldn't have asked."

"Ask anything you like." Rebecca sighed. "I'm aware of how confusing it must be to you. After all, you've been in school abroad through most of these past ten years."

The waiter brought her change, bowed, and left. Rebecca placed a half dollar on the silver tray and slowly returned the bills to her pocketbook. "Did Anson tell you about the house his father built on the Island, Ellen?"

"The house? No. I'm afraid we didn't talk about houses during our few minutes on the telephone. What about it?"

"A. G. P. D. built a beautiful house at the Mills. Rose Cottage, it's called, because he's planted a spectacular rose garden around it. A house big enough and furnished for a family. And the first I heard of it was the other night when Anson called us."

Even Ellen could think of nothing to say.

"Well, our tea's gone. Let's go tackle those berths, Ellen. No reason why you shouldn't get some sleep. We arrive in Savannah at the crack of dawn."

The storm was almost there, now, and the northeast wind slammed against the tabby barn; slammed in angry, relentless gusts, rattling the windows, shaking the wooden doors.

Anson poke more pine splinters into the tiny iron stove he had found in his father's closet, as Horace wrung out another towel in the pan of salt water kept hot on top of the little stove.

"I don't think Procter's leg is jerking quite as much as it did, do you, Anson?"

Anson helped Horace wrap the hot towel around the boy's leg. Procter groaned, half asleep, half awake to his pain.

"He seems quieter. And I think the chilling's stopped. Your sister saved this boy's life."

"I hope it's saved. We all love him like a member of our family."

Anson sat down on a box and leaned back against the barn wall. "Your sister is an amazing woman. I wouldn't have expected her to act as she did this afternoon."

Horace smiled. "Oh, Anna knows how to get along with the Island, all right. She's had to learn. Knows how to get along with the good parts as well as the snakes."

"I like the way you said that—'Anna knows how to get along with the Island.' I envy her."

"Sister surprises you, Anson. I think she'd laugh at the idea of you envyin' her, but I also think she'd know pretty much what you mean by it. She loves this Island so much, she can tell in a minute when somebody else loves it."

"Your father is like that too, isn't he?" He sat up. "So are you, Horace." Anson's eyes were almost black in the flickering lantern light. "I'm different with you and your family. I never let down my guard with strangers. I even thought it bad taste. But I don't feel that way with the Goulds."

Procter groaned and tried to turn away from the pain. Both men bent over him, as the boy began to convulse violently, his eyes rolling, his muscular young body jerking; blood ran from his mouth, and one arm struck the sharp corner of the box where Anson had been sitting.

"Shall I run for Miss Anna, Horace?"

"No, she told me what to do. He's chewed his tongue bad. Hand me that piece of pine splinter there, Anson." Horace wrapped the pine in a linen towel and placed it between Procter's strong, white teeth. "Wring out another towel, Anson, and I'll try to keep him quiet as I can."

Horace stretched himself over the boy's writhing body, to protect him, as Anson struggled to wrap the flailing leg; and both men waited through the next frightening minutes, as the storm broke above them, slapping the roof with heavy sheets of rain. The horses stamped and whinnied at the rear of the barn and pushed against the wooden slats of their stalls, protesting the rain that found the leaks in the old roof and streamed down over their withers and backs.

Anson did all he could do to quiet the horses and promised himself he'd have the barn made tight against the next storm. Through the small window above the stalls, he could see the live oaks tossing their mossy arms against the sky, and the palm trees his father had planted were bent almost to the ground. The thunder crashed flat and hideous over the helpless Island, and out of the low bank of clouds, fingers of lightning picked at it without mercy, hunting a high tree to strike. But the boy on the straw pallet mattered most of all, and Anson didn't take time to wonder whether he still loved the Island in a storm. He was a part of it this night, and death could come in on one of those angry gusts, and the boy on the pallet would not be able to escape.

"How is he, Horace?"

"Still bad, Anson," Horace gasped, balancing himself on his arms above the boy's jerking body. "Maybe not quite as bad as he was. One good thing, he doesn't know anything about it."

On his knees in order to see Procter better, Anson wanted to pray.

"Pray, Anson," Horace begged.

"I'm trying to, Horace."

Every word that came to his mind flattened before he could say it, as the wind flattened the sodden moss against the trees outside.

"I'll pray for Procter in a minute." Anson's voice was strained, but definite. And in that minute, he faced the guilt he had refused even to look at until now; guilt that stood blocking his prayer for the boy like a thick stone wall. *"God, forgive me for striking my father,"* he breathed.

And then he prayed for Procter.

Ellen unbuttoned the heavy tasseled curtains around her upper berth and saw that the oil lamp was burning in the lower where Rebecca was in bed.

"Rebecca?" she whispered.

"Yes, my dear—why aren't you asleep?"

"I'm coming down to talk."

Not bothering to call the porter for a ladder, Ellen climbed nimbly out of her berth and lowered herself until her toe found the iron bar under Rebecca's bed.

"My goodness, child, hold on until I get these buttons opened!"

"I'm part monkey," Ellen whispered, as she crawled into Rebecca's berth and curled up at her feet.

"I thought you'd been asleep for hours, Ellen! Couldn't you get the rhythm tonight?"

"I'm too excited. But isn't it fun to be shut away together like this with all our happiness? I wish we had something to make a party, don't you? What are you reading?"

"My old favorite, Wordsworth."

Ellen reached for the small, worn leather volume. "Hm, you're a romantic, Rebecca—you've been reading 'Tintern Abbey.' I wouldn't want some of my friends to know it, but I love Wordsworth, too."

"He isn't very fashionable now, I know," Rebecca said. "But I still need him."

Rebecca leaned back on her pillows, and spoke the beloved lines from memory.

"For I have learned
To look on nature, not as in the hour
Of thoughtless youth, but hearing oftentimes
The still, sad music of humanity,

Nor harsh nor grating, though of ample power
To chasten and subdue. . . ."

"What do you hear when you hear the 'still, sad music of humanity?' " the girl asked.

Rebecca smiled. "Not as much as I should. Not as much as your Grandfather Dodge hears, I'm sure. I sometimes feel he hears the very heartbeat of every human being in the world. Of course, he doesn't. Only God hears like that. But he listens, your Grandfather Dodge, for the 'still, sad music of humanity'—all humanity."

"So do you," Ellen protested. "Oh, so do you! I've often thought you are good and generous and kind and sensitive enough to have been my Grandfather Dodge's daughter."

"Thank you, Ellen. But I'm not. I'm a rather self-centered woman, and, as you say, a romantic. I'm afraid when I read 'Tintern Abbey,' I hear something quite personal."

"Do you hear the 'still, sad music' of your own humanity?"

"I suppose so. But—" It was night, and they were utterly alone and closed in together, and Ellen was Ellen. What good is my everlasting reserve? Rebecca thought, and then she said, "I also hear the still, sad music of my husband's—humanity."

Ellen remained quiet.

"He's not all bad, Ellen." Rebecca spoke after a long silence. "He began with hope and purpose, like his father and his brothers—like your father, Stuart. Somewhere along the years, he got lost from the others. Now, I don't think he even knows he is lost."

"Do you think Anson is afraid he might be like his father, Rebecca?"

"Why do you ask that?"

"You know I don't have the slightest doubt that Anson loves me, that he wants to marry me as much as I want to marry him. But—"

"But, what? Don't lead up to it, my dear, tell me!"

"It's nothing bad, dear Rebecca, it's good. The

night before Anson left for St. Simons Island, he got that solemn, serious look in his eyes, and said, 'Do you know I love you enough *not* to marry you at all, my darling, if I discover there is the slightest chance that I might do to you what my father has done to my mother?' "

Rebecca looked down at her hands a moment and then straight at Ellen. "Your Anson will not get lost as his father is lost because he will have *you*."

The train wheels began to grind beneath them, and the car lurched. They were stopping somewhere in the black night, beside a row of shacks or a drygoods store, closed and dark until morning. One or two passengers might get off, or perhaps they would only take on wood or water. Up ahead, the whistle blew; the train lurched again and bumped and stopped, its steam escaping noisily. They could hear the rain now, but neither woman bothered to raise the blind to look out.

"My son will never get lost, Ellen. He will have you." Rebecca looked at the small gold watch pinned to her nightgown. "It's almost four o'clock, my dear. We'll be in Savannah in two hours."

The rain had stopped falling on St. Simons just after Anna and Sibby relieved Anson and Horace at four in the morning, but the wind still battered the barn and trumpeted eerily in the high frame of the Big Mill like a lone, sad horn. Anna held Procter in her arms now. His convulsion was over, but he lay almost lifeless against her.

"He ain't gonna die, Miss Anna. Procter ain't gonna die." Sibby shook the scalding water from her hands and wrapped his leg in still another hot towel. "Procter gonna live, dat boy. Gonna run an' jump aroun' good as new. Did you hear what Sibby say, Procter?"

"He can't hear you. He's fainted again. But don't try to bring him around this time. Let's just let him rest. He's suffered so much."

"Yes, 'um," Sibby said, her cheeks wet with tears. "Yes, 'um, so *much*."

The women did what they could do for him

through one more convulsion, and then for two hours he was quiet.

"Two hours, Sibby, and he's still here."

"Procter ain't gonna die, Miss Anna." Sibby hoisted herself to her full five feet. "The boy gonna pull through. We prayed, an' Sibby's standin' on that. The Lord tol' me Procter ain't gonna die, an' Sibby's standin' on that. You stan' on it too, Miss Anna, you hear me?"

"Yes, Sibby. I hear you."

"You standin' on it, Miss Anna?"

"Yes, I'm standing on it." She tightened her arms around the boy's shoulders. "Procter is going to get well."

In Savannah, Ellen arranged excitedly for their trunks and valises to be transferred from the train from New York City to the tiny, dark-red day coach of the Southern line which would take them to Sterling, ten miles from Brunswick, Georgia.

"Two hours and fifty endless minutes, Rebecca— and then we can hop aboard that magnificent little chariot over there! But, at least, that should give them time to move our things. I didn't mean to bring so many bags, did you?"

"I never mean to travel so loaded down. But I always do."

Ellen laughed. "We may be going to some isolated little spot where we'll never dress! I don't care, do you? We're not going to dress up, are we?"

"No, my dear, *we're going to be with that boy*."

"And Rebecca Dodge, do you realize we'll be with him tonight? This very night, he'll meet us at the hotel in Brunswick!"

"Indeed I do realize it. But right now, in spite of my excitement and my poundage, I'm starved. Let's eat a huge, lumberman's breakfast."

"All right, with ham and eggs and—what do they eat down here?" Ellen snapped her fingers. "Uh—grits. Ham and eggs and grits."

"And biscuits," Rebecca added, patting her waistline. "After all, there'll be nothing but sandwiches—those dreadful dry bread sandwiches on that little train. And even after we reach Sterling we have a carriage ride to the hotel."

"Do you think he'll surprise us and be at Sterling instead of the hotel, Rebecca?"

"My dear, how could anyone possibly surprise you? You think of everything first!"

"Look, Miss Anna, the sun's comin' up again, same as usual, an' the wind's dyin' down. The Lord's still in charge."

"Yes, Sibby. And Procter's quiet now. No more spasms. No more chills. Sound asleep."

"That's git-well sleep he's catchin' now. Git-well sleep for Procter."

Anna laid the boy's head back on the big feather pillow and stood up to stretch her cramped body. "I feel as if I'd grown to that pile of straw."

"You a kind, good woman, Miss Anna Goul'."

"Hush up, Sibby, and go in and fix us some coffee."

"You need more than coffee, Miss Anna."

"No. Just coffee. I don't think I could swallow any food. Not yet. Not till Dr. Massey gets here and tells us Procter's all the way out of danger."

Chapter Seven

Rebecca and Ellen walked up the wide stone steps from the carriage entrance of the hotel in Brunswick, Georgia, alone. Anson had not met them at the station. And he was nowhere in sight now. Neither spoke, but both watched eagerly, shielding their eyes against the midafternoon sun, looking for the familiar energetic walk; one shoulder hunched a little higher than the other, the dark head tilted impatiently forward.

Inside the hotel, people strolled or swept past them across the ornate lobby, the men carrying bowlers and wearing spats, the women with bows on their bustles, bows down their flounced and bunched-up skirts—some with their skirts too full for the year 1879.

"The women are rather fashionable, Ellen. I'm somewhat surprised, and glad." Rebecca's mind wasn't really on the people around them, but she was putting off the inevitable moment when one of them would have to come right out and say that Anson was not there as he had promised.

"I couldn't be less interested in what the Southern woman is wearing, Rebecca." In the middle of the high vaulted lobby, Ellen stopped, stricken. "He's not here. He's just not here, and I was foolish enough to think he'd surprise us and take a carriage to the station!"

"Don't jump to conclusions, my dear." Rebecca was still looking around, watching both entrances to the hotel lobby. "After all, Anson had to come from a remote little island, and heaven only knows what their transportation is like down here."

"He's been here long enough to find out," Ellen snapped. "He could have made allowance for slow transportation, unless—" Her face clouded. "Oh, Rebecca, what if something has happened to him?"

A uniformed bellboy walked toward them, calling, "Missus Anson Dodge, paging Missus Anson Dodge."

"Here I am, boy." Rebecca took the telegram from his tray and handed it to Ellen to read.

The girl's hands trembled as she unfolded the yellow paper and read aloud: "DELAYED BY ILLNESS OF ONE OF THE SERVANTS GO TO YOUR ROOMS AND WAIT FOR ME ANSON" She read it again, her incredulity growing. "Rebecca, 'the illness of one of the servants'? Is this enough to keep him from meeting *us*? Isn't there anyone else in that whole magnificent lumber operation who could take care of a sick servant? Does Anson have to do that in person? 'Go to your rooms and wait for me,' indeed!"

Rebecca patted her arm. "Come, my dear, let's do just that, and then we can think what we want to think in private. I'm sure he's reserved our rooms. After all, we weren't planning to leave for the Island until tomorrow morning."

"I don't care when we go to that miserable Island. I want to see Anson!"

"No one can blame you for being hurt, but—"

"I'm not hurt. I'm furious. No woman wants to be more excited about seeing a man than he is about seeing her!"

Angry because she was beginning to cry, Ellen crumpled the telegram and threw it into a big brass spittoon.

Procter's pain was almost gone, and he had enjoyed every minute of his ride up Frederica Road. Bedded down in a big, roomy mill wagon on a pallet Sibby made, the boy loved looking up at the changing bright-dark sky and right into the branches of the red gum trees and the yellow nut trees, and most of all it made him happy that Miss Anna, herself, was driving him home, with his new friend, Mr. Anson Greene Phelps Dodge, Jr., riding along on Bessie to escort them. Dr. Massey had said he would be all right, and Miss Anna had cried, and this made Procter happy. Not that he wanted her to cry, but she had explained that sometimes a woman cries when she's glad.

"It won't be long now," Anson said, dropping back to trot alongside Procter, lying in the wagon bed. "We'll be there in no time." The boy already knew this, because he had been listening to the frogs singing in the savannah just below the Black Banks road.

"I sure am glad you rode with us, Mr. Anson Greene Phelps Dodge, Jr. I reckon you really had to protect me an' Miss Anna, didn't you?"

"Well, you were hurt working for me. It's my responsibility to be sure you get home safely."

"He shouldn't have come at all, Procter," Anna said. "We'd have made out fine."

Anson laughed. "Don't listen to her this time, Procter. I'll get back to the Mills in plenty of time to catch the *Ruby* at six o'clock, and I'll be in Brunswick in a little over an hour after that."

"*If* the tide's with you," Anna warned.

"The tide will be with me, don't worry. I think even the tide knows how much I want to get there, Miss Anna."

Rebecca poured more tea. They had ordered a light supper in their rooms, most of which sat on the table before them untouched.

"Help me, Rebecca!"

"Child, drink your tea, and try to calm down. I'm sure we'll hear from him soon."

"I don't want to hear from him—I want to *see* him." Ellen got up abruptly and began to pace the big sitting room. "Why didn't he tell us in that pompous telegram when he'd arrive? Don't these boats run on a schedule? After all, Reconstruction has been going on for thirteen years!"

"I know exactly what you know, Ellen—nothing. We'll just have to wait for him."

"But something in me hates having that beautiful

moment spoiled! Every mile of that long train trip, I'd been living for the moment when I'd see him again. Now it's gone."

"It isn't gone. Nothing is gone but your own preconceived idea of that moment. Anson will be here. Nothing but the circumstance has changed."

Ellen tossed back the curls from her forehead. "This is the first time he's done anything like this to me, Rebecca. How long did it take you to learn to be so patient?"

"Years. But you're quicker than I."

"How do you know I am? Maybe you're all wrong about me."

"No, I am not wrong about you. But this is not a matter for the years. Your problem is a readjustment for right now."

"Rebecca, help me. Don't let me cry. I spoil my eyes when I cry. Maybe I'll never understand him."

"You can learn."

"But shouldn't a woman know by instinct how to understand the man she loves?"

"It takes more than instinct to know a man as complex as my son. Which is one of the reasons you love him. He challenges you."

Ellen's face was wet with tears. "I wish we'd all three go right back to New York City!"

"My dear girl, you're angry with *yourself* for losing your poise. Don't be. Don't make the mistake of deciding anything on the basis of one disappointment."

There was a sharp knock at the door.

"Good heavens, Ellen, there's the waiter for our table, and you haven't eaten a bite."

"I'll tell him to come back for it later." Ellen dried her eyes. "Oh, Rebecca, Rebecca, can a woman love a man too much?"

"Yes, I suppose so. But that kind of love happens so seldom, any woman should hold onto it, no matter what."

There was another knock, and Ellen hurried to the door, opened it, hesitated for an instant, and fell weeping and laughing into Anson's arms.

Chapter Eight

The morning was soft and gray as a dove's wing when Anson followed Rebecca and Ellen up the narrow gang plank onto the *Ruby* at the pier in Brunswick. He had hoped for a brilliant sunrise, wanting Ellen to be captivated at once with St. Simons Island, as he had been, and all through breakfast at the hotel, he had not stopped talking about what it would be like when the sun broke through later on.

As the little steamer paddled away from the noise and confusion of Brunswick harbor, out into the Sound, following the channel through the quiet, marsh-bordered inlet past Brunswick Point and neighboring Jekyll Island, Anson settled his mother on a wooden bench on deck, then went to stand beside Ellen at the ship's railing. He was still telling her about the sunsets, and the light at noon on Frederica Road; about the giant, twisted oaks, the frosty-blue cedar berries, the Island birds, and his new friends, the Goulds of Black Banks. And over and over he said, "Ellen, wait till you see that little churchyard!"

He had laughed when his mother mentioned that Ellen was unusually quiet; not distant, no longer angry with him—the first sight of him had ended that—but quiet. "Don't overdo your travelogue, my dear," she had warned, but he only laughed again and kissed her.

"St. Simons Island isn't a little town, or even a village, Ellen," he was saying. "It's just—the Island, the most breathtaking part of Glynn County. Those

stretches of marsh out there are the marshes of Glynn,
and the Island is not only patched with them, in some
places they extend all the way to the sea. I haven't even
seen the ocean yet, I've been so—"

"*These* are the marshes of Glynn?" Ellen interrupted, her eyes wide. "Anson, slow down for a minute.
Did you say these are the marshes of Glynn?"

"Yes." He turned to her, puzzled but delighted by
her sudden enthusiasm. "Why, darling?" He laughed.
"You look transfixed."

"I am! Oh, I *am* transfixed. To think, just to think,
only last week I discovered that poem, and now here I
am floating among 'the length and the breadth of the
marvelous marshes of Glynn'!"

"What poem?" He watched as she spread her arms
toward the marshes and the sky, oblivious to everything
but her discovery.

"An obscure poet named Lanier, darling. I found
him only last week, and *these* are his marshes!

> "*Ye marshes, how candid and simple and noth-
> ing-withholding and free Ye publish yourselves to
> the sky and offer yourselves to the sea!*"

"That's beautiful," he said, "but you can do even
better. *You* write an Island poem for me!"

"It's been *written*, Anson. I've just told you. Sh-h,
let me try to remember more of it:

> "*As the marsh-hen secretly builds on the watery sod,
> Behold I will build a nest on the greatness of God:
> I will fly in the greatness of God as the marsh-hen flies
> In the freedom that fills all the space 'twixt the marsh
>   and the skies.*"

Hers was the kind of beauty that touched and per-
plexed him: her gallant, nearly boyish figure, whipped
by the freeblowing wind off the water; her grace, un-
consciously sensuous for one so young; her thick, dark
hair welcoming the flying wind, as Ellen welcomed every vital thing. But she was unaware of his eyes upon
her, utterly taken up with remembering the poem and
responding to the marsh.

*"By so many roots as the marsh-grass sends in the sod
I will heartily lay me ahold on the greatness of God:
Oh, like to the greatness of God is the greatness within
The range of the marshes, the liberal marshes of Glynn."*

He studied her face. Why did her beauty baffle him? he wondered. Was it because Ellen had laid "ahold on the greatness of God" in a way he didn't understand? Was this the reason she seemed at home anywhere? Was this the secret behind her ready laughter and her capacity for joy? Did Ellen possess some secret path to the Source of all joy? She seldom spoke of God, but standing beside her, on this soft, cloudy morning, he realized how often he related his joy in her to his concept of a joy in God which so far he had missed.

"Oh, darling, you've found the marshes of Glynn for me!"

She hugged him, laughing, her dark eyes full of lights, even without the sun.

Wanting them to have time alone, Anson suspected, Rebecca had demanded some rest, and by late morning of their first day on St. Simons Island, he and Ellen were riding through the spangled light and shadows up Frederica Road toward Christ Church. The insistent sun had routed the clouds, and with her beside him, sitting her horse as only Ellen could, the long, full skirt of her riding habit as black as her mount, Anson was even more captivated by the beloved road.

For the first mile or so, he had issued exuberant commands: "Look at the yellow grape leaves, Ellen. Look at the moss in the sunlight. Look, darling, at the red gums and the butternut trees and the ferns growing right on the branches of the oaks. Look anywhere, anytime, and you find beauty enough to make you weep."

Half an hour later, trotting slowly along the narrow white shell road, under the roof of tree branches tangling colors over their heads, they were not talking at all: Ellen content to be with him, Anson feeling vaguely uneasy that she had loved the marshes more than she seemed to love his woods.

"The marshes are nothing compared with this, are they?" he ventured.

Ellen laughed. "Is that what's bothering you, Anson Dodge?"

"There's nothing bothering me!"

"Oh, yes, there is. Let's stop—right here."

They reined in their horses, and she was on the ground first, holding out her arms to him. There could be no more glorious spot on earth for a man to kiss the woman he loves, Anson thought, and she read his thoughts.

"Even you do not have a mind capable of concentrating on these woods *and* me at the same time. I love you, sir. Kindly concentrate only on me for just a few minutes?"

And he did.

"Now, you may go embrace a tree, if you like." She laughed breathlessly, still holding his face in her hands.

"Why did you say that?"

"Wouldn't you like to hug a tree now, my serious beloved?"

"I did hug a tree," he said simply. "The first day I rode up here, I hugged a live oak tree."

She stopped laughing. "Dear Anson, did you?"

"Yes."

"I do love you," she murmured. "Anson Dodge, I do love you with all my being. I love all the ways you are, and all the ways you can ever be."

He wanted to tell her about his father, about what he had learned of himself in the past days on St. Simons, but she was kissing him again, laughing again.

"I love your Island, too, Anson. But you must give me time to get as excited as you are. You get in my way. It's difficult for me to see anything else when I can look at you."

"You saw the marshes." He grinned.

"But we were in public on the deck of a boat!"

"I'm jealous of this Lanier fellow."

"Oh, but he wrote about your woods too, darling—in the same poem! He called them 'beautiful glooms, soft dusks in the noon-day fire,—Wildwood privacies, closets of lone desire.' " She smoothed his eyebrow. "He also called them the 'dim sweet woods, . . . the dear dark woods.' "

Anson brightened. "He did?"

"Yes, he did. Now are you happy?"

He held her and held her there on the empty little road, in the "beautiful glooms," in the "soft dusks in the noon-day fire. . . ."

They hitched their horses at the same tree across from the churchyard, and now she was there as he had wanted her to be the first time he saw it. She was there now to hear him say, "Ellen—look at that brave little church!"

"I'm looking, darling, I'm looking. Tell me about it. What battered it so?"

He told her all that Horace Bunch Gould had told him about the desecration of little Christ Church, and Ellen's eyes filled with pain as she listened.

"Let's mend it, Anson! Let's you and me mend it."

He stared at her.

"Why not? We can do it. Let's make a gift to these new friends of yours of a beautifully mended little church—or a new one."

He had meant to lead up to this carefully, and Ellen's sudden offer disturbed him. His caring for the people of St. Simons Island had grown too deep for what he called typical Dodge *largesse,* no matter how sincerely it was given. They were both rich in their own right; rebuilding the church would be simple. But instead of joy at her impulse, he was troubled. "What is it, Anson? You're frowning. Didn't you have this in your mind already?"

They stood in the churchyard hand in hand, Ellen looking at him intently, Anson looking away toward the guardian trees.

"Anson Dodge! Look at me. Did I say the wrong thing? It seems to me the least we can do is rebuild the church for these poor people."

Afraid of saying too much too quickly, he said

nothing. Ellen began walking alone toward the church; and then he hurried after her.

"I've gotten off the track somewhere, darling." She smiled bravely. "Give me a chance to understand where." Then she took his hand and led him toward the little cemetery. "In the meantime, let's read every inscription on every single stone, and make up the people."

Ellen ran toward a small, tilted granite slab, and read: *"Children of Theodore and Catherine A. Dodge.* Darling, had *we* gotten down here too? In the year 1827?" Her voice grew tender. "Two infants . . . *Theodore, aged two months, born and died 1827, and Cornelia M., aged two months, born and died 1828.* How sad, Anson. But they missed ever having a heartache, didn't they? And even if they'd lived, they couldn't have been as happy as we are. No one ever has been!"

They walked on, Ellen unmindful of the prickly burrs her long skirt gathered.

"Look here!" She laughed merrily. "Here, under these mossy bricks, lies *Lt. Colonel Wardrobe. Died 1812.* Now, what do you suppose were the viewpoints of stalwart Lt. Colonel Wardrobe, aged fifty?" She folded her arms and looked solemn.

Anson could not laugh. "He must have died in the War of 1812," he said. "Horace Bunch Gould was born in 1814. It was a terrible war. Even after the armistice, the fighting went on. Hundreds of men died for nothing."

Ellen tried again. "Stevens, Postell, Armstrong . . . acres and acres of them. They must be *the* aristocracy."

Anson failed even to manage a smile. The Postell descendants were still on the Island, among the few remaining communicant families of Christ Church, Horace Bunch had said. The Postells were people, not "aristocracy."

"Anson," she called, running ahead, then kneeling to read the lengthy inscription cut into a large, squarely impressive marble monument. "Listen to this: *John Couper, born at Lochwinnoch, Scotland, 9 March, 1759 . . .*

died at Hopeton, Georgia, 24 March, 1850. Endowed with a fine intellect, a cheerful and amiable disposition, and most liberal and benevolent feelings, his long life was devoted to the duty of rendering himself most acceptable to his Creator by doing the most good for His creatures. Darling, this worthy gentleman could easily have been a philanthropic Dodge! Doesn't all that benevolence sound familiar?"

But still Anson could not laugh. John Couper had been a dear friend of Horace Bunch.

Ellen turned away, puzzled by his silence. As she stooped to read a solidly lettered word *Resurgemus!* on the base of a marker to someone named Margaret, she smiled up at him weakly and then forgot the old markers. "Darling, what am I doing wrong? I'm lost."

He walked toward her and took her in his arms. "I wish we could get inside that church!"

"So do I, but we can't. What is it, Anson? What have I done wrong?"

"If we could kneel together at that broken altar, we would be all right again. I know we would."

She pulled away from him.

"What's wrong with us? What's happened? Don't be cruel, Anson!"

He reached for her hand, but she wasn't finished.

"It's something about this place. We were happy until we walked into this churchyard. What is it? I think it's lovely and sad and important—I didn't meant to be making fun of the people buried here. You've laughed with me before at funny, quaint old mottos and epitaphs. What have I done wrong?"

Anson stared at the ground.

"Did it happen when I wanted to rebuild the church?" She paused, studying his face. "Yes, it did."

"No, Ellen, I want to do that too!"

"Then why be angry with me when I agree?"

"I'm not angry."

"Then what are you?"

"I don't know. Something changed in me in this churchyard the first day I came here alone. And I've been terrified ever since that you wouldn't understand it just exactly the way it was."

"And now you think I don't." She sighed. "Well, I don't. But it isn't because I don't want to understand. You haven't told me anything. You've just been peculiar. Anson, please tell me. This isn't fair."

They sat down on the sagging wooden church steps, and Anson told her how he had felt the people in this churchyard belonged to him, and he to them. He grew excited again, as he talked, reliving the hour he spent there alone, running from plot to plot, coming alive inside as one comes alive after a long journey, when home is in sight. He told her of his fears of being like his father; he told her what his father had said the evening he left.

"Mother and I are no longer a part of his life in any way. He's through with us. He's gone."

And then he told her of striking his father, and of his prayer for forgiveness when Procter Green lay in the Rose Cottage barn, near death. He told her about Anna Gould's courage, and her brother's kindness to him. He told her he had a new father in Horace Bunch Gould. And then, he tried to make her understand the most difficult part.

"Up here that first morning, I felt clear with God about myself. I knew then, for the first time, that it was safe for me to marry you."

Her hand tightened on his arm, but she said nothing.

"I went back to the Mills that night, after my visit with Mr. Gould at Black Banks, feeling hopeful again. I was so free of myself, I even felt hopeful that the four years he lived here had changed A. G. P. D. too. And then"—he clenched and unclenched his hands—"he said what he said, and I struck him."

"He drove you to it!"

"But Ellen, this frightened me more than his leaving. I ran out of the house and walked and walked. Then I sat by the marsh until I heard the whistle when his boat docked in Brunswick. I stayed there a long time, trying to find again what I'd found here that morning. All I could think of was that when he had hurt me, I had hit back. I was like him again, and afraid for you. I had trusted myself for one short day! And I failed. I tried to blame him for what I did. I did blame him. But it didn't help. I got up to start back to the Mills and suddenly, somewhere near a big live oak tree where I stood, God was there. It came as clear as a bell to me there beside that oak tree that it needn't matter any more than I was A. G. P. D.'s son. What mattered was that I am also God's son."

"You became your true self." Her voice was quiet.

"How did you know that?"

"You just told me, and you're much more persuasive than you realize, dear heart. You'd make a far greater preacher than my father ever could be, sweet as he is."

Anson jumped to his feet, and stood looking down at her. "Don't joke about that, Ellen," he said hoarsely. "Don't say anything—just tell me you *are* going to marry me."

"Yes, Anson, I'm going to marry you." She stood up and slipped her arms around his neck.

Instead of kissing her, he held her head against his shoulder, not daring to look at her as he spoke. "I want you more than I've ever wanted anything—except to become the minister to the people of this church."

She didn't move.

"Ellen?"

Still she clung to him, her thoughts rejecting what he had said, rejecting the life her mother had known with her father as a minister's wife, rearing her children almost alone, waiting for him through all those long trips while he served God and missed knowing his family. She saw the self-righteous faces of the church members who had tried to run her mother's life, down to criticizing her children's behavior and the way she dressed them—"as unbecoming the children of a man of God." Anson on this lonely, isolated Island, parish priest to a handful of country people? Her brilliant, dynamic Anson a country parish priest?

"Ellen?"

"I acted like a horrible spoiled brat last night before you finally reached the hotel. I knew I'd have to confess it sooner or later."

He held her away from him and studied her face.

She was trying to smile. "What does that have to do with this?" he asked.

"More than I like to admit. I was jealous last night of the poor little boy with the snakebite. I was jealous of this whole Island."

"Ellen, a minister's wife can't be jealous."

"Give me a minute, Anson!" she flared. "Give me time to take this in before you begin to lecture me."

For a while neither of them said anything, and then he asked a question no one had ever asked her before.

"Ellen, is God real to you?"

"*God?*"

"You have always been so full of life and—joy. I know you were a lonely little girl, away from your family for such long periods because of your father's work, but it hasn't marked you. I want that kind of joy, too. I don't find joy anywhere, but in *you*. Is God more real to you than He is to me?"

Why was he forever catching her off guard? Why couldn't he be predictable just once? Why must he force her to think things through when all she wanted was to love him and laugh?

"You can teach me to laugh, Ellen. You can untangle me from all the graveclothes of my old fear of myself. I'll believe you if you tell me right now that God is your secret."

For the first time since she had begun to love him, she wanted to escape his piercing eyes. What right did he have to turn the questioning on her? Wasn't he the one who thought God had called him?

"Teach me to laugh, Ellen. Show me how to know joy, the way you know it. If a minister is to help his people, he must help them to find joy."

Hadn't he noticed her struggle at all? Was he so set on becoming the shepherd of this straggly little Island flock he couldn't see what she was going through?

"Ellen, is God real to you?"

He would never be put off. Never. Ellen looked away from him toward the tall oaks and faced herself with his question. Yes, God was real to her. She had not been able to admit this to her father and mother. To do

that would have seemed like defeat. All her life she had
been a rebel against what she thought was too much
religion, not enough joy. God to her was someone she
could hum little songs with, someone to listen to her
poetry. She had refused to insult Him by putting on a
Sabbath manner with Him. God was her Friend, but to
have admitted He was the same God her father
preached about in sepulchral tones, banging the pulpit
with his fist, would have meant defeat to her. Her God
was a God of joy and laughter and music. And not always hymns, either! It had surely been God, looking
like Jesus Christ, to whom she had talked, alone in her
bed at boarding school in Switzerland, away from her
family. He had always listened to the news of her heart-
aches and triumphs. It had been His voice reaching her
in the exultant thunder rollicking across the sky. Ellen
had never been afraid of storms because, for her, God
was in them. His voice had reached her in the wind that
blew on the mountains she had climbed, off the oceans
she had crossed. She had been alone much of her short
life, but it startled her when Anson called her childhood
lonely. She had seldom felt lonely; there had always
been her Friend who loved her. Their friendship was
such a happy habit, she had almost never stopped to
think about it. And He had always been as natural with
her as she had been with Him. Just this morning, His
voice had come dear and familiar to her in the wind
across the marshes of Glynn.

He spoke now, in the deserted little churchyard: *Be
not afraid, it is I*. Whether or not Anson was off on an
impetuous tangent, God was in this with them. She had
never quite realized it before, but it was clear to Ellen
at that moment, that more truly than she had ever
known, she had built her "a nest on the greatness of
God." Dear, beloved, serious Anson had forced her to
look into her heart, into the self she had always taken
for granted, into the Friendship she had been content
merely to accept and not evaluate. The precocious,
carefree child rebel was gone. In that breath of time,
Ellen, the woman, recognizing the Source of her joy and
her strength, had been born. She could thank her parents for teaching her always to include God even though

she had rebelled at what she called their stuffiness. She could thank them too, she supposed, that His presence had remained real to her, so that she hadn't minded too much that they had been off serving Him for most of her life.

She looked at Anson steadily, her head high. "Yes, darling, God is real to me."

Ellen held out her arms, but he took her hands. "What does He tell you about this place—and us? Do you want to be here as much as I do?"

He was pushing her too fast again. "Oh, Anson, I adore this dear place. But, please, if you love me, give me time!"

Chapter Nine

At mid-morning of their first Sunday on St. Simons Island, Rebecca Dodge rode with Anson and Ellen in A. G. P. D.'s splendid buggy, up Frederica Road to share dinner and Evening Prayers with the Goulds at Black Banks. They were nearing the Black Banks road when Rebecca forced herself to stop thinking.

Anson had come to her room that morning to tell her his father had lied about the telegram calling him to handle a labor crisis in the Pennsylvania operation: A. G. P. D. was leaving the country. Canada, he had said. Anson had put it off for a night and a day, dreading to be the one to bring this final blow to her; hating to be the one to tell her they were cut out of his father's life at last. There would be no more pretending, no more forced encounters, no more reason to hope.

Her sons's tenderness when he told her had broken her reserve. He was no longer the indulged boy, depending upon her to fix it somehow. Rebecca had wept on his shoulder for the first time. Then, deliberately, she had shut off her tears. "I love your Island, Anson, but I do wish it had a church. I need to go to church today."

All the way from Rose Cottage to the Black Banks turnoff, both young people had been unusually quiet, in deference to her, she knew; sensing her painful, awkward, anticlimactic grief over her husband. They had not made her uncomfortable in their silence; they had held her in it. But now, she must release them. This day

meant too much to Anson. They were going to meet his
new friends, the Goulds, and it was obvious how important this was to him. She must enter into whatever lay
ahead. And so she stopped her thoughts and gave her
attention to Ellen, who was saying something about the
narrow, winding Black Banks plantation road, curving
mysteriously back through a half mile of Island woods.

"What a sense of drama these people have, giving
one all this delicious time to anticipate what's at the end
of the road." Ellen shivered with delight and reached up
to trail her fingertips through the hanging moss as the
buggy rocked along under the low branches of the big
trees.

"There's a treasure at the end of *this* road, all
right," Anson said, so seriously that Rebecca hoped
nothing would occur today to cause any more tension
between him and Ellen.

Ellen had told her what happened in the churchyard at Frederica yesterday, and his mother prayed he
would take one day at a time. She had fallen asleep last
night trying to imagine her son the rector of a small
Island parish; but since her talk with Anson this morning too much of A. G. P. D. had crowded her thoughts
to allow room for anxiety or even confusion over what
Ellen had told her.

"I'm sure there's treasure at the end of this road,
darling," Ellen agreed, but Rebecca caught her look of
apprehension.

Then, around the last turn in the road, the Goulds
were waving from the piazza of the Black Banks house,
and the gate in the white picket fence stood open to welcome them.

Sunday dinner at Black Banks was fried chicken,
gravy, biscuits, rice, collards, berry cobbler, laughter at
James's jokes, good talk, and—Rebecca realized—for
her son a new kind of joy. It amused her that Ellen had
obviously startled them all somewhat by her utter lack
of shyness, her knowledge of politics and history, her
humor with James. But, she thought, Anson is almost
too delighted that his friends had accepted Ellen. More
than accepted, she had completely charmed them. Even

that rather phlegmatic Anna. Rebecca found them all most agreeable, except perhaps for Anna. Poor girl. Though what chance did another young woman have with Ellen in the room? I do like the parents, Rebecca admitted, especially Deborah Gould's quaint way of addressing her husband as "Mr. Gould, dear."

Yes, it's good to be here, she decided, entering the parlor with the others. Extra chairs had been placed in a small, careful circle, and a skinny young man in his Sunday best brown suit and striped silk shirt sat straight as a ramrod on a spindle-backed kitchen chair, waiting, his Prayer Book already open in his lap, a yellowing straw sailor hat set squarely on his head. When he saw them, he laid his hat quickly on the floor and stood up. The Goulds greeted him warmly, thanked him for fixing the chairs again, and, as they introduced him to the Dodges, explained that Mackbeth Postell hadn't missed a service of Christ Church since he had measles on his twelfth birthday.

"An' I'm twenty-four, goin' on twenty-five, now." He grinned proudly, pumping each of their hands straight up and down. Two missing front teeth gave Mackbeth the look of a six-year-old when he smiled, but it was more than the front teeth, Rebecca realized. He had the simple, eager mind of a small boy. Moving precisely from one to another, he shook each hand with enthusiasm, twice around. James Gould slapped him on the back affectionately and called him St. Mack.

"I legged 'er up to the Basses ag'in this week," Mack announced, and by the way the Goulds responded, Rebecca sensed this had become Mack Postell's self-appointed mission. His grin vanished, and he dropped his head. "They ain't comin'."

Deborah Gould told them it had broken Mackbeth's heart when P. D. and Emma declared themselves no longer members of Christ Church. "They went up north on a trip," she explained gently, "and now they think they're 'saved' and we're not. Seems they attended a revival meeting up there."

"Ha! If they got revived, I don't want any of it." James laughed.

"That's no way to talk, son." Horace Bunch grinned in spite of himself.

"If their brand of religion changes people as much as P. D. and Emma have changed, I'll just go on in my evil ways, making others happy—like now."

"Are they really so different, James?" Anson asked.

"Oh, they were always the biggest gossips on the Island—or almost—but at least they didn't look down their holier-than-thou noses at the rest of us."

"Now, Emma still comes to Auxiliary meeting with us," Deborah said. "Bakes the best spice cakes you ever tasted. Makes one every time we have a meeting."

"They'll eat with us, Mama, but they won't set foot inside an Episcopal church any more. Not even when good old Mack here invites 'em. Don't you worry, Mack—you're a better Christian than they'll ever be."

Mackbeth grinned, relieved, and after they were all seated in the circle Mackbeth had arranged, he grinned again and pointed unself-consciously at Ellen with his thin, shaky forefinger. "Pretty girl!" And his look of simple joy included them all, so that everyone smiled, and Ellen thanked him. That was a lovely gesture, Rebecca thought, like a child pointing at a pretty flower.

"Well, we might as well begin," Deborah said. "It looks like you're the only one coming, Mackbeth."

Mack grinned again. "Oh, they can't anything hardly keep me away, Miz Gould."

After a moment's silence, in which everyone opened his Prayer Book and got settled, Horace Bunch read quietly: *"The Lord is in His holy temple; let all the earth keep silence before Him."*

This Island keeps His silence, Rebecca thought. Silence so deep she found it difficult to remember the jarring rumble and clatter of horses and carriages over the New York streets. Noise that frayed the nerves was totally absent here in this silence kept by these simple people before God. Some of the peace entered her own heart, as she prayed the Lord's Prayer with them.

"O Lord, open Thou our lips," Horace Bunch read.

And they answered, *"And our mouth shall show forth Thy praise."*

Then Horace Bunch's low, gentle voice: *"Glory be to the Father, and to the Son and to the Holy Ghost."*

And they answered, *"As it was in the beginning, is now, and ever shall be, world without end. Amen."*

Rebecca had longed for a church. Here, with the parlor windows open to the warm December afternoon, she was finding what she had seldom found in a church; here there was no haste, no routine formality: the very atmosphere was new to her, and life-giving.

Young Horace stood up to read the First Lesson from the Old Testament, his soft, southern drawl unaffected and sincere, not arresting but enlarging the peace.

Then, at Horace Bunch's request, Anson also stood and began to read the Second Lesson from the Gospel of St. John, clearly, crisply, his voice almost matter-of-fact, in command of every word. Rebecca saw Mack Postell look around the group and smile, as though to say, "Isn't it nice we have somebody new to read to us?" She saw Ellen struggling to look thoughtful and attentive, as though she were listening and not loving Anson more than what he read. He does read better than young Horace, Rebecca thought, and felt a little ashamed of herself.

"I seek not my will but the will of the Father which hath sent me," Anson read, and then stopped abruptly and looked at Ellen.

James Gould uncrossed and crossed his long legs. Everyone pretended not to notice, except Ellen, who looked back at him, puzzled, trying to smile. But then Anson looked over Ellen's head, away from them all, out into the bright sun slanting through the trees. Rebecca sat on the edge of her chair, watching the color drain from her son's face. Why had he stopped reading? Was he ill?

Finally Horace Bunch spoke. "Son?"

Anson turned to him and said in a strange, flat voice, "I'm sorry, sir. If I can have just a minute, I'll go on. I want to finish. I really do."

The minutes dragged by, and Anson reminded

himself there was no rush, no formality, no restless congregation, just his friends and his mother and Ellen. He could take his time. He wiped the perspiration from his upper lip and coughed nervously. "Thank you, sir. I'll begin again, if I may."

"Certainly, son."

He read slowly this time, almost faltering, as though he were deciding something within his own mind and heart: "*I seek not my will, but the will of the Father which hath sent me . . .*" It was not the end of the sentence, but he stopped again, this time without panic.

Somewhere deep inside him, he had simply experienced a turning around. A definite reversal in the mainspring of his being. He didn't understand it, and it was all right that he didn't. He had reached a destination.

He exhaled almost leisurely. These *were* his friends, they loved him, they would wait. It was all right if he took his time getting accustomed to this new thing that had happened to him.

When he began to read again, his voice had a new quality: no longer matter-of-fact, no longer merely crisp and decisive, certainly no longer faltering. As he read, he saw Horace Bunch lean forward, and all the way to the end of the Lesson, he felt himself freed with every line, freed and settled in the deep places of his soul. From his first time alone on Frederica Road to this moment, he had been recognizing within himself the certainty of having come home. In spite of the torment with his father, and the misunderstanding in the churchyard with Ellen, that conviction had not left him. Now, it was complete. He was where he belonged, doing what he, Anson Dodge, was meant to do. He was handling the Word of God.

"Did you mind coming for a walk with me, Anna?"

"No, Miss Dodge. I didn't mind."

That was a lie, and Anna knew it. For the first time in her life, she dreaded a walk in her beloved woods. What would she talk about with an uppity young woman like Ellen Dodge? That was a lie, too. Ellen was anything but uppity, and Anna liked her. That was the trouble. She didn't want to like Ellen or Anson. Least of all did she want to like his mother. Rebecca Dodge frightened Anna, made her uneasy, sure that if everyone else in the room missed one of her social blunders, Mrs. Dodge would see it. Mrs. Dodge *was* uppity, she decided. And even if that was judging, she didn't care. Anson seemed different too, with his mother around. Oh, not that you could put your finger on the reason, and goodness knows, no one else seemed to notice. But, except for Ellen, she wished they'd never come at all.

She'd felt nervous as a cat while he read from the Scriptures, too: stopping and starting and stopping, forcing them all to wait with nothing to say. It was as if her own privacy were suddenly being invaded, and this made no sense whatever to her then or now.

"Anna, I don't see how these trees can stand still! I couldn't. I'd be dancing all afternoon, if I were adorned with tassels and banners full of sunlight. Don't you sometimes feel your whole Island is dressed up in its waving moss and grapevines for a special gala occasion?"

Anna looked around at the trees, their moss streaked with rose from the fire of the sunset, and smiled. "Yes, I expect so."

After another burst of enthusiasm over her discovery of the coral and blue and green lichen growing on the trunk of one old oak, Ellen laughed at herself and said she sounded like Anson shouting look, look, look at all of St. Simons Island.

"I reckon Mr. Dodge likes our Island a lot," Anna said, leading the way deeper into the woods along the sandy footpath, thick with last year's narrow brown oak leaves that crackled as they walked.

"*Likes* it, he's wild over it. It's almost all he talks about." Anna heard Ellen sigh, and when she spoke again her voice had changed. "I don't really feel like exclaiming, even over your beautiful woods, Anna. I don't feel gay at all. Could we just walk and be still?"

"Oh, yes. I'd like that."

And for several minutes, they said nothing. Of course, Anna was glad when anybody loved her Island.

But these people were outsiders, and they loved it the way outsiders love a place. She couldn't have told you at all why she loved it. Ellen's rhapsodic outbursts left her feeling mute and awkward. Still, if a person had lived in a place all her life, she didn't need to talk about it. She just belonged. It was nice having the Dodges at their house for dinner and Prayers, but she felt better when Horace or Papa read. The Dodges had their own world; the Goulds had theirs.

Ellen stopped by a mossy, fallen log. "Anna, let's rest. I want to talk."

Anna watched her sit gracefully on the low log, handling her skirts as though she were in the Rose Cottage living room on that green velvet chair.

"Did you feel anything strange when Anson read this afternoon, Anna? I don't mean just because he stopped, but after he seemed to recover his poise. Did you think he was different after that?"

Anna would never get used to the way Ellen just came right out with things that people usually didn't mention, but all she said was, "Yes."

"So did I! I felt suddenly like a stranger with him. And, Anna, I love him more than any human being on earth. Do you think I could be imagining things to make me feel that way?"

"I reckon not." Ellen looked so helpless, Anna had to think of something else to say. "It—well, I wanted to get up and run outside."

"Honestly? You've no idea how that relieves me." She clasped her hands around her knees and studied the thick green moss at her feet. "Anna, something's happening to him, and I'm—afraid."

Ellen looked up at her, and Anna wanted to put her arms around her and comfort her. Instead, she pulled a yellow grape leaf off a vine and folded it over and over into a hard, brusied wad in her hands. "I don't believe there's anything for you to be afraid of," she said.

"Do you like me?"

Ellen's directness shocked her again. "Yes, Miss Dodge. I like you."

"I mean, could you imagine yourself being my

friend? My real friend? For exchanging confidences?"

"I guess I never thought about that, Miss Dodge."

"Look—I'm only seventeen, can't you call me 'Ellen'?"

"I reckon so. If you want me to."

"I do. I need a friend now. I prefer you to anyone else I've met here."

Anna knew Ellen had already met everyone who was anybody in the little Mills settlement, and so she answered gratefully, "All right."

"I have dear Rebecca, but I need a friend who isn't his mother." Ellen stood up. "Anna, Anson told me yesterday in the churchyard at Frederica that he wants to become the rector of Christ Church."

"No!"

"Why did you say *no* like that? Anna, why?"

"Well, I—I don't know why I said it. I guess I said it without thinking." That was another lie. She *had* thought. "You couldn't live stuck away on this Island, Ellen."

"Oh, yes. I could live anywhere with him. I don't think that's what frightens me. I don't know what it is." She turned away, and then right back. "Yes, I do, too. He's so in love with this place and so distressed over what's happened to all of you since the war, I'd lose him if we lived here. I'm jealous, Anna. Just plain jealous. He wouldn't belong to me any more, he'd belong to all of you."

Anson heard the clock in the Black Banks parlor strike four. He had been sitting with young Horace and his father at the opposite end of the big piazza from Rebecca and Deborah for almost an hour. His friends had respected his need for time to think, and he was grateful. He had said nothing about what had happened during Evening Prayers, and they had asked no questions.

Now, after the fourth chime from the parlor clock, young Horace stirred, stretched, and mused, "I wonder if Mackbeth will wait for five today, like last Sunday?"

Horace Bunch chuckled and explained to Anson that one of the things Mackbeth Postell enjoyed most was staying after the service to listen to their clock strike. "He just stays in there all by himself and waits. Well, he's welcome to stay and listen all night, if he wants to."

Anson saw that his mother and Deborah were still rocking and talking; Ellen and Anna had not come back from their walk, and for a few minutes he put off facing the fact that they would have to leave soon in order to reach Rose Cottage before dark. He would cling as long as possible to the glow of what he had experienced that day, what he was still experiencing. He could sit here a little longer with his friends, in the strong last light of the sun, and realize the strength and the movement of the light within him. The new light, the clarity which had been coming almost steadily ever since he set foot on St. Simons Island. Light like a steady wind, pushing him outside the familiar chaos of his restless nature, setting him free on a high place, a wide plateau, from which he could look quietly, without fear or haste.

For the first time he did not doubt himself. In the years ahead, as he moved step by step to carry out his dream of becoming rector of Christ Church Frederica, it could seem to his mother, to the rest of the family, even to Ellen, that he was driven by a foolish impulse, enjoying the drama inherent in the idea of rescuing the old church, of being thanked by the people of the Island for his Dodge benevolence. All right, he would enjoy it! But not in the way they might think. He would enjoy it the way Ellen enjoyed God. His will had passed into the will of God as he read from the Scriptures today, and God's will was that he should restore the shattered church and become the minister to these people. He could go ahead now, not minding any obstacle, because he had it straight with God. Uncle Norman and his Grandfather Dodge could build a church at the Mills, but he would rebuild Christ Church Frederica, and he would live beside it with Ellen, in a house they would build together under the big trees. She would come to see and to be part of his dreams. She would bear his children here, and, unlike him, they would have both a father and a mother and a place to live away from the distorted values and confusion of the city. Their children would grow up like Horace and Anna, understand-

ing the Island, because they were a part of it. They
would not be outsiders, as he and Ellen were. They
would belong from the beginning of their lives to the
place their father loved more than any other place on
earth. And for this, he would spend every waking hour
showing his gratitude to the handful of people on St.
Simons, comforting them in their sorrows, sharing their
joys. He would marry their lovers, baptize their children, and bury their dead. And they would come to
love him some day, as he already loved them.

He had planned to tell Horace Bunch right away.
Now, there seemed no need to talk about it with anyone
. . . not yet. Before he and Ellen and his mother went
back to New York, yes. But not just yet. Still, he felt the
need to say something to his friends, and maybe now
was the time, because Mack Postell was walking across
the porch toward them, his face shining. He had heard
the clock strike three, three-thirty, and four.

Anson stood up. "Gentlemen, I don't know how to
thank you for today."

Mack pumped his hand up and down several
times.

"We're the ones to thank you, Anson." Young
Horace smiled.

"Yes, sir!" Mack grinned and shook his hand
some more.

"You brought a whole new spirit to our service,
son." Horace Bunch looked up at Anson. "God was so
close while you were reading to us, I felt I could reach
right out and touch Him. We hope you'll come every
Sunday for as long as you're here." The older man got
slowly to his feet. "We need you more than you realize."

"You do, sir?"

"Yes, we do."

"Yes, sir!" Mack said.

"I need you, too." Anson threw his arm around
Mack's shoulders. "I haven't told my mother or Ellen
yet—in fact, I've just decided. I'm going to stay on
here, at least until spring."

Chapter Ten

The Wagner "Palace" sleeping car lurched and swayed through the rainy night over the uneven tracks between Savannah and New York. Ellen had tried for more than three hours to sleep, to control her tumbling, chaotic thoughts. This, she decided, was ridiculous and futile, and since Rebecca's lamp was still burning, she slipped into the lower berth with her.

"I knew you weren't sleeping, Ellen. I'm glad you came down. Oh, child, child, what can I do to help you through this bad time?"

"I don't know, Rebecca. I wish I did know."

She pulled the extra blanked around her shoulders and sat at Rebecca's feet in a dejected heap. Anson had been kind, even gentle, when he told her he was not going back to New York with them, but he had also been firm, and nothing she said made him waver in his determination to stay on the Island until spring.

"Rebecca, I've *lived* for this winter with him."

"I know you have, my dear. After all, it's your first full winter in America since you two fell in love. But—"

"But what? What is there to say except that he prefers to stay on that remote Island? Away from me. What's happened to him, Rebecca? Do you think he has the vaguest idea how I feel? Is he so wrapped up in his big dream that he dares to take a chance like this with me?"

She turned away from Rebecca's questioning look.

"*Is* he taking a chance, Ellen?"

The girl's shoulders sagged. "No, but this just isn't the way it's supposed to be. We'd planned all those wonderful week ends this winter—the concerts, the theater, visiting you in Alexandria—I won't even have you in New York. I won't have anything but school and classmates and grandparents."

"You can still visit me, and I can visit you. I will, often."

"But this isn't the way it's supposed to be!"

"For whom, my dear? For you? Or for Anson?" Ellen pretended not to hear.

"Perhaps it is the way it's supposed to be for him. When you made all those plans, he hadn't found the little church or the Island or these people."

Ellen sighed. "But why? Why did it have to happen?"

"I don't know. But I do know I believe that God is in Anson's dream."

"Not the God I know!"

"Is your God different from his?"

"Well, He doesn't go about spoiling things the way Anson is doing now."

"Do you think things are spoiled for Anson, too?"

"For Anson? Ha! Not in the least. He's happy as a bird. He didn't seem to mind one bit saying good-bye to me."

"I think he minded very much. He was trying not to show it, for your sake."

"Well, all he showed was how little he knows about women." Ellen wasn't looking at her, but she knew Rebecca was smiling. "Rebecca, this is all something he's dreamed up. He didn't have to stay. He could be right here in this car with us, going back to New York where he belongs—with me."

"Do you think you know better than Anson where he belongs?"

She didn't answer.

"I admit to you, my dear, that I too don't understand why he felt he needed to stay on until spring. I would think, knowing how impatient he is by nature, that he'd have hurried back to New York to finish college and get into seminary as soon as possible."

"Then you do agree I'm right!"

"No. I don't see it as being right—or wrong. I simply see this as your second big chance to make an adjustment. At the hotel our first night in Brunswick, you had an adjustment to make, and you made it."

"Oh, that. That was nothing compared to this."

"Yes, it was something. It was difficult for you, but you came through it."

"Only after I was in his arms."

"Well?"

"But I can't be now. Not for ages and ages. Three months, maybe four. I'm on a train going away from him. Farther and farther away!"

"I may sound cruel, Ellen, but this will give you a golden opportunity to learn to come to grips with yourself—to make use of your own inner resources. Let's face it, Anson will always require adjustment on your part."

The girl thought a moment. "I wouldn't love him so much if he didn't, would I? I do want to be right for him, Rebecca. You're helping me. I'm stubborn, but please keep on helping me."

"My dear, part of your dilemma is no doubt the same as mine—I'm actually in awe of what seems to be happening to that boy. There were times before we left St. Simons when I felt he was a stranger to me."

"Now, that helps me more than you know. I felt that way, too."

"Still, I cannot stand in the way of what he appears to be so determined to do. I wouldn't want to. Of course, I had other dreams for him. To me they were bigger, more important dreams. But no one dares stand in the way of what a man feels is a call from God. If Anson's dream is merely a dream of his own, you and I will have to trust God to show him, to stop him."

"At this point, I don't think anyone but God could."

"But God can. After all, it isn't as though Anson were doing something wrong. It's a good thing he wants to do, Ellen. A good and constructive and unselfish thing."

"Then why do I feel he's being selfish?"

"My guess is because of the way he's doing it."

Ellen saw the old cloud cross Rebecca's face. "What do you mean, Rebecca?"

"He's barging in headlong—like his father."

"Oh, but he isn't like his father! Not at all. I won't permit even you to think that about Anson." She hadn't meant to say that much, and she was relieved to see Rebecca smile.

"I'm glad you won't allow even me to think it, Ellen. And I agree completely. He's not like his father in his motives, but his—his methods are the same at times. We have to face this. He is his father's son."

"Oh, Rebecca, forgive me."

"Forgive you?"

"I'm the one who's selfish. How can I love you the way I do and go on piling my own problems onto the load you already carry?" Ellen wiped her eyes. "Anson is his father's son, but he told me in the churchyard that day that he had finally realized he was God's son, too."

"Did he say that?"

"Yes. I should have told you before. That just shows you how selfish I am."

"Not selfish, so much as young."

"But I don't want to be young any more. I want to be right. For you and for him." She sat up, and the blanket dropped from her shoulders. Her eyes were almost bright now. "Suddenly, it's all right about my lonely winter without him. I don't like it—I don't like it one bit. But suddenly, the fight's gone out of me. And you did that for me, Rebecca."

"I'm sure I don't know how."

"By being you. I forgot you, Rebecca. I forgot you, and I forgot Anson. I just sat here loving me desperately. But that isn't the way I want to be. I love you both best, and I won't be a burden to you this winter, I promise."

"Oh, my dear, you are always only joy to me. Except when you make me ashamed of my own laxity by not learning as quickly as you do."

"I won't be a burden to you or to him. And whatever it is he'll be doing down there this winter, even if I don't understand it, I'll back him up. I'll write beautiful letters to him and encourage him." She smiled. "If he wanted to spend his life in a bamboo hut in Siam, I'd go with him." She leaned back in Rebecca's berth. "You know something? I thought I was jealous of the Island, of the people, of how much he loves them. I told Anna Gould I was afraid he wouldn't belong to me any more if we lived there."

"You told her that?"

"Yes. When we went for our walk in the woods."

"I see."

"I like Anna Gould, don't you?"

"I'm—really not in a position to say. I don't know the girl."

"Oh, you would like her, Rebecca. She's real."

"I didn't find her particularly outgoing, like the others."

"Anna's shy. But I didn't have things straight when I told her that. It wasn't the Island I minded. It was Anson—pushing me. Now, you've helped me see that I can do something about that."

"It won't be easy. He won't always be right."

"But I can always remember not to fight back. I can learn to wait him out."

"That won't be easy either. You're as definite as he is."

"But I can learn, Rebecca. I can learn." She pulled the older woman toward her and kissed her on the cheek. "I think I'll climb back to bed."

"I hope you sleep."

"I will now. You too." She opened the thick curtain, then hesitated. "I'm not going to like being away from him this winter. But you can depend on it, things are going to be all right."

"Bless you, my dear. Spring will come."

Chapter Eleven

Anna kept trying to feel the same about spring as she had always felt, now that April had come to the Island. Procter Green was singing while he helped her pull moss from the budding pear trees with a long pole, his young voice clear and soft as rain water. In her mind, she checked off the familiar signs of spring: jasmine bursting thick and yellow up the limbs of the oak trees, sudden white clouds of wild Cherokee roses crowding among the tangled branches noisy with birds singing their heads off for joy at being back. The signs were all around her, but so was the anxiety. All the beauty was back, and the gentle, mild days and the spring light everywhere, but nothing felt the same since Anson Dodge had taken over.

Procter was singing a song he shouldn't be singing, and she must stop him; but she put if off because if she stopped his singing, he would begin asking questions, and if he did, she might fly to pieces.

> "Stay in the house an' drink good rum.
> Oh, pay me my money down."

"Proctor Green! What kind of a song is that?"

"It's a stevedore song, Miss Anna. I'm gonna grow up an' be a stevedore at the Mills. Ever' chance I get when I'm down there workin' for Mr. Anson Greene Phelps Dodge, Jr., I hang aroun' the wharf with the stevedores an' learn to sing."

"You can outsing them all right now, and you're not to hang around that wharf again."

Procter grinned. He enjoyed every minute of her lectures, and she knew it. "I was only teasin' you, Miss Anna. I'm gonna work full time for Mr. Anson Greene Phelps Dodge, Jr., when he comes back to the Island to live."

"You don't know he's coming back—ever."

"Oh, yes, I do!"

"How do you know so much? He could change his mind once he's back up north in school."

"No, he won't. I know he's comin' back because he said so."

She would have to be careful with Procter. The boy almost worshipped Anson Dodge. That was the way things were. People either worshipped him or they wished he'd never come to the Island at all. Nobody seemed in between.

"What's wrong with you today, Miss Anna? You sick?"

"Of course I'm not sick."

"You sure are grumpy."

"Go on, sing some more, Procter."

He grinned again, then burst out laughing. Anna could have smacked him. "You're just puttin' me off, so's I won't ask questions, ain'tcha?"

"I declare, Procter, you'll give me a headache."

"Miss Anna, you sweet on Mr. Anson Greene Phelps Dodge, Jr?"

"*What?*"

"Mr. and Miz Bass say it look to them like you got your cap set for him."

"That's a bald-faced lie, and you can tell P. D. Bass and Emma I said so."

"When can I tell 'em?"

"You can't tell them at all."

"But you just said—"

"I know what I said, but I was just talking." She gritted her teeth. "Procter, sing me another song, do you hear?"

"I don't feel like singin', Miss Anna. I feel like talkin' to you."

She felt like talking to P. D. Bass and his nosy wife, but they were too far away, so she fumed to herself. Just because Anson Dodge spends so much time at our house, tongues had to start wagging at both ends. Oh, it's more than the time he spends here, I reckon. Nothing would do Papa but I had to work at the church with him cleaning up that day, and I should have known better. I told Papa they would talk. But he's so quick to trust folks. Sending me up to Frederica right under their noses to help him sweep out before the Stevenses started patching up the old church.

Anna tugged too hard with her pole and brought down a tender limb off a pear tree along with a clump of moss.

"You sure do act mad, Miss Anna."

"Hush up, Procter, and sing."

The boy began to sing. *One o' these days, my people.* . . . Anna sighed with relief and returned to her own thoughts as she worked. Why couldn't we just go on having church at our house? Why couldn't he get interested in the new church they're building at the Mills? She jerked moss and her thoughts rocked and collided, and always Anson Dodge was to blame. Well, who else can I blame? Papa, maybe, but Papa is so happy these days. It looks like he's made Papa and Mama and Horace and Procter and Mack Postell as happy as he's made me miserable. Getting himself made lay reader, reorganizing the vestry like it was all up to him. Makes it look like Papa and Horace had been shiftless all this time since the Yankees tore up our church.

Yankees barged in and tore it up, now another Yankee's barging in. Nothing has been the same since he came, and nothing ever will be again. Even at home. All Papa and Horace talk about are his big plans to rebuild the church some day.

Anna sighed. What's wrong with me? Don't I care about our church? Of course, I care. I'll be as glad as anybody to have the church again, but we'd have managed by ourselves some day. It was the way he did things, too fast—like a king giving commands, and then acting surprised and even hurt when everybody didn't jump with joy and do just what he said to do. Her brother, James, had been her only ally.

"Even if I didn't want to go to sea, sister, I'd go, just to get away from all this Dodge religion."

She missed James, now that he was gone, and she hadn't really meant to.

It wouldn't surprise me a bit, she thought, if Ellen got tired waiting for him to come back to New York. Two letters from Ellen lay in her top dresser drawer, unanswered. Letters asking for some idea of what Anson's plans were, when he was coming back to New York, what he did with his time. Why is it my business to tell her when he's keeping her in the dark the way he is? Standing up there on our piazza yesterday telling Papa he was resting in God's will about everything, when all he does is rush up and down Frederica Road from the Mills to our house to the church, holding "meetings," as he calls them, with Papa, then Horace, then George and John Stevens—now he was even making a chart of the cemetery! Rode all the way back down Frederica Road to Black Banks twice yesterday, to ask Papa about the dates some of the Coupers died. You'd think they were all kinfolks of his, the way he wants to know every little thing. Mama says he touches her heart. I say he'll make a lot of enemies if he keeps it up.

"Why does Mr. Anson Greene Phelps Dodge, Jr., have to go to school some more to be a preacher, Miss Anna?"

She had almost forgotten Procter was there.

"It's a rule of the church. They can't have uneducated men preaching sermons."

"Are you edgecated, Miss Anna?"

"No."

"Don't women have to be?"

She thought of Ellen and wanted to resent her, too. It was impossible. She could resent nothing about Ellen Dodge; not her European education, her beautiful clothes, her wit, her beauty, her charm. She made Anna feel old and awkward and plain, but she loved Ellen Dodge and wanted somehow to protect her.

"Mr. Anson Greene Phelps Dodge, Jr., is gonna git me edgecated."

"Who said that?"

"He did."

There it was again! She should be happy for the boy to have a chance like that, but it only made her feel he was taking Procter away from her, too.

"How long does it take to build a big house, Miss Anna?"

"What kind of a question is that?"

"Didn't Mr. Anson Greene Phelps Dodge, Jr., tell you he bought a piece of land up at Frederica?"

"What for? Who told you he did that?"

Proctor grinned again. "Now it's you askin' me questions, ain't it?"

Anna struck at a strand of moss on a high limb and missed.

"Who told you he bought land at Frederica?"

"Mr. P. D. Bass. He say Mr. Anson Greene Phelps Dodge, Jr., is gonna—"

"Can't you just say 'Mr. Dodge' once without going through the whole thing?"

"I kin, but I don't like it as well."

"When did you talk to P. D., and what did he tell you?"

"I been helpin' 'em make garden. They didn't tell me though. They was tellin' Miz Taylor. Gossipin', the way you don' like. Then Miz Bass, she say they sure ain't gonna sell him the half acre of their lan' he wants to buy."

"I reckon he bought part of the Taylor's ground."

"Yeh, an' now he wants a half acre of Bass lan', but they ain't gonna let him have it. Why not, Miss Anna? Why did Miz Bass sound so mad at Mr. Anson Greene—uh, Dodge? She stamp her foot an' look kinda crazy when she talk about him."

"Emma *is* crazy, Procter."

"She is?"

"Well, no, I had no business saying that." Anna rubbed her forehead. "I'm talking out of turn. Guess I've been looking up too long, pulling at that moss."

"Is your head swimmin'?"

"Are you sure you didn't make all this up?"

"Cross my heart an' hope to die."

"When did he buy that land, Procter?"

"Is it gossipin' if I tell you, Miss Anna?"

"I reckon it is, but if you don't tell me, I'll whack you one with this pole!"

The boy laughed. "You don' scare me none. But I think he buy it day before yestiddy the way they was talkin'. He aims to build a big, big house up there for him an' Miss Ellen to live in after they get married up, an' then I'm gonna live right there on the place an' work for Mr. Anson Greene Phelps Dodge, Jr. He tol' me last night when he rode past our place just before dark. Same time he tol' me he was gonna git me edge-cated."

Anna threw down her pole, sat flat on the ground against a big live oak tree, and faced the fact that she had been hoping against hope that he might change his mind. Now it was settled. He was coming back.

From where she sat, she could look straight down the Black Banks road, and she remembered the day Anson Dodge rode toward her on Horace's mare, the morning he came hunting her father. She had been excited that day, happy that someone new had come to visit them. Little did she know. And little did she know how much she would change in so short a time. *Am* I the one who's changed? No, I'm not. I'm the same, it's that everything else has changed, and I can't do a thing about it. There was a time I could ask Papa what to do, but not now. Tears stung her eyes. It was *his* fault too, that she felt shut away from her father.

"Miz Bass say Mr. Anson Greene Phelps Dodge, Jr., is rushin' in where angels fear to tread. What did she mean, Miss Anna?"

Anna disliked agreeing with Emma Bass about anything, even in her heart. "Never mind what it means. What else did she say?"

"Said it looked like he could mind his own business an' that they didn't need no Yankee money. Said if God wanted the church fixed up, He'd fix it Hisself. Mr. John Stevens didn't agree with her, though."

"Were any of the Taylors in on the talk too?" She felt ashamed pumping the boy like this, but until now, she hadn't faced up to how deeply all the comfortable relationships on the Island could be disturbed by Anson Dodge's big ideas.

"Yeah—I mean, yes, Ma'am—they was several of the Frederica white folks standin' aroun' talkin' while I hoed. Mr. Taylor mostly just listened, like I did. But Mr. John Stevens, he thought it would be a good thing to build a whole new church."

Why not? He'll get paid for building it, Anna thought, and then felt guilty. The Stevenses and the Taylors were among their closest friends.

"You wanta hear some more gossip, Miss Anna?"

"Don't make anything up, now."

"Oh, I wouldn't do that. But they don' like it 'cause Mr. Anson Greene Phelps Dodge, Jr., put two of the Mill folks on the—uh, vesty. What's a vesty, Miss Anna?"

"Vestry, not vesty. And never mind what it is. Let's change the subject."

"There's a lot more I ain't tol' you yet."

Procter was going to squeeze the last drop of pleasure from his tale, she knew, and hated herself for letting him.

"They don' like Miss Ellen, neither, 'cause she's from up north, an' they don' like her bein' his cousin, an' they don' know what to make of Mr. Anson Greene Phelps Dodge's Papa goin' off so fas', an' his mother not comin' aroun' at all till after the ol' man was gone. They whisper when they talk about all that, but I hear mos' of it."

"I'd say you heard too much, and you're not to tell another living soul, do you hear?"

"Oh, yes, Ma'am. But do you think Mr. Anson Greene Phelps Dodge, Jr., is purty?"

"What *are* you talking about, Procter Green?"

"Mr. P. D. Bass says he's a purty preacher boy, then he spit tobacco juice, hard."

Anna surprised herself by laughing.

"What you laughin' at, Miss Anna?"

In the time it took the boy to ask, she stopped laughing, got to her feet, and made a big fuss about brushing off her skirt, to keep from crying. "I'm not laughing at anything."

"Now, your face is all red. How come?"

"I don't know, Procter. I guess I just don't know what I'm doing or why."

Her father was coming slowly down the back steps, his fishing pole in his hand, when Anna hurried around the corner of the house, her face still flushed. Papa's the last person I need to see right now, she thought. He'll know something's wrong.

"Anna!"

"Hello, Papa."

"You and Procter get the pear trees out from under the moss?"

"Almost. Procter's still working on them."

Anna started to run up the back steps past him, but he caught her arm affectionately. "Hold on a minute, young lady. What's the rush?"

"Nothing, Papa."

"Well, then, sit down a minute beside me—here on the steps in this nice, warm spring sunshine. We haven't had a good talk for a long time."

He looked suddenly old, old and tired and pale.

"You all right, Papa?"

He exhaled heavily as he set his pole and bait bucket carefully beside the railing, then lowered himself onto the step where Anna stood.

"Yes, I'm all right, Anna. Gettin' old, I reckon." He looked up at her, his kind blue eyes inviting her to be with him, and in a minute Anna sat down, too.

"Well, now, this is more like it." He put his arm around her shoulders. "You haven't given me a chance to have a heart-to-heart talk with you for a long time, daughter."

To save her, she couldn't think of a thing to say.

"Wish Anson would drop by for dinner. I feel lucky today. Think I'm gonna' catch some fish."

Anson Dodge again! Couldn't he talk to her about anything else after all this time? They used to talk about things that mattered to Island people, like the horses, or the berry crop, or how the Negros were getting along, or what birds had come back now that is was spring.

"I reckon Procter told you what the boy's plannin'

to do." Her father's face glowed when he spoke of Anson. "When he comes back here after seminary, Procter'll work for him till he's old enough for a trade school, then Anson's payin' his way."

"Procter told me." Her voice was dry and toneless; she could feel her father's eyes on her, and she knew the blood was rushing to her face.

In the oleander bush by the back door, a mockingbird shouted part way up the scale four times, and then tried it part way down the scale four more times. They had always laughed together at the abandoned way mockers sing; maybe this would help close the distance between them so she could feel comfortable with Papa again.

"Do you think that's the same mocker we laughed at last spring, Papa?"

Horace Bunch smiled. "I wouldn't be a bit surprised if he is." Then he chuckled. "I just have to laugh at Anson. He says he's never had a chance to really listen to how versatile mockingbirds are till he came here. He'll stop right in the middle of a conversation to listen. Says they remind him of Bach's music: always experimentin'."

Anna slapped at an imaginary mosquito. Wasn't there anything they could talk about without Anson Dodge butting in? Did Papa know what Bach's music sounded like? He acted as if he did, and the distance between them widened.

"I haven't heard any music of the kind Johann Sebastian Bach wrote since I was up at Yale as a lad. I don't reckon you've ever heard it, have you, Anna?"

She picked at a prickly burr on her skirt. "You know I haven't, Papa."

"Maybe some day you can hear it. It's the music of heaven."

"I'm satisfied with the mockers."

He took her chin in his wide, brown hand and turned her face toward him, so he could look right into her eyes.

"What's wrong with my girl?"

Crying was the last thing she meant to do, but suddenly she was sobbing like a child against the rough, nubbly cloth of his old jacket. For a moment she gave in to the pure comfort of the familiar, big arms, the gentle hands patting her shoulders. Then she pulled away and stood up.

"Anna, can't you tell me what's wrong?"

She turned her back and looked toward the river. "I could have, maybe—a month ago. But not now. You've been so taken up with him!"

When he didn't answer, she looked around to see her father pull himself slowly to his feet. "Now, if that's true, daughter, I owe you an apology, and I ask you here and now to forgive me. I had no idea you felt like this. You've been so good helpin' Anson at the church, and—"

"I did it for you!"

"Well, thank you, but I wouldn't want you to do any of it for me."

"For whom, then?"

"Well, for God—for all of us. Didn't you think it was mighty fine to be able to worship in the little old church last Sunday, patched up as it is?"

She had to admit she did. Anson Dodge had not only paid for all the repairs, he'd worked like a beaver himself, right along with the other men, cleaning up, putting in new windows, fixing the roof and the shattered old belfry, mending the altar. He had varnished the patched places in the old altar himself and, when the varnish dried, had rubbed and rubbed until it shone again, almost like before the Yankees came. Anson had made Papa so happy, why couldn't she be glad, too? Papa's happiness meant everything to her, and here she stood like a dumb ox unable to share it with him.

"Anna, won't you sit back down here with me?"

"I really ought to go help Procter finish the trees."

"Please, Anna."

She sat down.

"Now, daughter," he said, "I love you just the way I've always loved you, and that's all the love there is. When two people are as close as we've always been, there has to be a way for you to be glad for what God is doing for us through Anson."

"I'm not the only one, Papa. It's the way he lords it over everybody."

"I don't think the boy does that at all."

"But people are talking. They don't all feel the way you and Mama and Horace feel about him."

He took her hand. "Anna, we have to realize that some folks just can't stand change of any kind. Specially some of these folks here, if the change is brought on by a Northerner. Even if it's a change for the better, they'll fight it. Remember when the Mills first came?"

She remembered. Oh, as soon as the money showed up and the jobs became plentiful, the complaints mostly died down. But some people kicked on the whole idea at first. She did, too, until she saw it really wasn't going to change anything for her.

"But, Papa, what I want to know is why is he going ahead so fast? If he still has to finish school before he can preach, why can't he just leave well enough alone till then?"

"Folks don't stop to think about his side of things, Anna. I doubt if you have, have you?"

"His side of things?"

"Anson isn't just giving to us. He's receivin', too. The boy needs to do what he's doing now. It encourages him to see results right now, before he can actually begin to preach to us. Gives him a goal. And he's got so much energy, he can't help going as far as possible with his plans *now*. Makes him feel all the hard work and study he has up ahead will be for a reason. His work will go on now that he's helped get the church reorganized, even while he's gone. Maybe even more than that, he needs to feel he belongs to us. He can sit up there in New York, studying, and think about the Island and the trees that will stand guard around his own church and his own house at Frederica some day. He can think about us down here on Sundays, worshipping together in the old church because he helped fix it up. The trouble with folks being on the receivin' end of things, the way we've all been with the Dodges here on the Island, is that we don't stop to think where the Dodges stand. With or without money, Anna, people still have feelings, still have needs. Anson's needs are great."

Anna covered her face with her hands. "I've got a long way to go, Papa."

"We all have. Anson's got a long way to go, too."

"I thought you considered him just about perfect."

He patted her knee. "Daughter, listen to me. This boy needs a father. We don't discuss his own father, any of us, because we don't need to know why he left the way he did. If Anson wants to tell us some day, he will. But God has given the boy to me to father. And I aim to do the best job I know how to do. I figure no matter how much fuss the folks kick up—and some will, I reckon—I've got to go on doing the best I can to guide and encourage him, because if I don't I'll be disobeying God. One thing I know, just as sure as we're sitting here on these steps together, is that Anson Dodge is obeying God by preparing himself to become rector of Christ Church. He may be running ahead of Him here and there, but the boy's heart is in God's direction—and in ours."

She watched him get up and then steady himself against the wooden railing of the back steps. "Papa! You're pale as a ghost. You don't have to go fishing. We've got ham left over for dinner."

"I want to go fishing. I need to be by myself awhile." He reached in his jacket pocket, took out a ball of fishing line, and carefully rewound the loose end.

"I'm sorry I spouted off at you like I did, Papa."

"That's a fine howdy do. What do you think I'm here for?" He lifted her chin again. "Now, is everything all right with my girl?"

"I reckon it is."

"We need what's happening on our Island, Anna. You ruin the best pot of mullet stew if you don't stir it once in a while."

"Papa, I think I'll go fishing with you."

"You won't do any such thing." He smiled. "If you're not going to help Procter, I know Mama needs you."

Anna kissed him, then let him go. He walked slower than usual, but with his pole over his shoulder and his bait bucket in his hand, the way she had seen him start out for fishing ground for as long as she could remember. He turned when he reached the marsh, they waved to each other, and then he was gone out of her sight over the rise in the ground toward the Black Banks River.

A little before noon, Anna went back to the east piazza, hoping to see her father coming up his familiar path around the big stand of magnolia trees, a string of fish in his hand. Instead, she saw Anson Dodge running as hard as he could up from the river, toward the house, alone.

When Anna met him in the back yard by the kitchen door, his eyes were wide with shock.

"Miss Anna!" he gasped. "I went looking for your father, down by the river, and—"

Anna backed away from him, "Don't say it! I already know. Don't you dare come here an' say Papa's dead." Then she screamed, "Papa's dead! I know he is—but don't *you* tell me!"

II

Chapter Twelve

The bare, lofty limbs of the big trees that lined the campus of General Theological Seminary in New York were slowly coming to life on an unusually warm spring afternoon, as Anson walked toward his quarters, totally unmindful of his classmates loafing on the grass. He walked slowly, a thing he seldom did, his head down, thinking about death. April had come again, April, 1882, and he knew that spring, coming on with life after winter, would now always remind him of death: Horace Bunch Gould's death in April, two years ago. He walked faster, wanting to shake off the paradox. Spring should not be related to death in a man's mind, he chided himself. I am a man in love, and spring reminds me of *death*.

Two years, and I can still see him lying there face down in the shallow water among the reeds at the edge of Black Banks River, his old felt hat floating beside him, his fishing pole in his hand . . . his great heart stopped forever. Six months at college and now a year and a half of seminary behind me, and I can still see him. I still miss him.

Except for the time spent with Ellen, when they could both escape school, Anson faced the fact that he had lived through hours and days and months like a man digging in darkness, desperately and alone. Digging for a treasure which had to be there, a treasure he had not found. God *had* to have an answer to the human suffering of those left behind when a loved one dies. The answer could not be merely submission—that was Islam. It could not be merely a resolute going on—that was Stoicism. God must have a creative answer. Not necessarily an easy one, but one on which a grieving heart could lay hold.

Inside his small room, he stood looking out the window at the hard green buds on the elm trees. Anson knew there was no darkness for Horace Bunch Gould. No darkness forever. His faith told him this was true, or God was false. And now, two years later, once or twice, late at night, when he had put out his lamp, he had sensed his friend more alive than he had been when his physical presence had steadied and blessed them all. But the gentle voice was silent; he had stopped chuckling and encouraging and loving them in ways they could see or hear or understand. Deborah Gould slept alone in the big, empty bed; Horace carried the full responsibility of the family on his thin young shoulders; James was back from the sea this spring, living painfully through his first days at Black Banks without his father.

And Anna . . . Anson could cope with his thoughts of the other Goulds more easily than he could cope with any thought of Anna. Until the day of her father's death, he had taken Anna almost for granted. He admired her courage, her resourcefulness. He would never forget that she saved Procter Green's life. He was grateful for her help at the church, for serving his meals when he visited Black Banks, but aside from that he had thought little of her. Now for two years he had been haunted by his inadequacy with her, who had been from the first moment, somehow, more stricken than the others. *I had nothing to say to her that day.* After two years of searching I still have nothing to say.

In the leather letter file on his desk, he hunted for the courteous but reserved note she had written for the family after he sent the handsome granite marker for her father's grave. When he found it, he unfolded it slowly and read the careful script aloud: *"We could never have bought one half so nice for him, and we are all grateful to you for your kindness."* Why did her words still cut him so sharply? Did he only imagine she was resentful? Resentful of what? His money spent for the expensive tombstone? Anna was too real for that. Her values were too straight. Perhaps she had meant nothing but gratitude, but he had never been able to satisfy himself with that. Kindness and a granite marker were not enough for a priest to give at a time of grief as dark as Anna's grief over her father, and kindness and the marker had been all he could give. His belief in life after death had given him nothing usable to say to Anna Gould; nothing to heal her heart, nothing to break the shell of her bitterness. Night after night, before he slept, he saw her stricken face, heard her voice, harsh and desolate, the day he left St. Simons: "I just loved him too much. There's nothing to say to me now. I wish you wouldn't try. I just loved Papa too much."

Anson paced from the door to the window, from the window to the door. He refused to accept the fact that anyone could love too much. If God is love, he argued, this cannot be. If God is love, then God is somehow responsible for Anna's shattered heart. If human grief brought on by love goes unanswered, then God is a fiend, and there is no comfort and no sanity.

If the death of a loved one could twist a kind heart like Anna Gould's against a friend who only meant her well, then somewhere there had to be help for her. *Papa's dead. I know it, but don't you tell me.* To Anson's mind, her open resentment until the day he left could not have been personal. She did not resent *him*, Anson Dodge. Her grief had made her say things she didn't mean. Somehow, somewhere, he must find help for the Anna Goulds of this world.

I must study more, he prodded himself. Then suddenly he knew this was not true.

He stopped pacing. Maybe scholarship does not hold the answer. Maybe there is no bridge between the learned phrases in the thick books and Anna Gould's broken heart. He sat down at his desk, his body tensed. I should be terrified that all this searching might be futile. But I'm not terrified.

"I must think this through," he said aloud. Why had he always thought of Anna in his moments of darkness? Why not Deborah or young Horace or James? They also loved Horace Bunch. Why had he not

stormed heaven for an answer to his own grief? His father's death could not have scarred him as this man's
death had done. For two years, even during vacations,
he had not been able to return to St. Simons Island because Horace Bunch Gould would not be there. And
yet, for some reason he had not demanded an answer
from God for himself, only for Anna—perhaps the light
lay there! Why Anna? He had liked her, but they had
not been close. They had little or nothing in common.
Why was it always Anna? Why Anna's need? His mind
raced toward what seemed a rim of light: *It wasn't
Anna, it was Anna's need.*

Need.

*Blessed are they that mourn, for they shall be com-
forted.*

"How?" He made his demand aloud. "Oh,
Christ—how? What do You mean by that? Do You answer only when our need is great enough?"

He buried his face in his hands. The rim of light
faded as swiftly as it had come. After a long moment
back in the old darkness, he pounded his desk with his
fist. "I won't settle for a theory. Anna Gould would
scoff at a theory. She needs comfort, the kind of comfort her father gave her. If You're sending me down
there to comfort these people, You've got to show me
how. I can't find it in the books, Lord. I can't find it
anywhere!"

"What would I do if you refused to come with me
when I need you?"

"Ellen waited to answer him, wanting first to grasp
his mood, the reason for his need. Anson had rushed to
her school, demanding that she leave a class to come
with him. She studied his solemn face, sitting beside him
in the rented carriage as the horses trotted briskly
through Central Park. Always before, they had driven
slowly through the park; he was urging the horses today, and she knew he was deeply troubled.

"I'll always come when you need me, Anson. Forever and ever and ever. Even if I were dead, I'd come."

He jerked his head toward her. "Don't say that!"

"But I would. I'd find a way."

She wanted to grab him by the shoulders and shout, We're *young*, Anson! We're not going to die. We have so little time together while we're both in school, why must you always have such dark thoughts? Instead, she took his right hand in hers and held it tightly.

"I would come to you, Anson. I'd find a way."

He reined in the horses at their favorite spot in the park and turned to her. She looked steadily back at him, but neither of them spoke, and he helped her from the carriage. Still silent, they began to walk slowly toward the big granite boulder where they always sat.

"You're still struggling, aren't you, darling?"

"Just be with me."

Ellen slipped her arm around his wrist. In the bright spring daylight, ignoring the people who passed on foot and in carriages, he held her close to him for a moment before they sat down in the wide curve of the rough, friendly rock.

"I suppose it was unthinkable of me, snatching you out of class."

"I was delighted. I hadn't studied, and we were just about to have an oral examination. You rescued me."

"I half lied to the Dean."

Ellen laughed. "What did you say?"

"Simply told her I was your cousin—"

"Well, you are."

"—and that a member of your family needed you."

"And he did. Isn't it marvelous that you needed me, Anson? That's the loveliest, most important thing in all the world. Relatives are so dull, I forget you're one, too." She handed him a dandelion and settled closer to him, as he kissed her fingers one by one and held her hand hard against his cheek. What, she thought, can I do to help him—really help him?

"Aren't you going to ask me why I had to see you?"

"No."

"You're perfect, aren't you? No woman is perfect. How can you be?"

"Because you love me."

She waited for him to smile, but he could only look at her, and look and look, until she stopped smiling.

"I never mean to pry, Anson. I respect you so. Even your conflicts."

"Ellen, your mother's death didn't make you bitter. Why? She was only in her forties—she's been gone just a little over a year. Don't you fight it sometimes when you're alone?"

Ellen had already recognized that death had become a separate thing to Anson. A dark thing that pushed them apart as nothing else had ever done. "No, Anson. I don't fight my mother's death. I miss her. I miss her letters. I miss writing to her even more, I think. But, darling, I'm too grateful to fight."

"Sometimes you frighten me, Ellen."

"Because I'm such a trusting soul?"

"Because you don't react like the rest of us. I don't understand at all how you can be so at home on this earth with me and still react to all the ugliness and horror as though—as though you had found another dimension. A kind of heavenly dimension earth-bound people—can't grasp."

She felt the gulf widen between them, again, and fought back her fear of it. "Don't worry, dearest. I'm as much of the earth as you are. And I'm at home here, utterly at home. I respect your searching mind, but I simply can't search. I just happen to *feel* as though God is my Father, and I can't be anything but a child with Him."

"I can't see what that has to do with it."

"With what?"

"With death—with grief."

"Being a child with God has everything to do with everything, Anson Dodge. I'd be bored stiff with your theological tomes, but I know what I know about God."

"Then tell me!"

"That day in the churchyard, Anson, you forced me to find out what I really believed. How simply I believed in Him. I don't know as many theories about Him as you know, but since that day I find it possible to go along through everything *assuming* God's love for

me. God *is* my Father, Anson. He understands me the
way my earthly father never will. I intend to move
through every change in my life, happy or sad, depending on the fact that God knows me as I really am—and
still loves me."

"But can't a man find out God's particular answer
to human sorrow? Don't we have a right to know?"

"Maybe. But I doubt that man ever will find out
the intellectual particulars his mind demands. Faith is
being a child with God. Look, darling, you trusted
A. G. P. D. until you found you couldn't trust him, didn't
you?"

"Yes."

"No one will ever find that out about God. The
only answer I know is living with Him in the kind of
total trust a child wants to place in his father. Your
wonderful, analytical mind reaches toward Him in one
way, my mind reaches in another." She pressed her
hand against his chest. "Please don't push, darling.
Can't you just live? God knows your fine mind as thoroughly as He knows my funny one. He won't be late in
letting you discover what you need to know. He's never
late, is He?"

"But, Ellen, as a priest, I must know! How does
one explain 'living' to other people? How does one look
at Anna Gould staring down into the grave of her father
and say 'Just live, now, Anna—live.' "

"Can you define loving me?"

"No."

"But you do love me. No one can define living or
loving. I think we help people learn to live or love by
giving them the courage to try it. You're my life and my
love, Anson, but I can't explain it."

"Is that putting me before God?"

"What a ridiculous question! I don't worship you,
but I don't love you any less than I love God. I just love
you in a different way. It's a difference of *kind*, not *de-
gree*."

She saw his frown fade. "Now, that makes sense."

"God uses my love for you to get at my heart with
His love. God has never acted independently of the human race. He acts through us. He was even born into

human life, of a woman. He's *in* the whole thing with us. He's here!"

Ellen waited. He closed his eyes and leaned his head against the big rock. "Thank you," he said.

After a moment, he opened his eyes and smiled at her, like a man smiling for the first time after a long illness.

"Do I depend on you too much, Ellen?"

"Too much for what?"

"Now who's being analytical?"

"I'm not. Kiss me."

"There's a carriage coming."

"I don't care."

The carriage clattered past and on down the road before either of them spoke again. Then Ellen said, "That's better. After all, I do have to wait a long time between kisses."

"A whole week sometimes," he whispered. "Unless I get desperate—like today."

"I wish you'd get desperate more often, sir."

"Ellen, why are we waiting?"

She pushed him away far enough to look at him. "I haven't the slightest idea. There seemed to be reasons for a while. But I forget them."

"Your mother's death?"

"Enough time has passed now."

"Your father?"

"He's not going to like it no matter when we get married, Anson. I've accepted that. Nor is Grandfather Dodge, nor Grandmother Dodge, but dear Rebecca will like it and—oh, darling, *we* will! I don't know why we're waiting."

"For us both to finish school?"

"School is adjustable."

"Would you need time to have a wardrobe made?"

"My wedding gown has been finished for three months." She laughed. "And you'll want to marry me the minute you see me in it. It's a ravishing white velvet."

"You're not twenty-one till February. We'd have to elope."

"Even the word excites me!"

"Oh, Ellen. . . ."

"Darling Anson, I don't want to wait a minute longer."

"Now who's pushing?"

She hugged him. "I am!"

Chapter Thirteen

"He's coming with news of A. G. P. D.," Rebecca said aloud to herself, as she watched from the high front windows of her home at Alexandria for the carriage that would bring her beloved father-in-law.

She had read and reread his brief, warm letter, written from St. Simons Island, Georgia, where he had spent a month with his son, Norman.

> I am coming to Virginia especially for a heart-to-heart talk with you, Rebecca. And, of course, to see your home there. Melissa regrets our decision that I should come alone this time, but she is looking forward to a visit in the near future. I will arrive in the early afternoon on Tuesday in the first week in May. And now, my dear, relying upon your common sense and our sincere regard for each other, I beg to assure you that our talk will be of value to us both.

She read it again, folded it, and put it back in her Bible. Like everyone else, she thought, I find it impossible to throw away even a note from him. He would be gone one day, and she would miss him so much, she would keep even this casual message among her treasures. He would surely be coming with news of her husband, whom she hadn't seen in four years; not since that day in June, 1878, when she and A. G. P. D. had kept up appearances by attending the golden wedding celebration of Melissa and William Dodge at their country place in Tarrytown, New York.

That day pushed again into Rebecca's mind as she watched for her father-in-law; for her a day of wonder and agony. Wonder at the fresh, vital love of the senior Dodges; agony at seeing A. G. P. D. again, at being forced once more to endure his gallant attentions, so blatantly insincere. That day had changed many things. Her real hope of reconciliation with A. G. P. D. had died. And hope had been born for Anson and Ellen. The center of everything shifted then from her life to theirs.

She saw the carriage stop. Her father-in-law climbed out and mounted her front steps, his kind eyes looking for her at the window. He waved, and Rebecca hurried to open the door herself.

Seated with him in the library, she picked up the silver teapot with a steady hand to pour their tea. Already her fear over what he might have to say had begun to fade. Fear couldn't live around this man, she thought.

"We haven't seen enough of each other these last few years, Rebecca. I've missed you. Melissa and I have both missed you."

He smiled, and Rebecca hoped for his sake she would be able to accept whatever he had come to tell her.

"With all my heart, I wish I could say I had only come for a friendly visit. I have, my dear, but there is more."

Rebecca sat straight in her chair, her head high. "What word is there of *him*, Father Dodge?"

"He is in Canada—has been since he left the Island."

"I know that. I know he lied about his reason for leaving. Anson knew at the time he was not called to the Pennsylvania operation."

"What a blow for the boy."

"He seems to have accepted his father now, as he is. This has helped me, of course. But we know he went to Canada. Is that all you've come to tell me?"

"I'm afraid not." He sighed. "He wants money settled on you in your own right. The boy, of course, is already in possession of his share of his father's wealth. You see, my son is not coming back to this country. He's become a Canadian citizen, Rebecca, and a member of Parliament."

"Is that all?"

"Yes. He said nothing about a divorce, my dear."

Her smile was bitter. "I rather think a divorce would spoil things for him. Remaining legally married to me gives him a perfect reason for not acquiring the responsibility of another family. Forgive me, Father Dodge. I know he's your son, but I would be deceitful not to admit my bitterness."

She saw the old man's eyes fill with tears, and his cup rattled in its thin saucer. I hate A. G. P. D., she thought, as much for what he has done to his father as for what he has done to Anson and me.

"I'll handle the transfer of the property and stocks to you, my dear, so as to make it as convenient as possible for you."

"Thank you."

"Now, there is one more rather difficult thing, Rebecca, not concerning my son, but yours." William Dodge set his cup down and leaned toward her. "I had a long talk with Norman before I left the Island. He told me everything Anson is planning to do there for the people. He's not like most young men of his age. These days, the average young man of twenty-two, with his means, is not considering any venture that won't in some way advance his own position in the world. I'm proud of the boy. This is undoubtedly your influence, Rebecca."

She spoke almost sharply. "No. He made his own decision. In fact, he made it so quickly, it took a while for me to adjust to it. I have now, fully. It's his whole life."

"Norman tells me the boy plans to build a new church at Frederica, finish his studies, take Holy Orders, and become its rector. I knew, of course, he was entering the ministry. But there seems to be some doubt among a few of the people at the Mills about the wisdom of having two churches on the Island, and—"

"Excuse me, Father Dodge, but if this is the difficulty you mentioned, I can assure you they need two churches."

"Is that so? Have you heard anything recently concerning the attitude of some of the Frederica folk about his plans?"

"Why, no, not directly. But I saw with my own eyes how grateful the Goulds were."

"That is the Mr. Gould who died, is it not?"

"Yes, but his son, Horace, has carried on with the work Anson began. They correspond regularly. Anson has sent money for the upkeep of the old church he repaired before he left. There's no difficulty among the Frederica people, I'm sure. If there were, Anson would have told me."

I doubt if he knows it, my dear."

"What kind of trouble could there be? I should think these poor people would only be grateful to him!"

"Many of them are. But as far as Norman can tell, it might be wiser to wait a while for the church at Frederica. Anson could become the rector of the Union Church at the Mills, and then—"

"Have you seen my son lately, Father Dodge?"

"No, but I plan to have lunch with him next Wednesday."

"I advise it. It would be helpful to you to hear his plans from his own lips. He's *going* to build that church at Frederica. God has not called him to become the rector of the church at the Mills. He has called him to Christ Church Frederica."

"I see. Thank you, Rebecca. I do need to hear all viewpoints. I don't get down there often, but the people of St. Simons Island seem to me unusually worthwhile."

"And a bit ungrateful, I'd say, from what you've just said."

"If I gave the impression that all the people are against the church at Frederica, I gave a wrong impression."

She took a deep breath. "Is that all you have to say about my son?"

"No, my dear, there is more. I learned something else while I was there which troubles me greatly. I know how young people change their minds, and it may no longer be true. But Norman told me—feeling he had an obligation to do so, mind you, and I believe he did— that Anson and his cousin, Ellen, are still planning to be married."

Rebecca wanted to stop her ears.

"I had hoped their 'romance' had ripened to a more suitable friendship. You know, of course, such a marriage must not take place."

Rebecca clenched her hands to stop their trembling, but she did not speak.

"Have you known of their plans, my dear?"

She could only nod. Their plans were her plans. Anson and Ellen were her life. As much as she loved and revered William Dodge, she would defy him before she would permit him to wreck all she had left to live for.

"And do you not agree with me," he went on, "that it is not acceptable for first cousins to marry?"

She had not expected him to put it into words. Her anger must be showing now, and it was anger—no longer merely anxiety or fear, but anger. She jumped to her feet and began to talk rapidly and too loudly. She paced back and forth, pouring out her pent-up bitterness and heartache and fury upon this gentle, well-meaning man who loved them all. "But love implies understanding, Father Dodge—and while you well know my own religious and moral convictions, I not only believe these two young people must be allowed to marry, I shall do all I can to help them! They are cousins, yes, but they met as strangers and fell in love as any two young people fall in love. Neither of them could ever find happiness without the other now. If the whole lot of you turns against them, I will not. I will not have my son's heart broken still another time by a Dodge—even you. Nor will I permit Ellen to be treated as an irresponsible, erratic child. She's had quite enough of that from her own parents."

He was standing now, reaching for her hand.

She went to him. "Don't do this to them. In heaven's name, not you, too! I've always believed you and I could talk reasonably about anything. I so counted on your understanding when the time came. If no one else ever sees this clearly, I so counted on your seeing. Help them, Father Dodge, I beg of you. Don't close your heart to them. Ellen's mother would have come to understand, I know, if she had lived. But only you can influence her father."

She watched him, alarmed that he had grown so pale and shaken, but she could not stop talking.

"Father Dodge, give yourself time to try to imagine what it would have done to you if someone had attempted to stop you from marrying Melissa! Anson and Ellen love each other as you two love. They make me think of the way you and Melissa must have been. The boy has had a lonely life—just the two of us. I've tried to give him everything, short of spoiling him. We've traveled together, read together, sung together, played together—"

She made an effort to laugh.

"I'm quite a marble shot, and when Anson was fifteen, I even took up target pistol practice with him. But he was still lonely. After all, I'm only his mother. He never had many close friends. He didn't seem to want any; he was so serious. Oh, not dull or stuffy. He teases me unmercifully. But until he met Ellen, he was alone except for me, and that's not good for a young man. He can't always have his mother, and even if he could, he needs someone his own age. She's just right for him, and"—she straightened—"what's more, he'll never be like his father as long as he has Ellen. Not that he would ever mistreat her or anyone else. There's no danger of that. But he does have his father's impulsiveness. He jumps to decisions. Thank God, Anson's quick decisions are motivated by an almost terrifying idealism. He's actually prejudiced in favor of the downtrodden. Sometimes, I think, unfairly to the rest of us. But like A. G. P. D., he rushes into things. There the similarity ends, and Ellen understands all this. All of it. She will be his balance, as well as his great joy."

Rebecca sat down, let him take her hand in both of his.

"I had no idea you felt this way, Rebecca. I'm afraid I simply took it for granted you'd see it as I do."

He took out his linen handkerchief and wiped his forehead. "I mean only good toward them, my dear. I love them both deeply. Neither Melissa nor I nor Ellen's father has any notion of ruining their lives. It's just that we feel this is against the teaching of the church."

Rebecca looked straight at him. "I respect my church and yours, sir, but both Episcopal and Presbyterian doctrines concern me not at all where the happiness of those two young people is involved."

"And what about our duty to protect them from acting impetuously?"

"Father Dodge, they've known each other for almost four years! I would stake my life on the fact that Ellen and Anson are not acting outside the will of God."

The front doorbell startled them both. And while they waited for Rebecca's maid to announce the visitor, they sat in silence. When she did not come, Rebecca rose. "Excuse me, Father Dodge."

In the hallway, she found her maid holding a telegram, undecided about interrupting her. Rebecca's hands shook as she tore open the yellow envelope, read it quickly, and returned to her father-in-law, smiling and cheerful, as though the anger and the darkness of a moment ago had never been.

"Good news, Rebecca?"

"Yes. Yes, Father Dodge. Very good news."

When he realized she was not going to share it, he got up slowly, wearily, and said, "I'm glad. You need some good news, my dear. And perhaps I'd better do as you say—give myself time to think from the viewpoint of the young people, too. I'm afraid I can never agree such a marriage is the highest way, but it's possible I was being overly protective of my own son Stuart. He's dead set against it, and I'd like to shield him from another heartbreak, so soon after losing his wife."

"I understand that. But Stuart, although he is a famous preacher, may have to learn to adjust like the rest of us."

"Preachers are human beings, too, Rebecca. Even dedicated ones like Ellen's father."

"He doesn't seem aware of it, but his daughter has

the makings of a great and wise woman, Father Dodge. You should be better acquainted with Ellen."

Rebecca smiled easily, as she walked with him to the door, eager now to be alone, so she could devour the shining, triumphant message in the telegram from Savannah, Georgia, which read:

> WE DID IT DEAR QUEEN VICTORIA   ON OUR WAY
> TO ST SIMONS ISLAND NO LONGER COUSINS BUT
> MAN AND WIFE HURRAH FOR OUR SIDE   ANSON
> AND ELLEN

Chapter Fourteen

Anna Gould sat in the wicker chair by the window in her room under the eaves of the sloping roof, staring out over the darkening marsh without seeing it; without seeing the marsh or the gulls flashing past in the last streaks of the evening sun. It was too hot to be in her room; she should be on the piazza with her mother. After supper was the time Deborah missed her husband the most, and Anna had made a point of sitting with her every evening since Papa had been gone.

She should be down there with Mama now, but she wasn't. Her grief was fresh again because Anson Dodge was back, and the old sickness rushed over her as she sat rigidly, her fingers twisting a loose strand of wicker on the chair arm. She had trouble breathing, the way it was during those first weeks when she rode almost daily to Christ Church to tend the flowers on her father's grave, to sweep the fallen live oak leaves carefully from the long, low mount of sandy earth piled in front of the impressive granite monument Anson Dodge had sent, with the words *Our Father* chiseled on its base, as though Papa had been his father too.

The mound of sandy earth was gone now. Two years had leveled it, and for the past few months, her heart had almost leveled out too. But Anson Dodge was back again, with Ellen as his wife, and Anna's fragile peace was torn up the way a plow tears up a cotton field in spring.

Papa would be so happy to have him back if he

were here, she reminded herself. But I'm not Papa. To me, he's barging in again, stirring things up, just when they were beginning to seem almost the same. Oh, he had touched her heart when he told them of his own grief for Papa. Tears had rolled down his cheeks. I felt for him, Anna admitted. He meant it. I should be thankful, but I'm not. Having him back is like losing Papa all over again. He changes everything when he comes, and we don't want or need any more change. We've all had enough.

From downstairs she heard her mother call good evening to someone. And in no time Anson's voice boomed from the parlor, and then she heard Ellen laugh and ask for her.

"Anna's upstairs in her room, Ellen. Why don't you go right on up?"

Oh, I could bump Mama, Anna thought, jumping up from the wicker chair, drying her eyes on her skirt. She stood trapped like a possum up a tree when Ellen's knock came at her door.

"This is marvelous, finding you alone, dear Anna." Ellen hugged her.

"My, but that's a pretty dress, Ellen!"

"Thank you, but I can't concentrate on dresses now. Anna, can you believe I'm his wife? At long, long last—can you believe it?"

"I hope you're happy all the rest of your life, Ellen."

"Oh, I intend to be. I mean to be deliriously happy right up to the day I die. And listen, Anson's just told me, we're going straight from here to Europe and then to India for the rest of our honeymoon. With all my heart, I've longed for just one glimpse of the Taj Mahal. Anson's already seen it, with Rebecca when he was a little boy, but isn't he dear to want to go back with me now?"

"I reckon he wants to be with you the same as you do with him."

"But it's a sort of sacrifice, I think."

She sat down on the edge of the wicker chair, looking for all the world, Anna thought, like a serious child.

"The only place he really wants to be, Anna, is right here on St. Simons. Do you know he's already got the lumber delivered to Frederica for our house? We've settled on the architecture, Mr. John Chapman is drawing plans, the Stevens men are ready to begin work, and we've retained Sibby Jackson to be our cook—all in the three days we've been here!"

"You mean P. D. and Emma gave in on that half acre he wanted?"

Ellen frowned. "No. But we don't have to have their half acre to start building. We'll need it later, goodness knows. One side of our house will be right on the present property line with no room for the stables. But Anson is blithely sure the Basses will change their minds later."

"He ought to know P. D. and Emma better than that by now."

"Anna, the Taylors were so nice to sell to us, why are the Basses difficult?"

"P. D. wouldn't be, I reckon. Maybe Emma would be all right, too. But you have to know how to handle them. They don't like to be pushed."

"I know Anson seems to be pushing. But he doesn't mean it that way."

Anna sat down on her bed, and Ellen leaned toward her.

"Anna, Anson and I need you."

"I don't know what for."

"To be our friend. I doubt if you realize how he has grieved for your father, how much of the happiness went out of his plans when your father went away."

Anna studied her hands.

"This is part of why I came up here to talk to you. Do you know that he hasn't stopped for all this time trying to find what he calls God's answer to *your* grief over your father? He seems to have no idea that you—resent him."

Anna jumped up and went to the window, her back to Ellen. How did Ellen know how she felt. Did it show that much?

"Anna, why do you resent him?"

"It hasn't got anything to do with you, Ellen."

"Help him, Anna. Anson's good. He's even noble, like Grandfather Dodge. He means everyone so well. He wants to give his life to your people here, and he's brought me around so I want to give my life right along with him. But he doesn't want gratitude—he isn't trying to be important. He just has a big dream, and some of your people misunderstand him. Almost everyone at the Mills has been charming to us—but you can influence the Frederica people, Anna. There's no reason why the Basses should refuse to sell their little half acre. They don't need the land, and they do need the money. I'm afraid Mrs. Bass might turn the Stevenses and the Taylors against him, too. And this must never happen. Those Frederica people will be our neighbors."

"They're all good neighbors, too. The Taylors and the Stevenses understand P. D. and Emma."

"But it's desperately important that they understand Anson. It's Frederica he loves. With all his heart he wishes he had been born right here, so no one would ever think of him as an—intruder. Oh, I think I've noticed the opposition, the suspicion, more than he has. He trusts everyone and just goes forging ahead expecting them to be able to see right into his heart. I know this makes it seem as though he's trying to take over. I used to think that. But he isn't. He's just taking good will for granted. Yours, too."

"I don't know of anything I've done to stop him."

"Neither do I. But I've got a sixth sense about how you feel. Oh, Anna, give him a chance! You're a sort of key now that your father is gone. The people trust you."

"I don't know that anybody could change P. D.'s mind, or Emma's. Least of all me."

"I'm not asking you to change their minds. I'm just asking you to be Anson's friend. You're my friend. I know this, the way a woman knows things. But can't you try just once to put yourself in Anson's place? To see from his viewpoint and help him?"

Ellen went to stand beside Anna at the window.

"I've heard that ridiculous gossip the Basses started, Anna."

This was the last thing Anna expected her to say. How could Ellen plead with her to be Anson's friend, knowing that? What kind of girl was she? And because she could not find her tongue to answer, Anna confronted herself with a thorny question: was she determined to fight Anson Dodge just to prove the Basses' story was a lie? It was not that simple, though, and she knew it. Nothing would ever be simple again.

"I don't believe a word of their stupid talk, Anna, and I beg you to ignore it. I only brought it up to help clear your mind of it. Anson hasn't heard it. He's so full of his dream, I doubt if he'd pay much attention anyway. He doesn't understand malevolent people. Or their threat to his work here. He needs us both to help him."

Anna wanted to laugh; how ridiculous to think for one minute that Ellen would have minded if she *had* set her cap for Anson Dodge.

Ellen touched her arm. "When we come back from India, Anna, we're going to need *you*. Can I count on you to be his friend by then?"

Chapter Fifteen

Arthur Murray Dodge stood a little back from the ticket window of the Coney and Parker steamship office in Brunswick, thoroughly enjoying the conversation in progress between the imperturbable agent and two irate passengers.

"Now, we're just as sorry as we can be, Miz Bass," the agent drawled, "but there ain't a blamed thing anybody can do about it."

"What kinda service is this, I wanta know? Folks comes to Bruns'ick of a mornin' in good faith, expectin' to git home to the Islan' at night, an' you stand there sayin' the *Ruby* ain't makin' the trip!" P. D.'s voice rose, and Arthur Dodge decided to get his money's worth before he interrupted them.

"She's got a leaky boiler, P. D., an' you know as well as I do a steamboat won't budge without a boiler full of steam."

"But me an' Emma's got to git back to St. Simons tonight!"

"They's a big party at the Mills!" The rolypoly, thickly bundled woman was near tears, something Arthur Dodge felt sure happened only in moments of extreme frustration.

"She's got a leaky boiler, folks. She won't run."

"Then Coney an' Parker oughta hire a boat to carry us back!"

"Ain't nothin' printed on the ticket to say that."

"Once a year Emma an' me comes to Bruns'ick an' this is the kind of service we git."

The agent yawned. "Ain't nothin' stoppin' you folks from hirin' a skiff to carry you over. Cap'n Sims's right outside. I can git him for ya in five minutes."

"Yeah, for six or eight times the price of a ticket!"

Arthur Dodge stepped toward them, tipped his derby to Emma Bass, exposing a thatch of red hair, and said, "Excuse me, please. Perhaps we can work out something. I planned to take the *Ruby* to St. Simons Island this evening myself."

He watched P. D. and Emma turn around slowly and look him up and down, taking in his custom-made suit, his topcoat folded over his arm, even his shoes.

"I'll gladly hire the boat for our trip over. After all, we do need to get there, don't we?"

"Well, I know we do," P. D. said, squinting at him.

"I'm on a rather urgent mission. I may already be too late. But I've come this far, so, late or not, I'm determined to go all the way."

"You a Dodge, are ya?"

Arthur laughed and shoved his derby back on his head. "Yes. Is that bad?"

"To some it is, an' to some it ain't," Emma said.

"I'm Arthur Dodge. My brother, Norman, runs the Mill on St. Simons."

"Yeh, yeh, we know all about it."

"Is there a lot to know?" He grinned at them. "I hope there is. After all, if this gentleman will do whatever it is he does to enable one to rent a private launch, we'll have plenty of time to talk on the way. Will you join me?"

He saw Emma nudge P. D. "I reckon so. Much obliged."

Arthur Dodge settled himself in the stern behind P. D. and Emma, as the small naphtha launch chugged slowly out into the channel, past the schooners *Rhondda* and *Champlain* at anchor in Brunswick harbor. The pine tar flare lighted the shell of the boat more than it did the black water ahead, but Captain Sims had assured Arthur he could navigate the channel to St. Simons with his eyes shut. Emma and P. D. sat straight as ramrods, annoyed somewhat, Arthur felt, because they had to turn around when he talked. Already he knew perfectly well they were not people to miss anything, even a look.

"So you're attending a party on the Island tonight, eh?"

"Yep. Big shindig for young Dodge an' his bride."

"Did you say 'bride'?"

"Yep."

Arthur Dodge began to laugh, forcing Emma and P. D. to fidget and turn, nudge each other, fidget, and turn some more. When he stopped laughing, Emma said, "We didn't know it was so funny."

"No, of course you wouldn't know. It's a tremendous joke on me, really. But after that long, extremely uncomfortable train trip from New York, I think I'm entitled to at least a laugh. My friends, I have just ended one of the wildest goose chases of the century."

He waited for them to turn around and stare. They both did.

"Do you know why I was sent packing from New York all the way to Georgia? To stop those two youngsters from doing what I am now happy to learn they have already done!"

On the front porch of Rose Cottage, Ellen threw her arms around her Uncle Arthur and kissed him on both cheeks. "There, I've decorated you for perfect timing! I've never been so happy to see anyone turn up late."

"I'm happy to be late, too, dear girl, and that's all we need to say about my journey tonight. Let's not spoil your splendid party. Your guests will miss you. After I freshen up, I'll have a marvelous time just mingling."

Anson rejoined them from the house, rubbing his hands together energetically.

"I've sent your valise upstairs to your room, Uncle Arthur. You may go up whenever you like. But do come back down. We've a million questions to ask." He frowned suddenly, and his manner changed. "On second thought, sir, I don't think I can wait. Ellen doesn't seem anxious, but I confess I am. How much trouble will Uncle Stuart make for her?"

"Not any beyond my surprise arrival, Anson. I even suspect he knew I'd be too late."

"Then why did he send you?"

"To ease his conscience, I imagine. Oh, I doubt if the old boy was aware of that. I had a feeling your Grandfather Dodge agreed for me to come on principle only. But he did agree."

"When did they find out?" Ellen asked.

Arthur grinned at Anson. "You forgot to cancel your luncheon date with your grandfather, my boy."

"It hadn't once crossed my mind. Not till this minute!"

"Then they didn't miss us for two days. Your date with Grandfather was for last Wednesday, wasn't it, darling?"

"You should have reminded me, Ellen."

"What possible difference can it make now, Anson? It's all right. Grandfather has humor to spare."

"She's right, Anson. That frown does not become a bridegroom. Not the groom of a lovely creature like this."

Ellen took Anson's hand. "Daddy will be all right, Anson. I know that's what worries you, but I can handle him. After all, we'll be gone over a year. He'll calm down by the time we're back. He loves me. No one will be able to resist my sorcery by then, anyway. A woman grows more charming when she's happy, and I shall no doubt end up being the world's most charming woman! Uncle Arthur . . . we *are* happy."

"I can see you are, my dear, and neither of you is to give a thought to what I'll say to them when I get back to New York. I'll simply tell them I was too late, that you are the perfect bride and groom, and—besides that, it would have been worth the whole long, gruesome journey just to have had that interesting trip in the little boat from the mainland."

"Isn't the marsh breathtaking at night?"

"The marsh? Yes, Ellen, I suppose so. But I confess I was too entertained by my traveling companions

to notice the marsh. I shared the launch with a Mr. P.
D. Bass and his wife."

He stopped smiling when he saw their expressions
change.

"Are they making trouble for you already, Anson?"

"Why, no, not exactly, sir. I believe the Basses are
really good people."

"Everyone on the Island is good, according to Anson, Uncle Arthur. That's because he's so good." She
patted his cheek. "The Basses *are* causing him trouble,
but he's too kind to admit it."

"Be kind, my boy, if you want to, but don't be a
fool. These people are amusing, but be careful of them.
The woman especially. It wouldn't surprise me one bit
to find them eavesdropping right now, out there in the
shadows of those oleander bushes."

Chapter Sixteen

The morning sun woke Anson, and he lay in the big colonial bed in the yellow room at Rose Cottage beside Ellen and felt something very like pain in his heart. This isn't pain, he told himself, it's joy—too much joy for one man to contain.

He raised himself on one elbow carefully, so as not to waken her. No one could be that beautiful, and yet there she was, her quiet face bathed in the Island light . . . the dear face, full of life even in sleep. He could feel her warmth, smell the fragrance that always surrounded her. He studied the straight, proud nose, the full red mouth he had kissed until they both fell asleep last night. Even her feet were beautiful: slim, straight, graceful like her hands. He touched her hair and then took his hand away, wanting another moment to look at her before all that life came rushing back toward him.

Ellen was more alive than anyone he had ever known, and she stirred life within him. Life, with joy at its center, the way love is at the center of all one knows of God. He smiled. God is love. Ellen is joy. My joy, he reminded himself, and she's going to be the center of my joy for all the rest of our lives together. I'll never live long enough to be with her as much as I need to be. No man could live that long.

"Darling," he whispered. "Wake up! We're losing time."

She stretched, smiled, and reached for him. Then she lay back and opened her eyes. "Good, good morning, my husband. What a beautiful sight for waking up! Oh, Anson, I *do* love you with your hair mussed."

Suddenly she pushed him away and sat up.

"Grow a beard!"

"What?"

She turned his head this way and that, one finger on his chin. "I just this minute pictured you with a lovely, curly, glossy black beard. Not too long, not too bushy. Just right."

Anson laughed and tried to interrupt her with a kiss, but she went right on.

"You'd be so handsome, so distinguished, I'd demand to be your wife forever!"

"You're going to be my wife forever, anyway. And who would guarantee proper barbers along our route from Georgia to the Taj Mahal?"

"I would. I guarantee you everything. I'm serious, Anson. I love the way men look with beards. I'll bet you do too, secretly. Come on, admit it."

He tried to kiss her.

"No, no more kisses until you admit you'd like to have a beard."

"Can't I have even one private conceit?" He grinned. "All right, I confess. I've always wanted to wear a beard."

"Good," she laughed. "I've won my first argument." She gave him a kiss, threw off the coverlet, and bounded out of bed. "Now, get up, beloved, we're going on our honeymoon—*today*."

Anna and her mother rode in the Gould buggy up to the edge of the crowd at Steamboat Landing just as the *Ruby* was about to dock. They had ridden down Frederica Road to say good-bye to Ellen and Anson, and for once Anna hadn't found the drive beautiful. Her heart was as heavy as a green oak log, and she hoped Mama hadn't noticed.

"Anna, look—isn't this fine? Everybody's here to wish them a happy trip. Even the folks from Frederica came. There's Belle Taylor, and Rossie Stevens." Deborah waved happily and called, "Morning, Belle. Morning, Rossie."

Anna waved too, forcing a smile she didn't feel. "Looks like P. D. and Emma are the only ones who didn't make it, Mama. Reckon nobody's surprised at that, though."

"Well, Anna, it's a long ride for them in that old buckboard. I wish we'd had room with us."

Anna didn't wish there'd been room. All she wished was to be as far as possible from this laughing, waving, chattering crowd of Island folk. But she was here, right in the thick of it and, she had to admit, puzzled by her own heavy heart. She ought to be glad for the peace and quiet they'd have while he was gone. *I don't know what I'm glad or sad about any more,* she thought. *Don't know why I'm here, except I had to bring Mama. And—I had to see Ellen again. I have to let her know what I'm aiming to try to do. In all this crowd and hullabaloo, though, how am I going to get to her?*

Climbing down from the buggy, Deborah waved and nodded at her neighbors and friends, Anna joining in because it was expected of her. But mostly she was pushing her mother along toward the edge of the crowd at the dock where she supposed Ellen would be—with him. She could see Arthur Dodge and her brother Horace directing the loading of the luggage. Anna had liked Arthur Dodge, what little she saw of him at the party last night. He seemed so easy and natural in his ways, and downright glad he'd been too late to stop the wedding. Funny he'd come at all, though, feeling like that. The Dodges were funny people, the ones she'd met. His grandfather, William E. Dodge, had said nice things about Papa, the one time she saw him, but Anna still felt that Rebecca Dodge had looked right through her, as though she wasn't even there. Everybody at the Mills seemed to like Mr. Norman Dodge, but Anna had only seen him once or twice, and he was such a Northern-mannered man, he made her feel uncomfortable. Only Ellen always acted the way she really felt inside. And just then she saw her, laughing and shaking hands with Mack Postell and then with other people, bending down to talk to their children but, at the same time, edging through the crowd obviously looking for someone.

"Anna!"

Anna's heart warmed. Ellen had been looking for her. "Morning, Ellen."

"I'm so glad I found you. Good morning, Mrs. Gould. Isn't this the most glorious day for beginning one's honeymoon?"

She hugged Deborah and then took Anna's hand.

"Would you excuse us just a minute, Mrs. Gould? I have something secret to say to Anna, and there's such a little time left."

"Of course, my dear. I want to visit around anyway."

When her mother moved off with Mrs. Wright and Mrs. Young, Anna stood smiling at Ellen, her own eyes smarting with the tears she vowed she'd keep back.

"Anna—I have something for you."

Anna watched her dip down into her large handbag and bring out a small box, wrapped in white tissue paper and tied with a white satin bow.

"This is a treasure of mine. Maybe, outside of my wedding ring, my dearest treasure. I bought it in Switzerland when I was about twelve years old. Ever since we've been friends, it's reminded me of you. You're like this *inside*. Not everyone knows this about you, but I do. And I want you to have it, because I love it and because I love you."

Anna reached for the small, heavy package. "Thank you, Ellen," she managed. "But, if you love it so much, you ought to keep it yourself."

"That's backwards, Anna! Because I love it so much, I want to give it to *you*."

The *Ruby's* shrill whistle cut through the laughter and the shouting and the noise of the saws at the Big Mill, and Anna's heart tightened. She would have to start talking fast, because in minutes now, Ellen would be moving away from her across the water and then it would be too late.

"Ellen, I—I want to say something."

"Oh, so do I, Anna. There's so much I wish we had time to say, but in a year, or maybe a little longer, I'll be back to stay right here forever. We can be together and talk as much as we like."

"I know, but—after the other night in my room up home, I've been thinking. I oughtn't to have been the way I was with you."

"Friends should always be the way they really feel with each other, Anna."

The Negroes had begun playing *O, Susanna* on their banjos, and Anna had trouble talking above the music and the singing and the laughter.

"I'll try to do what you asked me, Ellen. I reckon that's about all I can say. I remember what you said, and I want you to know I'll try."

"You'll be his friend, too, when we come back, Anna?"

Anna nodded, and Ellen hugged her, gave her a good-bye kiss, and started away toward the crowd at the dock. On impulse, Anna pulled her back.

"I'm much obliged for whatever it is you gave me, Ellen. I hope you have a real nice trip."

"We will, dear Anna, we will! Is it all right if I write to you?"

"Oh, yes. I didn't even hope you'd have time to do that."

"Of course I will. I love to write letters, and when I come back, I expect to be in attendance at *your* wedding!"

Anna watched her dart through the crowd and join Anson at the foot of the *Ruby's* narrow little gangplank. The banjos struck up *Blest Be the Tie That Binds* and Anna watched them run up the gangplank, hand in hand, then stand laughing and waving at the rail with Arthur Dodge beside them, Ellen blowing kisses at everyone on shore. The *Ruby* whistled again, the people shouted good-bye, the banjos plunked, the Negroes sang, and as the little steamer moved slowly away from Steamboat Landing, the whistle at the Big Mill boomed a thunderous farewell.

Anna turned her back, unable to understand why she felt grief almost like the grief she felt when she walked away from her father's grave on the day of his funeral.

Supper was over, and Anna stood by the window

in her room, holding the white ribboned box still unopened in her hand. In a few minutes she'd go down to
sit with Mama on the piazza to watch the sunset. All
day long she had waited for time to open the small,
heavy package.

"What in the world would remind her of me?" She
spoke aloud in a half whisper, as she often did in her
room where she always felt free. "Like me *inside*, Ellen
said."

Anna turned the package in her hands, then carefully slipped off the white satin ribbon. She folded the
tissue paper and laid it alongside the ribbon in her top
dresser drawer. Now, all she had to do was lift the lid
on the small wooden box. Only Papa had ever seemed
to notice what she might be like *inside. You're our
Anna,* he would say. But what was it really like to be
Anna Gould? All she had to do was lift the lid on the
wooden box, and she'd know what a girl such as Ellen
thought she was like.

The catch stuck momentarily, then the lid was
open, and there on blue-green velvet lay a crystal gull
with its wings spread in full flight.

Anna looked out at the marsh where the gulls
wheeled and flashed in the Island sunset. Wheeled free
of the earth, free to be part of the air and the sky and
the light.

She sank into the wicker chair, staring at the small,
exquisite bird, turning it so the light glinted off its wings
and its back.

"Me—like a gull? Me?"

Chapter Seventeen

Rebecca Dodge settled herself on the chaise longue in her bedroom and looked at the bulky travel-worn envelope postmarked Yokohama, Japan, June 22, 1883. Slowly she tore it open, unfolded the tightly written pages, and began to read.

Steamer *Oceanic*

Dear, dear Rebecca,

Anson has just had a marvelous idea! Do keep my letters, because he wants to combine them with the others I'm writing to some of the Murray Hillites back in New York, and turn them all into a book of our travels when we come home again. You know how flattered I am that he thinks my efforts of sufficient literary merit to be made into a book.

Just at present we are tossing in a steamer that lies within a few miles of Yokohama. This side of the deck is the windiest and more than a little damp where the waves dash over. It is also rougher than rough. Never mind; Japan is worth a touch of seasickness. Just now, if you were here, you could see, off there in the west, a gray cloud forming a part of the dull haze that lies over the sea; they say Japan is behind it, and that we are going to get a very pretty view of the land presently, when the mist clears away. Already, to the south, a delicate rose flush, like the inside of coral, is growing out of the clouds, and there are what seem to be hills, with trees covering them, partly hidden in a haze of golden light, where the sun is setting. We have determined to spend all night on deck, watching for the first sight of land as we sail into the harbor; but if, after two or three hours of patient watching and deepening darkness, we do turn in, Ah Chung has explicit directions to call us as soon as the steamer is fairly anchored in Yokohama Bay.

Rebecca read through page after page, smiling at their doings, particularly that they did turn in and, because their Chinese boy forgot to awaken them, were both sleeping soundly some six hours after their boat had anchored in Japan.

Anson is well and, I think, happier than I've ever seen him. Oh, now and then he worries that we were too far away to come home for dear Grandfather Dodge's funeral last February. We have written often to Grandmother, and our hearts ache for her. Grandfather Dodge would be so hard to lose from one's life. Such a good and great and loving man. I've purposely never asked you how he reacted to our marriage, but perhaps if Anson could know he had accepted us, it would help him forgive himself for being on his honeymoon!

Rebecca had hoped they wouldn't ask until they returned. The few minutes she had spent alone with Ellen's father still depressed her.

"Father would never have admitted it," Stuart Dodge had said. "but the two young people added immeasurably to his heavy burden at the end. God will surely punish them both."

Rebecca had held her tongue out of respect for the dead. Out of respect for Ellen's father, too, for whom she felt deep sadness. "Can't you try to enjoy their happiness, Stuart, as I do? You're missing so much."

"How can a man enjoy a shattered heart, Rebecca?"

Sometimes she felt Stuart enjoyed his sorrows, he clung to them so devotedly; but he was already hard at work on a book on *Memorials of William E. Dodge.* Perhaps this would help the poor man put things into perspective.

"I still feel their marriage was not the highest way, Rebecca," William Dodge had said, the last time she saw him. "But the children have my blessing and my prayers for a long and happy life together."

She could tell them that much, anyway. She had heard their grandfather say it, and Ellen had asked about him, not her father.

Rebecca went to her desk and began to write. They would be looking for a letter from her when they reached Tokyo.

> Tokyo, Japan
> August 20, 1883

My dear friend, Anna,

How I wish you could see the streets of Tokyo at night! I am in love with the Orient and the lovely, brown fairies who could be called neither "woman" nor "girl." The Japanese female is too lovely, too fragile, to fit either word. They move and dance like the lights in their narrow streets at night. Perhaps the word "maiden" suits them, or better still: Mädchen, the German.

Arson and I rode in our jinricksha tonight, through the narrow, shadowy streets lined with small and large houses, huts, and shops, and suddenly out into a wide avenue of lights that took my breath away. Hundreds of moving figures in bright dresses and colored sashes, each carrying a lantern. It was gay, Anna, the way your Island is gay in the spring sunlight under its moss-tasseled trees roped with Cherokee roses and grapevines. I am loving every minute and trying to contain my joy that every minute is bringing us closer to the moment when I will at last look on the Taj Mahal. China, Ceylon and then—India!

Anson is happy with it all too, although I could be irritated now and then that the mind of the man with whom I share my honeymoon is to be found time and time again thousands of miles away on an island off the coast of Georgia, U.S.A. This man of mine does not live here, but there, and neither I nor the dancing girls of Japan keep his mind long away from Christ Church Frederica and all of you there. I hope you are learning to be glad about this, dear Anna.

One more thing before I close. Have I taken too much for granted to have our purchases for the new house sent in your care? They will come to the dock at Frederica, and you will have the bother of carting them down the road to Black Banks to keep until we come back. Somehow I believe you will not mind, and that you will want to help me arrange them all in the house some day. We have found literally dozens of things: nests of hand-carved and hand-painted Oriental tables, vases, rugs, figurines, silks—open them all, dear Anna, and enjoy them. And accept my thanks. They will be arriving for a long, long time, I'm sure—and often. Some will take six months, we are told.

Anna finished the letter, warmed by Ellen's friendship, proud that she wanted her to receive the treasures she was buying for her new home. She was folding the pages carefully, to tuck in her dresser drawer with the other letters from Ellen, when she heard low, angry voices from downstairs. She shut the drawer and tiptoed to the door of her room to listen.

Her mother's voice, usually gentle, came sharply through the closed door. "Emma Bass, I'm ashamed of you!"

Anna opened the door and slipped into the upstairs hall.

"If you don't know your own daughter any better'n that, Deborah Gould, it's high time somebody told you. Why, everybody on this Island knows she had her cap set for Anson Dodge, an' I don't intend to let her go on sufferin' for the rest of her life, thinkin' nobody cares that her heart is broke."

Anna gripped the stair railing, unable to believe what she was hearing. Emma was right below her now, not ten feet away, standing arms akimbo at the foot of the stairs; so close Anna could smell her fat, bundled, sweaty odor—she had always hated that.

"I aim to go right upstairs and tell that poor girl she's got one friend on the Island, anyway!"

Horace stepped forward and Anna saw her mother grab Emma's arm. "You'll do no such thing, Emma Bass!"

Hold onto her, Mama! Don't let her come up here, and don't you dare call me to come down.

"Looky here, I'm on Anna's side, Deborah!" Emma's voice grew louder, and Anna could picture her sucking her thick lower lip in and out. "I aim to make life so miserable for him an' that high-toned wife, they'll be glad enough to git on back up north for good!"

"Emma Bass, hush up!"

"You hush up, Deb Gould, an' ask the good Lord to forgive ya for bein' such a no-count mother to Anna. Just because she ain't purty to look at like Miz Dodge ain't no reason why her friends oughta leave her to fend fer herself."

"But, Emma, Anna isn't in love with Anson Dodge. They're friends, that's all. Nothing more."

"Ha! Friends, she says, P. D. Didja hear that? Friends, she says. I'll 'friend' them when they git back. Jist you wait an' see. An' if her own family ain't gonna help, P. D. an' me'll do it ourselves."

Anna saw her brother turn to the older man. "What about that, P. D.? Are you aimin' to make trouble, too?"

P. D. looked blank, confused. He scratched his head and thought a minute. "Why, no, Horace, we ain't aimin' to make no trouble. Emma an' me's tryin' to help out, that's all. The Lord tol' Emma He don't want them Yankees here, an' if He don't want 'em here, we don't want 'em neither."

Deborah sighed. "P. D., Emma . . . we know you mean to do right. None of us doubts that for a minute. But God hasn't told any of us that He doesn't want the Dodges here, and you'll just have to give us the right to hear from God, too. After all, we've been neighbors for such a long time, and—"

" 'I come not to bring peace, but a sword'!" Emma shook her fat forefinger at Deborah.

"Now, we don't have any intention of arguing the Scriptures with you, Emma. And right now the thing that concerns me most is that you *act* and *talk* as though you're our friend."

Emma crossed her arms on her stomach and leaned back on her heels. "Deb Gould, didn't I come here to protect your girl?"

"No, it seems to me as though you came here to stir up trouble for Mr. Dodge."

" 'The Lord loveth an 'umble and a contrite heart,' an' if you kin find an 'umble bone in that man's body, I'd be glad to look."

"It is not your place to judge Mr. Dodge, Emma."

"It's our place to see to it that no Yankee comes down here pushin' us offa our property an' breakin' the heart of a Island girl whilst P. D. an' me jist looks on like some others I know!"

For a long moment, Anna watched them all stand below her in silence. Then Emma marched out of her sight toward the front door, P. D. behind her.

"Would you folks like some tea before you ride home?"

"No use 'n trying' to butter us up, Deb," Emma said. "We had hopes you'd help, but if you won't, we'll jist go 'er alone."

Anna heard the front door bang, and then Horace said, "Sorry this had to happen, Mama."

"So am I. Emma's always been troublesome, but I declare I never saw her like this before."

"I reckon the new house at Frederica's closin' in on her. John Chapman says she gets more cantankerous every day. The higher the house goes, the meaner Emma gets. Refused George Stevens a drink of water yesterday."

"But Anna—this is so unfair to *her*, Horace."

"Emma's taken a funny turn with that notion of hers. For a while she was tellin' it in a way that poked fun at sister. Now she's twisted it around to sound like she's sister's best friend."

"Do you mean Emma's told that before? About Anna and Anson?"

"Yes, Mama. But I thought she'd forgotten it long ago."

"Oh, Horace, I wish your father were here."

"So do I, Mama. So do I."

Chapter Eighteen

Ca had fussed steadily at Anna all the while they hung the heavy, wet, freshly washed blankets over the lines in the back yard.

"You gotta go to Frederica yet today, Miss Anna. Why you keep on helpin' me like this? Don' you reckon Ca knows how to hang up blankets? It gonna be too late to start out all that way up there by yo'self. Now, git on in that wagon an' go."

Anna laughed. "I'm stalling on purpose, Ca. The gums and the sumacs and the wild grapes have started to turn color. I want to be driving along in the late afternoon when the sun shines on all that red and yellow, like fire."

It was late October again, and nothing pleased her more than riding up Frederica Road with the woods turning crimson and gold above her and around her. She would ride up the road every day if she had her way about it, watching for every change that came on in almost every tree with the passing of each day. It would be dark before she got home, but she didn't mind. The moon was full, and she liked thinking all that color was there, even though it didn't show at night.

Bumping along the narrow shell road in the Goulds' wagon an hour later, Anna smiled at herself. Here Ellen thinks she's imposing on me, asking me to make these trips to Frederica after the things she bought. I wish I had to come oftener. She thought about the lovely nest of black lacquered tables she had un-

161

packed last week. They looked like tables Ellen would pick out: teakwood—graceful, hand-painted in gold and green and red, one table fitting inside the next just as pretty as you please.

She wondered what would be at the Frederica dock today, and how much farther along the big house was by now. The last time she saw it, all three stories were up and part of the siding on. George Stevens might be adding the fancy scroll trim by now. Anna admitted to herself that she had also timed her trip when Emma and P. D. would be having their supper; and, to put all thoughts of Emma out of her mind, she began to sing as she rode along, eager now to have another look at the splendid Dodge house. The most beautiful house she had ever seen: sixteen rooms, each with tall windows and hardwood floors. It would look like a castle when it was finished, high and turreted and gabled under the pines and oaks and cedars. Then she frowned. Out of place, though, standing alongside the Bass cottage, which needed paint and a new roof. Out of place alongside any of the Frederica houses, even the Stevens and the Taylor places. The Stevens house, built on top of the Old Fort by the river, had been the nicest one. Now it looked like a shack. Anson Dodge could have built a smaller house. None of the Island plantation homes had ever been big and fancy like the ones on the mainland. Yet some of the plantation owners had been well-to-do before the War. Like the Kings at Retreat. And the Hazzards at West Point and the Hamiltons at Gascoigne Bluff where the Mill now stood, or the folks at Butler's Point. I reckon our house was about as nice as any, she thought, and it looks like a shanty alongside what he's putting up. The architect, John Chapman, says it's simply the kind of house a Dodge builds. Well, lording it over us won't work, I can tell him that.

Still, she wanted Ellen to be happy in her house, and, hating conflict, Anna pushed her thoughts away and tried simply to enjoy the red gums and the sumac and the grapevines. The sun was behind a cloud, though, and she wished she had minded Ca and started earlier.

John Stevens and two of the Taylors' Negroes had helped load the three crates. Now Anna hitched the horses in front of the big house. The siding was all on and most of the gingerbread scrollwork. A modified Queen Anne house, Mr. Chapman called it. "With lots of glorious, wasted space to give it the kind of elegance only Queen Anne can have," he explained in his high-pitched British accent. Anna liked Mr. Chapman, and so did everyone else. He had stopped at St. Simons off a boat from England but, instead of going on to New York as he had planned, had stayed at the Mills to draw the plans for the new church there. Now, he was the architect for the big Dodge house at Frederica and no doubt would stay on, since he had become lay reader at Christ Church to serve with Horace until Anson Dodge returned.

"I've searched for this Island all my life," he told Anna one day, as he showed her from room to room in the big house. "I do hope I'm as welcome as you people make me feel."

Anna didn't think of John Chapman as an outsider, yet he was, even more than Anson Dodge. But there was a difference. She wished suddenly that John Chapman were there now, to walk around the big house with her.

The men had quit work for the day. The big, unpainted house stood silent and empty in the shadows under the tall trees. Anna walked slowly toward the opening where the front door would be. The porches were in place, extending around the house, and almost all the French doors were hung—tall glass doors that would lead from the two dining rooms onto the porches. Anna pictured Ellen walking through these graceful doors, leading her dinner guests outside for coffee; Ellen laughing, at ease, belonging here.

Inside the house, Anna stood in the long hall that ran the length of the building and inhaled the pungent smell of fresh-sawed pine lumber. To her left was the parlor, small and proper. To her right, the little dining room and, a few steps farther on, the large dining room.

What in the world, she wondered, do they want with two dining rooms? The big dining room mantel was in place, and Anna stepped inside to admire its carving, heavy and ornate, all the way to the ceiling. Across the wide hall from the dining room was his study. She peeped in at it, marveling at the solid oak paneling. One thing she knew, no one could ever find carpenters up north or anywhere else to match George and John Stevens when it came to working with wood. She rubbed the panel nearest the door but did not go in. With Anson Dodge on the other side of the world, she still did not feel free to enter the room that would be all his.

Back in the hall, she was uneasy for no reason. It was almost dark outside, and the only lantern she had was in the wagon. I'd better get on home, she thought.

And then she head a clatter at the front of the house. The long hall was too dark now to see to the end of it, but someone was coming toward her from the front porch. Anna didn't move. She smelled the sharp, acrid odor as Emma Bass walked past, her arms full of pine knots.

The ride home by moonlight held nothing of what Anna had hoped for. Tom and Daisy lumbered along, unmindful of her urgings, and when at last she reached her room and lay back on her bed, her heart still pounded as it had during the panic of those moments in the big house. She felt sick at her stomach, sick with fright, sick from the stench of Emma's bulky figure pushing past her in the hall as though she were not there.

Why can't I talk to Mama about bad things? Why do I always try to protect her? As the wagon rounded the corner from Frederica at the churchyard, she had wanted to call out to Papa, but what was the use calling out to a grave?

Anna sat up in bed. "Emma Bass is planning to set fire to the Dodge house!" The sound of her own words chilled her. "I ought to tell somebody. But who? Who would believe me?"

Chapter Nineteen

The heavily loaded train from Agra to Allahabad rattled through the countryside of the United Provinces, and Ellen felt almost sad. She could have stayed at Agra for a month, taking the carriage ride every day and every night to look at the Taj Mahal in every kind of light. She was going on to Allahabad with Anson because he wanted to go; the Bishop of Calcutta was there this week, and it gave Anson as much pleasure to sit and talk church affairs with a Bishop as the Taj Mahal had given her. She was going with him, but her mind was still captive to the enchanted place, the glowing marble monument to a man's love for his dead wife. Anson sat beside her in their compartment engrossed in a Church of England journal, and she was relieved. For the first time, she found herself wishing he wouldn't talk. Eighteen years, the Mogul Emperor Shah Jahan had spent guiding the building of his white marble dream: a dream motivated and kept alive by the love in his heart that would not die. Ellen pictured him in her mind: tall, wide-shouldered, a fine-featured, brown-skinned face, with eyes that saw into the most minute detail of every lacy minaret; dark, burning eyes that haunted the nights of the men who skillfully and patiently carved the shimmering white marble, every curve and crevice to his demanding taste. A man who loved a woman as Anson loved her. She smiled. I'm sure I've pictured the Mogul Emperor as an Indian Anson Dodge. Why not? The picture fits them both. She would describe the Taj for

Rebecca and Anna later. She had no words yet. Only strange, almost holy stirrings in the depth of her being at having looked on it with her own eyes. At having "looked on beauty bare." Throughout most of the night she had sat in their hotel room at Agra, staring toward where she knew the Taj stood glistening under the full November moon, just a mile away, out of sight of eyes, but not of her imagination. The moon would be moving, she imagined, across the white marble spires, the perpetuation of a man's heart in stone and jewels.

She longed to take the church journal out of Anson's hands and pull him into the peace that wrapped her around, almost separating them. "I enjoy watching you look at it more than I enjoy looking at the Taj myself," he had said as they stood together in the moonlight. Now, on the rocking Indian train, she wondered at the peace she was experiencing apart from him. Peace that could not be disturbed, as though she were realizing for the first time that somewhere for her, for Anson, for everyone—beyond time—lay more beauty, more pure beauty than they had looked upon last night.

It's all right. Don't talk yet, dear Anson. Not yet. I am seeing something new, and I may never, never be able to tell you. Not that I won't long to. I will. I long to tell you now. I long to interrupt your reading and tell you. But what would I say? How could I reach across from *this* to your preoccupation with the growth of the church in India? She smiled again. Dear, church-minded Anson, looking forward to his meeting with the Bishop of Calcutta, a man with the earthy name of Edward Ralph Johnson. To Anson, she knew, there was really no distance at all between St. Simons Island and Allahabad. The church stood central to both places. The Emperor Mogul had not been a Christian, yet Ellen had sensed the presence of God in the glittering white beauty of his Taj. Her God was everywhere, just as the catechism declared Him to be: in the moonlight on the Taj, in the sunlight on the red gums and the yellow grape leaves on Frederica Road.

She leaned her head against the tufted leather back of the train seat. Did the Mogul Emperor find his dead wife nearer as the marble poem took shape? Did it help heal his anguish? Did he sometimes find her close by when he walked there in the moonlight over two centuries ago? How could death really seal off earth from heaven?

From her handbag, Ellen took a scrap of paper and began to write:

> *I have lain in the breast of a star, and danced on the lips of a rainbow; I have been caught in the laugh of the moon, and tossed my limbs in the yellow hair of the sun and the white hair of the old, old moon. I have slept on the edge of a blue and gold cloud; I have drunk the purple wine from the sky, and heard the love of the thunder. I have seen the Spirit of God flying through the air in the lightning. I have lain in the light that flashes from a man's eyes to a woman's; I have seen the morning hanging in the arms of the night; I have touched the verge of all eternity and found it one unending pleasure. And yet, I have found something newer and sweeter than all—I have found death.*

She scanned the lines, made a few changes, and returned the paper to her handbag.

Anson looked up, his finger marking his place. "Aren't you going to let me see what you wrote?"

"Not now, darling. It's very rough."

"About the Taj?"

"No, I think it's about a dream."

He touched her hand, smiled, and went back to his journal.

That's right, dear Anson. I need time to make the bridge from wherever it is I've been, from whatever it is I've just seen, to Allahabad and your Bishop Johnson of Calcutta. She sighed. I go gladly, though, beloved husband, because I love you the way the Mogul Emperor loved his wife.

Anna knew, when she first saw them coming at full speed up the Black Banks road, that Belle Taylor and Rossie Stevens were not just making an afternoon call. Her mother had joined her on the piazza by the time the old buggy rocked and jolted around the curve in the road and rattled across the yard, both women holding on for dear life, Belle to the seat and Rossie to the reins.

Belle was out of the buggy and halfway up the front steps before Rossie managed to hitch the horses at the big oak tree.

"What in the world, Belle?" Deborah called.

"Something terrible has happened, Deb. It's awful—just awful."

Rossie Stevens' ample figure puffed up the steps now, her usual dignity missing, her maroon bonnet askew, her chubby face red and hot.

"What in the world, Rossie?"

"We just had to ride down," Rossie gasped. "Wait'll I catch my breath."

Both women collapsed in the wicker chairs, fanning themselves with their long skirts.

"Anna, go tell Ca to bring us some tea."

"Not till I hear, Mama. Is anybody sick? Or dead?"

"You tell 'em, Belle. You're not as hot as I am."

Rossie untied her bonnet.

"The Dodge house!" Belle gasped. "Somebody tried to set it afire!"

"Oh, my land, Belle, did it burn?"

"No."

"Well, who did it?"

"P. D. Bass an' Emma say it was Procter Green."

"Well, I say it wasn't!" Anna snapped.

"You do, Anna?" Belle looked from Anna to her mother. "How can you be so sure it wasn't Procter? You way down here when it happened."

"Because I know Procter, that's why. That boy would no more set fire to the Dodge house than I would! He worships Anson Dodge. Procter's living for the day when he goes to work for him. It's all planned."

"That's what we thought too, isn't it, Rossie? Isn't that what we thought?"

"Yes, indeed. That's what we all thought."

Anna looked at her friends coldly. "Well, what do you think now?"

The two women stopped fanning.

"I said, *what do you think now,* Rossie? Belle?"

"We don't know what to think, Anna," Belle whimpered. "We just flew down here as fast as we could to see what you'd think. You an' your mother."

Anna flared. "I can tell you what *not* to think. Procter Green had nothing to do with—"

"Let them talk, dear. Why don't you tell us about what did happen, girls—as much as you know?"

"Well"—Rossie began to fan again—"I was on my back porch hanging up my tea towels when I heard this terrible yelling from over toward the Dodge house. Somebody was shouting, 'Fire! Fire! Help! Help!' "

"Who was yelling, Rossie?" Anna demanded.

"It was Procter."

"If Procter yelled for help, it doesn't make sense that he set the fire, does it?" Anna made no effort to hide her anger.

"But Anna, P. D. says the boy was tryin' to cover it up!"

"Tell us the rest, Rossie," Deborah urged.

"Well, Procter ran yelling an' hollering to the Basses' backyard and began jerking Emma's blankets down from the line. She musta just hung them up a few minutes before, because they were still dripping wet. Procter ran with the wet blankets and began smothering the blaze—and Emma right after him!"

"Was Emma trying to stop him from putting out the fire?"

"No, Anna—no! Emma was yelling, too, trying to help the boy. She made two trips to her back yard, along with Procter. Used up all her winter blankets."

"Was there much damage to the house?" Deborah asked.

"No, thank the good Lord. Just the west corner charred black. John says he can fix it easy. When it's painted, it'll never show. But isn't it the craziest thing? Deborah, isn't it the craziest thing?"

"We don't want you to think we really think Procter did it, Anna," Belle offered helplessly.

"I hope you mean that, Belle."

"Why, Anna, of course I mean it!"

"Who else heard P. D. blame it on him?"

Belle Taylor thought a minute. "Let me see now, there was Mr. Chapman, John, and George—and my Will. I reckon that's all."

"Then you and Will had better see to it that it stops with them."

"Well, for pity sakes, Anna, you act like we were planning to tell it around."

"People tell things before they think," Anna said. "And I happen to know Procter Green was *not* the one who did it."

"Well, who did it then, Anna? Who else would have done it?"

"Maybe it was an accident," Deborah said.

"No!" Rossie fanned faster. "Didn't we tell you? John found a pile of pine knots under the east corner of the house. They were wet from the rain last night, or that house might be burned to the ground by now."

Chapter Twenty

All through the lavish dinner given in their honor at the home of the British precinct official in Allahabad, Ellen hid her boredom. She had always found British food uninteresting, and tonight her dinner partners—a blond, pasty young British officer to her right, and ancient Dr. Hayworth to her left—matched the food. Conversation lagged, in spite of Ellen's gift for it; three times Dr. Hayworth had turned to her to exclaim, "By Jove, now, isn't this a coincidence? My offices right in the same hotel where you and your husband have rooms!" If a company of Englishmen were sent on a colonizing expedition to heaven, she decided, in six months they would find a way to turn the celestial mansions into ugly stone fortresses and transform heavenly manna into flavorless beef and dry potatoes.

Perhaps I'm not being fair, she thought. Look at my husband. He's so taken up with his new friend, Bishop Johnson, he has no idea what he's eating. The tall, angular Bishop had seemed stuffy when she met him; now he was beaming at Anson's interest in the history of the church in India.

"Will you and your husband be here to attend services in Allahabad on Sunday, Mrs. Dodge?"

Ellen turned to the young officer beside her. "Oh, yes, we plan to stay at least a week. Is it an interesting church? I mean—architecturally?"

"Oh, I'm afraid not. It's really not much to look at. In need of everything, one might say."

And then she escaped back to watching Anson again, who was now deep in telling of his own plans for building missions across southern Georgia. She could hear a snatch of his talk here and there: something about there being many Episcopalians in Georgia, but mostly Baptist churches.

Through dessert she amused herself by thinking of adjectives that described Anson: intelligent, patrician, dynamic, commanding. Allahabad was going to be Anson's part of their trip. Agra and the shimmering Taj seemed a universe away. Had the Bishop come out of his historical facts concerning the Indian Church long enough to sense her boredom? It seemed he had, and Ellen found herself drawn to the tall clergyman when he held her hand a moment as they said good-bye.

"Your husband is convinced you are in his plans with him all the way, my dear. I pray that you are."

He was quite human after all, she decided, and felt grateful to him for the courteous admonition. She vowed to forget the Taj now and concentrate on the rundown little church in Allahabad, on Indian church history, on Georgia missions—on anything that made Anson happy.

He was still glowing as they rode toward their hotel in a rented victoria. "Stimulating evening, wasn't it, darling?"

She moved closer to him. "I was foolishly proud of you. Only let's get out and find something to eat. I'm sure you didn't notice, but the food was vile, and I'm starved! Maybe we could find some fresh fruit and cheese. Doesn't that sound like a tempting idea?"

Ellen lay in bed, the mosquito netting well tucked in, head and foot, watching Anson read a month-old New York newspaper by the flickering oil lamp near the easy chair.

"Comfortable, dearest? Any mosquitoes getting through?"

"Not a one, Anson." She sighed happily and stretched her arms over her head. "I'm so glad to be right here in this room with you, I'd have trouble being inhospitable even to a mosquito tonight."

He smiled to her. "Not still hungry, are you?"

"No. My tummy is full of huge, glorious, deliciously juicy purple grapes. Do you know I ate a whole bunch myself? You didn't get any, did you?"

"Grapes? No, I much prefer those yellow plantains."

"Go back to your newspapers, darling. I'm utterly happy."

She leaned on her elbow, so she could look at him. He was reading again, the paper hiding his face.

"Anson . . ."

"Hm?"

"Am I being a nuisance?"

He lowered his paper, grinning.

"That's better. I do want you to know everything that happened in New York a month ago, but I can't see your face when you're reading. And with that beard, you're too handsome for me not to look at every minute."

"Still like it, eh?"

"I adore it."

She watched him resolutely try to go back to his papers, but he had lost interest. In a few minutes the lamp was out, and he was crawling under the mosquito netting beside her.

In his arms, she thought again of the Taj. The Taj Mahal, built by a man who loved a woman, as Anson loved her.

"What would you build in my memory if I died, Anson?"

He was silent a moment, kissed her nose, then laughed. "Two Taj Mahals, one upside down on top of the other!"

She made a face in the dark. "I don't think you take the Mogul Emperor's grief seriously enough."

"How can I with you here?"

He was kissing her mouth, her eyes, her cheeks, his hands caressing her; and suddenly, for the first time, Ellen found it difficult to respond. She felt dizzy, and a heavy restlessness grew like a tidal wave about to pull her under and away from him. She felt more and more trapped, more and more horrified that she seemed to

want to be pulled away, that, even in Anson's arms, a
kind of panic was all but engulfing her. I must think of
something beautiful, she thought, and white, glittering
marble minarets and silvered pools and delicate mother-
of-pearl patterns swirled and vanished and reformed inside her aching head. Then the chills came, and she
could feel her body cold and damp against his. Perspiration poured down her face and back and legs. Dear
God, don't let him notice. This is just some kind of reaction to all the pent-up excitement at having seen the
Taj at last—with him. Don't let Anson notice, God.
Then a spasm of pain tore a cry from her.

Anson sat up. "Ellen!"

She tried to laugh, gritted her teeth, trying.

"Ellen, are you ill?"

"No, Anson. I'm sure I'm not ill." She had to gasp
for breath now, so intense were the pains. "I'm sure it's
just—excitement."

She had never been ill in her life, except once in
boarding school in Switzerland when she and two classmates had eaten some green plums. Green plums!
Grapes! It was just a plain old-fashioned tummy ache
from too many grapes.

"Grapes, Anson. Just a plain old—tummy ache—
from too many—grapes."

He had lighted the lamp, was bathing her face,
soothing her. "I'll get Dr. Hayworth, darling. The old
gentleman who sat next to you at dinner tonight. He'll
be in his rooms downstairs now."

"Anson, no." She clung to him. "Don't leave me.
Please, please Anson, don't leave me. . . . Anyway,
darling—I had enough of old Dr. Hayworth—at—"
She began to cry. "Anson, I'm so—c-cold. Hold me,
Anson. Hold me . . . warm me."

He held her and held her, his heart calling, Oh,
God, God . . . God!

Perhaps an hour passed; perhaps it was only ten
minutes. Anson didn't know. Ellen, chilled, wept and
kept trying to encourage him. At last he made up his
mind. *Those were Indian grapes.* In India any fruit
might have been grown in cholera-infected ground; all

fruit must be carefully cleansed. They had bought the grapes at a side-street café! He wanted to curse himself for not making sure. But he could no longer focus on either a curse or a prayer. Ellen was ill. Ellen, her features pale and pinched, her body twisted with pain. After one siege of retching, so violent that blood appeared, she fainted. Anson lifted her in his arms and ran, stumbling and calling out, down the wide, sagging wooden stairs.

"Dr. Hayworth! Dr. Hayworth! I need a doctor. I need a doctor!"

The terrible, early hours of the November dawn, coming slowly to Allahabad, brought no change, Ellen lay all night on the cot in Dr. Hayworth's office, her skin cold, dry, her thirst intense, and as the sun filtered through the drawn curtains Anson could see the sick blue color of her face, could feel the once soft skin parched and wrinkled under his hands as he worked hour after hour with the old doctor, massaging her stomach with turpentine, applying ice packs to her arms and legs, in an attempt to ease the knifelike cramping that continued through the morning and into the afternoon.

Sometime after darkness came, she grew quiet, and Anson began to hope again. She stopped asking for water, her sunken eyes met his once with recognition.

"Her pulse, Doctor. Please take it again."

Dr. Hayworth hunted for her pulse, found it slow, barely perceptible, and shook his head.

Anson was bending over her, smoothing her hair back from her forehead, when she opened her eyes.

"Ellen? Oh, darling, you're better, aren't you?"

Her lips moved, but no sound came.

"Fight, Ellen, fight. I'm here with you. Fight!"

She nodded her head and tried to reach for his hand, her eyes drawing him closer, her voice a hoarse whisper. "Anson, don't . . . leave . . . me."

"I'm not going to leave you, dearest—not for a minute. And you're not—" Her features contorted, and the hard struggle began in his arms. He looked frantically toward Dr. Hayworth, who was hunting her pulse.

Anson was still holding her when the doctor dropped her lifeless hand: still holding her. . . .

The weary doctor tried to lift him to his feet, tried gently but firmly to disengage Anson's arms from the limp body.

And then he sat down across the room, to wait for daylight and to pray for the young man who held his dead wife in his arms . . . and who, now and then, startled the old doctor by crying, "No, God! No!"

Chapter Twenty-One

*I am the resurrection and the life, saith the Lord:
he that believeth in me, though he were dead, yet
shall he live: and whosoever liveth and believeth
in me, shall never die.*

Anson remembered Edward Ralph Johnson, the
Bishop of Calcutta, paraphrasing the words of Christ:
". . . though she were dead, yet shall she live." The
remainder of the brief Anglican Order for the Burial of
the Dead was a blur. He was on a Indian train, alone
with a big box, going to another place, unexpected, not
planned: Bombay, to take a boat, a faster boat, not
scheduled for lovers—instead of Calcutta and the leisurely return home under wide skies, across the blue
seas, laughing—Bombay now, and across in the hold of
a ship alone with a big box. . . . But first, eight
hundred miles on this train, Indian and slow. No one at
home knew she was dead. Not even Rebecca. This was
still his honeymoon.

The baggage car lurched, and his hand flew out to
steady the box where she lay inside the white casket,
sealed in a lead-lined ebony box, inside the wooden
crate. The heat pushed around him, an ocean of heat, to
float the swarms of flies drawn to the filth in a wall of
chicken coops stacked around him, three deep. His Indian boy tried to persuade him to ride in the first class
section, reminded him that he had paid for it. "I did

that from habit," Anson said. "I'm riding right here, all the way to Bombay."

The frightened chickens in the wobbly coops could screech their fear. Grief *was* very like being afraid, but he could only sit there in the cramped space, bearing it. Slowly he began to form more detailed plans: I will write to Mother from the last boat, Liverpool to New York. She should get the letter after Ellen and I are safely on our way to Georgia by train. Safe from family interference with my plan to take her back to Christ churchyard . . . safe even from Mother's grief.

The Bishop's voice came to him again, as though through deep water: "The Lord giveth, the Lord taketh away. . . ." No! God did not take her away. He could never believe that. They were simply careless about the grapes. Dear Mother, the accident happened on the evening of November 19: after dinner with the Bishop of Calcutta, Ellen ate a bunch of grapes and died of cholera in my arms. She lay on our bed laughing while I read the papers, and then she died of cholera.

He pressed the side of the box until his knuckles whitened. Ellen in there? Ellen in there in the filmy blue dress, still lying on the white silk pillow as she lay before the plain little altar in the Allahabad church a day ago? Not smiling, not even able to move her hand? Ellen making no sound? Offering him no help? Not even wondering why she was there instead of roaming the streets of Allahabad searching out ancient temples and shrines, laughing beside him in a *bandi*. . . . "We must take one ride in a *bandi*, Anson, before we leave India. After all, some of the Island folk still ride in oxcarts very like these buffalo *bandis*. The King girls do."

Anson had laughed, picturing the daughters of the once wealthy owners of King's Retreat Plantation bumping around the Island in an oxcart. Ellen had become better acquainted with the Island people and their ways than he. Miss Frances Buford King in an oxcart? "Certainly, darling, she told me herself. She rides up close to the animal's tail, just the way the *bandi* drivers do, and when she wants more speed she simply gives the tail a twist! So, we must ride in a *bandi*, because I intend to learn the trick." Ellen in an oxcart? Ellen in a buffalo *bandi?* Ellen going home in a baggage car motionless inside a big, solid box. . . .

I am the resurrection and the life . . . though she were dead, yet shall she live. If she's living, where is she now? How far along on her journey? Are you alone, darling? Do you know I'm here? . . . A coop of shrieking chickens tumbled to the floor end over end, and he sprang to his feet to set them upright, then tried to nod in a civilized manner to the Indian baggage man, who merely glanced over his shoulder, caring no more for the battered, terror-stricken chickens than for this crazy, bearded young man who insisted on sitting in the hot, crowded baggage car beside a coffin.

Anson's head throbbed with the heat and the stench and the grieflike fear that had come to stay with him. He had not yet found courage to sleep in a bed. Not in the three nights since she had gone away. He reminded himself that he could sleep sitting up in the train again tonight, and some quiet came, and a blank where all the other nights would be. "Your mind is in shock, son. Do only one thing at a time." Thank you, Bishop Johnson. I mean to. I'm thankful to have travel plans to make and carry out. Things to do that directly concern her. I will do one thing at a time, and the days will pass. . . . Now we are on the train, then Bombay, and the first boat to England. I will go on doing one thing at a time. She asked me not to leave her, you know, and it is good to have a promise to keep.

The hold of the big ship out of Bombay was roomier than the baggage car had been, and there were no chickens. Here the engines throbbed separately in his head, and the heavy water roared as the ship's bow split and hurled it against the hull not three feet from where he spent twenty hours out of every twenty-four.

"I sleep some down there, Shankar," he told his cabin boy. "Ever since you found that chair for me, I've really been quite comfortable. You see, it helps to sit there. My wife and I were always up on deck in the sunshine. I am trying to think of this as a new experience for us both. I suppose the other passengers pity me, as you say, but really I think this long voyage is helpful. As long as I'm on the high seas, I'm spared having to live a daily life again before I've had time to learn how. Do you understand what I mean, Shankar? Oh, not that I will refuse when I reach my destination. I have work to do there, work enough to last me the rest of my life. But now I am still on the bridge, passing over from one life to another. I think these things through down there beside her, and I feel I'm making a little progress. I'm really quite comfortable since you found the chair for me."

Sometime during the third or fourth week, he came to feel almost at home with the engines and the crash of the water against the hull. Two days passed without a headache; and tonight, December 19, one month after Ellen went away, he had taken his place for the first time at the Captain's table. He was maimed, he would always be a cripple, but he had gone to dinner, had tasted what he ate, had managed to ease the discomfort of the other passengers whose sympathy created an awkwardness only he could relieve. He had sat with them talking about America under President Arthur, after Garfield's assassination, sharing his thinking about the future of the South now that the era of the carpetbaggers was at an end. He had found his mind still retained its store of facts and figures, he had been energized once more by his own desire to be a part of the new South, to contribute to its people, his people: the Taylors, the Stevenses, the Kings, the Postells, the Goulds. Over and over, as the conversation flowed on, his mind twisted back to his pain, *but he had done it.* He had experienced society at a dinner table without her. And he had hurried from the dining room at the conclusion of the meal, to run almost excitedly down the steep, ladderlike steps to the hold of the ship. For what? *To tell Ellen?* He stood beside the box, mute and stunned. This he would have to learn: he could no longer tell her everything. From this moment, he must learn to live, keeping the big and the little things inside. She would be better, happier, no matter where she was on her strange journey without him, if she knew he had gone to the ship's dining room, had made the effort.

Though she were dead, yet shall she live . . . she was somewhere, living. He believed she did know, but he would have to learn to weigh his small and large accomplishments alone. He could believe she knew, but he would have to learn how not to run to tell her. Not to that box, not to her grave in the churchyard. Somehow he would go on believing she knew, no matter where he was. No matter where she was on her journey, he would learn a new way of being with her. Ellen was apart from the dear body now, and he would need time to absorb this: her new way of being with him wherever he was.

Where would they put the big box on the *Ruby,* he wondered, for the trip across St. Simons Sound? On deck, he was sure. He and Ellen would make the last part of the long voyage up on deck, under the piece of bright Island sky, in full view of the marshes of Glynn.

His hand smoothed the box from habit, as naturally as it had smoothed her hair and her face. The days were going by: the steamer *Royal Crown* from Liverpool, then New York and the train for Georgia, then the *Ruby* and Steamboat Landing, then a Mill wagon up Frederica Road the way he and Anna Gould had taken Procter home that day after the snake bit him, and, at last, the churchyard and the guardian oaks, and then he could breathe again . . . out of this dark place into the light of the Island days for all the rest of his life.

"There will come a day," the Bishop of Calcutta had said, "when you will begin to see that you can build for the second period of your relationship with your wife, much as you built for the first, with your whole heart, creatively." Anson leaned his head against the crate. The second part of my life with Ellen? "Mrs. Dodge would be expecting it of you. It is God's way not to waste anything. Even grief." It had taken him all these weeks to recall his friend's words. Words that seemed to mean there might be a way for him to *do* something beyond enduring the severed stump of his life . . . something beyond accepting the mere comfort of God . . . beyond attending to the mere medication of social contact with other human beings . . . beyond the solace of work to be done. He lifted his head from the big box. A way to build for the second part of his life with Ellen? Creatively? This in no way excluded her. She would be actively *in* a concept like this—she would revel in it!

In his stateroom on the British liner, *Royal Crown,* bound for New York, a few days out of Liverpool, Anson sat down to write the letter to his mother, carrying out the next step in his carefully laid plan. It was Christmas Eve, and he had cabled her holiday greetings from them both from London. Her Christmas would not be spoiled, and now he sat with the blank piece of paper before him, the pen in his hand. And with this moment, the realization of the depth of his mother's grief brought his first physical release: he wept, abandoning himself. Until now, he had only dared concentrate on the *fact* that somewhere, in some light-surrounded manner, Ellen was still alive. He had found this quite possible to believe, as a child believes, because it was impossible not to believe it. But now he faced what he had forced back for thirty-five days and nights. He would never kiss her again, never feel the warmth of her body against his, never smell the familiar cologne in her hair, never hear her laugh. He permitted the crash all at once . . . the big new house at Frederica would never be their house now, he would live there alone among their treasures—treasures that would keep coming to the dock at Frederica for months.

He half lay across the small desk in his stateroom, aware of nothing but his grief, not caring if someone heard him sobbing, unmindful of the tears that soaked the writing paper, his coat sleeves. And then the weeping stopped. Too black for tears, the final realization slashed across his mind, bringing him bolt upright, to cry out loud: *"Now I will never have a child by her!"*

I will bury their dead and marry their lovers and baptize their children, *but I will not have a child by Ellen.* Whatever I build on St. Simons Island will now end with me. I will leave no son to carry on my work. I will leave no daughter to grow to be like her mother. My children's mother will be lying in her grave at Christ Church Frederica where their father preaches every Sunday.

He sat in the dark and the pain and the finality and the despair, the letter to his mother unwritten.

Then, across his mind, slowly, like the growth of color in an Island sunset, spread a picture of the churchyard at Frederica. His eyes were open. It was more than a memory. He had catalogued every grave, he knew every foot of ground, every crumbling family plot, every holly tree, every pine, every smooth-barked myrtle trunk and every thick grapevine twisted around every oak. He looked at it all for a long time, the vision remaining clear. Calmly, almost restfully, he selected the spot where Ellen would lie first: behind the old church, near one tall pine tree. Ellen would wait there for the next step in the plan that was forming: with the money she had left him, and with some of his own, he would build the new church in her memory, a finer building than he had planned. He would tell John Chapman that Christ Church Frederica was to be the most beautiful country church in America: cruciform in design, paneled with cedar, and built of heart-of-island pine. It would be painted white, and it would stand with its stained-glass windows catching the sun journeying daily through the tops of the guardian oaks, and when it was almost finished, he would move Ellen inside, to lie under its altar.

The little church, like a surprise jewel in an unexpected place, would stand to the memory of Ellen, whom he would love, as he had always loved her, to the end of his life. *Though she were dead, yet shall she live.* Above her resting place he would preach, to the end of his life, what he now knew and believed as he never had before: *Because I live, ye shall live also.*

He picked up the pen again. *Dear Mother. . . .*

Chapter Twenty-Two

Anna stood between her mother and James at the brief, graveside service for Ellen in back of the old church.

"This grave will be temporary," Anson Dodge had told them, in a manner that to Anna seemed almost businesslike. "When the new church is finished, Ellen will lie under its altar."

He's got that new church on his mind, even now, Anna thought, and couldn't take her eyes off him, as he stood solemn, quiet, his head up, his face older and heavier behind the thick, black beard; more determined-looking than ever, pushing his way into her own grief now, with his shocking calm. Making her feel ashamed of her weeping as the rector from Brunswick prayed.

"O merciful God, the Father of our Lord Jesus Christ . . . who hath taught us, by his holy Apostle Saint Paul, not to be sorry, as men without hope, for those who sleep in Him. . . ."

Anna missed the rest of his prayer, but when Horace put the symbolic shovelful of sandy earth into Ellen's grave, she sobbed aloud. And when Anson turned to give her a small, steadying smile, she wept helplessly. She was weeping for him too, she supposed, but how could he try to comfort her at a time like this? He wasn't their minister yet. It seemed to her he could leave them alone to their separate feelings for a while. He didn't need to challenge her. Why was he afraid to act human like everybody else? Anna thought of the exquisite length of white silk brocade which had come for her only yesterday to the dock of Frederica . . . from Ellen.

"Unto Almighty God we commend the soul of our sister departed, and we commit her body to the ground; earth to earth, ashes to ashes, dust to dust. . . ."

One dry sob escaped Anson's lips.

Emma Bass hurried to catch up with Anna and her mother as they left the churchyard. "Didja see his face?" she panted. "A body pert near felt fer him, but he's jist as high an' mighty as ever! I thought sure this would bring him down to humility—an' what right's he got to bury her here in this churchyard?"

Anna and her mother kept walking.

"The Lord is speaking, Deb Gould, loud and clear! If none of you'll help me, it's plain as the nose on your face the Lord's takin' this man into His own hands. You mark my words, the Dodge punishment has jist started."

Chapter Twenty-Three

People didn't stop talking about Ellen's death for the six months he was away finishing seminary. Ellen was too young to die, and whatever they felt about Anson's ideas, they all talked about what a tragedy it was. All but Emma and P. D. Every few days Anna rode up Frederica Road to the churchyard to tend the temporary grave, taking fresh flowers from her mother's garden. Rossie Stevens went too, after they figured out what Emma was doing at night. Anna would fix the flowers and sweep away the fallen leaves, and the next day Rossie would walk around from her house, to find the flowers turned over, the petals pulled off.

Emma hadn't set fire to the house again, but the suspense and the wondering had almost been worse than if she had.

"What's going to happen to Emma Bass, Mama?"

"I don't know, Anna. It would be terrible if P. D. had to put her away."

"Is she crazy? Or just ignorant?"

Deborah sighed. "That's not for us to say."

"What good does it do Emma to tear up the flowers on Ellen's grave?"

"I don't know. It just looks as though the poor woman is caught in something she can't control."

"Anson Dodge is coming back next week, to stay. What do you suppose she'll do then?"

"I don't know that, either, Anna. But God does

know. And, even if things don't seem like it, He's still in charge."

Anson walked slowly across the campus of General Theological Seminary in New York. It was May, 1884. Six months had passed. In his hand he held the last letter his mother would write to him at seminary. She would go first to Atlanta with him where he was to be ordained into the Diaconate, then to the Island, to help settle the big house. He was ready: graduation was over, his trunks packed, his desk emptied. The unopened letter from his mother would contain words of encouragement, details for their meeting, and the inevitable last line: "We will learn, Anson. Somehow we will both learn how to live without her."

Yesterday Horace's letter, telling him that Ellen's body now lay under the altar of the new church, had filled him with a strange quiet. He had slept rather well last night, after forcing himself to pack away all of Ellen's letters, her journal kept on their honeymoon trip, her brown leather notebook in which she had written poems about the Island, the Swiss Alps, the sky over St. Simons, the dancing trees, her essay on Carlyle, written when she was nineteen, her short stories, and the strange, prophetic piece he had found in her handbag, written on the train as they left Agra, not about the Taj Mahal, but about—death. Her writings were all packed in a rectangular rosewood box in which he had kept his books as a boy: not to be unpacked or looked at again until he knew he could face reading them. There would come a time when they would strengthen, not destroy, the peace he was striving to keep for the sake of the Island folk who were at last going to be his people.

He climbed the steps to his room. Horace Gould had said the new church would be ready for services early in January. This was just right. Reverend Lucas had done a remarkable job, coming by boat from Brunswick every Sunday to conduct Evening Prayers in the old patched-up church. When it had been torn down that summer so that the new one could stand in its place, the services were held under the guardian oaks where the Wesleys had preached during the last century, when Georgia was a colony of the Crown. Anson studied a photograph of the new church. It stood with its foundation deep in American history: a symbol of the kind of peace and harmony God intended His children to enjoy. A small, graceful, carefully constructed house of God, designed by a British architect, built by Southern hands, paid for with Yankee money. His and Ellen's . . . in memory of love.

He walked to the window. The gaunt northern elms bent a little under a cold wind. Their leaves were in bud; they would unfold soon. He wouldn't be here to see them, but they would come.

His valise lay open on the bed, packed except for the last things: his toilet case, the silver hairbrushes Ellen had given him on his last birthday, and his Bible. He laid these in and snapped it shut. "Well, darling— I'm ready. I'm coming home now, to stay beside you forever."

III

Chapter Twenty-Four

Each November 19 since 1884, when he began his life on St. Simons Island, Anson had stayed in his room, refusing to see anyone but Sibby. But on that day in 1888, he was up and dressed before the birds were fully awake, before the light had spread all the way across the Island sky, long before Sibby was due to come to work. Today, he would not refuse anyone anything. From the tall, glass-doored bookcase beside his desk in the big study, he selected two books—his leather-bound Book of Common Prayer and Ellen's volume of Carlyle—stuffed them in his coat pockets, and walked briskly toward the church.

Five years ago he was holding her lifeless body in his arms, waiting for dawn to come to Allahabad. . . . Five years without her. . . . Five years of beginning each day on his knees beside her grave at the altar of the church, the grave marked with a flat granite slab bearing only her initials and dates: E. A. P. D. 1862–1883.

Today he was on his way there once more, but he would not return to his room to live it all again alone. Today, he might even go to the new church being built at Burnt Fort, to check on its progress. The roof should have gone on yesterday. If he went to the mainland to check the Burnt Fort building, he might just as well stay and visit his mission churches in Waycross and Valdosta and St. Mary's. The man he had hired to serve the new congregation at Waycross needed supervision. It would do no harm if Anson dropped in unexpectedly.

"You makes work fo' yo'self, man," Sibby would nag. "Ain't no man can think up so many extrys as you. Ain't nobody chasin' you, Mist' Dodge."

He stood in the quiet, gentle beginning of the November day, looked up at the tall gums, glistening crimson, the dew still shining on their leaves, then turned to glance toward the rundown cottage where the Basses lived, and wondered what more he could do to win them over. They had stubbornly held to their half acre of land, so that a buggy discharging passengers at his house had to circle the entire acreage to reach his barn. He sighed. At least Emma Bass had done nothing more than gossip, and Anson believed that Maimie Gould, James's blue-eyed, pretty young wife from Augusta, had been the one to keep her under control. It was Maimie who had the nerve and the good sense to tell him that Emma had once tried to burn down his house.

"I hate gossip, Mr. Dodge, but you shouldn't be in the dark about Emma. P. D.'s all right, but he minds her like a child. Whatever she says, he does."

"Maimie, doesn't every minister have his own Emma Bass? Unless the woman's insane, and I don't think she is, I feel I must go on expecting her to change."

"Who knows about Emma's mind? There are those here who think she's ready for the asylum now. And then there are those, who've known her all their lives, who still put some stock in what she says. It's your business, Mr. Dodge, but as far as I know, there's nothing in the Bible that says we should trust people too far."

Anson had come to depend more and more on Maimie Gould as time went by. In a sense, she was an outsider too. He respected her devotion to her sometimes erratic but lovable husband, James, and prayed that one day he would come to care about the things of God, as Maimie cared.

Anson turned from the Bass house and listened for a moment to a wren in the myrtle tree above him. Now that he's home from seafaring, perhaps we should make James a vestryman, he thought.

Pulling his coat collar up against the chill November morning, he quickened his steps. These were his people, the good and the bad, the kind and the unkind, the friendly and the enigmatic, and he thought about them deliberately and thanked God, as he entered the quiet, fresh green of the churchyard on the fifth anniversary of the day Ellen went away. He had hurried here during those first desperate months each time he felt himself falling into the darkness, and today, standing on the path watching the light break into the shadows over the crumbling stones of the little cemetery, he remembered that darkest day—the day he had moved closest to despair—when Anna Gould had found him slumped over the altar, exhausted from weeping. It was November 19, the second year, and Anna had come alone to bring flowers for Ellen's grave beneath the altar of the church. For a long moment, Anson had not turned to see who had entered. He had not heard her open the door, and only after she had walked through the vestibule and stepped on a creaky board at the rear of the little sanctuary did he realize someone was there.

"I'm sorry, Mr. Dodge. I'll come back later."

"No, Anna."

His movements were slow and stiff as he pulled himself to his feet beside the altar and faced the rear of the church where she stood. Anna had turned her back.

"Come on down here," he said hoarsely, making no effort to hide his agony. "It's good of you to come. Thank you."

She made no unnecessary protest, or apology, but walked swiftly down the aisle, laid her armful of yellow chrysanthemums on the granite slab covering Ellen's grave, knelt for a moment, and turned to leave.

"Did I say thank you, Anna?"

"Yes, you did."

"Oh." He wiped his swollen eyes. "You—you loved her, didn't you?"

"Yes."

For a moment, he studied her face. "Anna, it's just occurred to me—you and I may miss her more than anyone else on the Island."

"I expect you're right."

And then she had looked again at the grave, straightened the bunch of flowers a little, and walked out. Listening to her buggy rattle away down Frederica Road, Anson felt somehow that it had been an important meeting. She seemed almost relieved to have found him weeping. Neither of them had spoken of it again, but Anna had been less remote since that day.

Today, he started, as usual, for the church to pray beside Ellen, and then turned abruptly off the path and across the wide expanse of lawn stretching toward the tall oaks, their branches hushed like the morning, their moss barely waving in the hint of breeze coming across the marshes from the ocean. He walked to his favorite oak, older and thicker than the others, standing apart. Surely, he had decided, this one was old enough for its wide limbs to have sheltered the handful of colonists to whom the Wesleys preached, when they had come with General Oglethorpe to wrest this part of the Atlantic coast from Spain for the Crown of England. His mind reached back toward the hardy folk from Fort Frederica who had stood under this tree, their heads bowed in prayer: the folk who had been the first congregation of Christ Church, his church.

Standing close to the big tree, he laid his face and both his hands against the moist, light-blue lichen flattened along it's gray bark, allowing the resurrection ferns to caress his cheek. My tree, he thought. My tree, in my churchyard, on my Island.

After he had sat on the big, half-exposed root at the foot of the tree for half an hour, he knew he had changed his mind about going to the mainland. There was no real need for him to go, and now the sun was out, the full day of November 19 was upon him, and he was finding it more than bearable.

He had not yet been able to unpack her writing, but he had begun to read her books, marked freely by her hand, underlined and notated in her swift, lilting script. He took her volume of Carlyle from his coat pocket and opened it at random to the end of the essay on *Labour*; *Reward*. Ellen had underlined part of the last paragraph and in the margin had written: *Anson has discovered this—more deeply, perhaps, than most Dodges. If he ever forgets it, I pray I will be there to pick up the pieces!* He closed the book quickly and held it so hard the boards cut his fingers.

Even if I were dead, I'd find a way to come to you, Anson.

Still gripping the small volume, he felt, rather than saw, the sun inch above the tall pines behind him so that the church and the entire churchyard were bathed in full light: perhaps the one moment of the day when no shadow fell.

"She has found a way to come to me!" he said aloud, and his voice sounded young again, not restrained like the responsible priest-in-charge at Christ Church Frederica—like Anson Dodge in love with Ellen.

His fingers trembled as he reopened the book and hunted the passage she had marked. When he found it, he looked deliberately away toward the church before reading, wanting to savor the wonder of the first moment of what seemed to be clear contact with her after five long years: as though they were about to meet again, as though he were on the verge of a needed discovery about himself. And then he read her first underlined passage:

> *My brother, the brave man has to give his Life away. Give it, I advise thee—thou dost not expect to sell thy Life in an adequate manner? What price, for example, would content thee? . . . It is thy all; and for it thou wouldst have all.*

" '*Give* it, I advise thee,' " Anson read aloud. Was Ellen right? *Had* he discovered this? Or had he given his wealth, his energies, his time, his comforts on some emotional impulse? Had he given *himself* without a price? At the beginning, perhaps, but now that his work was under way with some success and much praise from those who seemed sometimes almost to worship him, had he begun, unknowingly, to exact a price? A price evident in his impatience with the tempo of the Southern folk to whom he ministered? In his almost grim determination to win back the Basses? Was his reputation as a priest—was his *pride*—at stake when month after month P. D. and Emma went right on in their hardheaded aloofness from the rest of the parish? In their disdain of his efforts to be friendly? Was he expecting to be paid with visible success because he had been willing to live as his neighbors lived on the primitive Island? Was he proud that he refused to have a newfangled bathroom built into his house? That he refused to drill an artesian well because none of his parishioners could afford one? Was he proud that he wore his shoes until they cracked? Did anything warm him more than that most of his people thought him humble? Brave, to have gone on without Ellen?

Anson has discovered this—more deeply, perhaps, than most Dodges. Had he? Had his Grandfather Dodge struggled the way he struggled now in the blazing clarity that flooded his mind as the sun flooded the churchyard? Did he expect the islanders to be more grateful because he received no salary? Because he paid the salaries of the missioners in charge of the other churches he had begun on the mainland? Because he had built the church at Frederica from his own and Ellen's money and had left the bulk of his fortune to the work in perpetuity?

" '. . . the brave man has to *give* his Life away.' " He frowned. All right, if I've been guilty of expecting payment, he thought, I can stop expecting it. There need be no pieces to pick up. If somewhere Ellen was conscious of him now, this minute, he would see to it that she knew him from this day on as a brave man who dared to *give* his life away. She had underlined another passage:

> *Thou wilt never sell thy Life, or any part of thy Life, in a satisfactory manner. Give it, like a royal heart; let the price be Nothing: thou hast then, in a certain sense, got All for it!*

He caressed the page where her hand had touched it. "Give it, like a royal heart," he said aloud. "Let the price be Nothing. . . ."

Nothing. Not even a sign that Anna Gould had grasped what he still longed to show her about God and human grief. He would keep a royal heart with Anna, no longer fearing defeat if she failed to see that God was teaching him, one painful step after another, how to live with his own grief. Anna would one day come to see, if he cared first, *not* that she learned it from him as her priest, but that she learned it.

He took a deep breath and exhaled slowly. . . . *He who loses his life for My sake, will find it.*

Give it, like a royal heart. . . .

On his feet, he put the Carlyle back in his pocket and was about to walk toward the church to pray when a buggy rattled up the road and stopped across from the church. Hidden from view by a big oleander hedge, Anson waited until he knew who was coming to the church at this early hour. In a moment, Anna appeared, a bunch of red gum leaves in her arms, walked straight up the path, and disappeared inside. Another November nineteenth, and once more Anna had remembered.

As Anson waited, giving Anna time alone in the church, P. D. Bass galloped his old nag barebacked around the bend in the road from Frederica, shouting, "Mr. Dodge! Mr. Dodge—you here?"

Anson ran to the road to meet him.

"It's Emma—she's turrible sick. 'Bout to die, I reckon, an' she's beggin' fer you to come an' pray over her. Wouldja come, Mr. Dodge? Wouldja come quick?"

Anson was about to swing onto the old horse behind P. D. when Anna called from the church door. "What's the trouble, Mr. Dodge?"

"Emma's dyin'," P. D. yelled. "We ain't got no time to talk. Hurry up, Mr. Dodge!"

Anna ran down the path toward them, calling, "No, don't go with him!"

Anson stepped back, surprised. "Why, Miss Anna? It's my duty to go."

"I know that, but not by yourself." She was un-hitching her own horses at the pine tree. "Hop in the buggy with me. I'll take you. Won't do for you to go by yourself. Not to see Emma."

Chapter Twenty-Five

"The minute I walked in Emma's bedroom with Mr. Dodge, I knew she wasn't really sick. She had old P. D. fooled, but not me—or Dr. Massey."

"But what did Dr. Massey say, Anna?"

"Yes, tell us what he said about Emma."

Her mother and Maimie Gould peppered Anna with questions.

"He didn't say anything much, except that she'd better stay in bed a few days and simmer down. When we walked in, she was lying there perfectly quiet, but the minute she saw us, she took on something fierce, rolling and tossing and clutching her heart and moaning that she was about to die right on the spot."

"Now, Anna, maybe Emma did have a slight heart attack."

"Mama, she had an attack of meanness."

"Did Mr. Dodge believe she was really ill?"

"Of course he did, Maimie. You know how he is."

Deborah said she was certainly glad Anna had gone with him, but hoped she wasn't jumping to conclusions about Emma.

"Mama, Emma got just what she wanted. Mr. Dodge has promised he'll come every day now and pray with her."

"Well, he's been asking God for a chance to win her friendship."

"I know he has, Maimie, but both of you mark my words—Emma's up to no good. If he's smart, he'll take

Rossie or Belle with him every time he goes to visit her."

Emma stayed in bed a month, with P. D. waiting on her hand and foot. Anson went faithfully every day, to pray with her and read from the Bible. P. D. never left her side, and toward the end of the week before Christmas, Anson was so surprised to see the old man drive past the Dodge house in his buckboard, he ran out to ask if his wife was feeling worse again.

"Nope. Jist the same. Nothin' would do her, though, but I had to ride in to the Mills to buy some groceries. She thinks I'm not eatin' right, I reckon."

"Is Mrs. Bass alone?"

"Yep. We knowed you'd be droppin' by soon, so I let 'er talk me into goin'."

"Glad you told me, P. D. I'll go right over."

Anson hurried inside for his coat and his parson's hat. Five minutes later, he was sitting beside Emma's bed, opening the Book of Common Prayer to read from the Gospel of St. Luke.

" 'And it came to pass in those days, that there went out a decree from Caesar Augustus, that all the world should be taxed. (And this taxing was first made when Cyrenius was governor of Syria.) And all went to be taxed, every one into'—"

"What book you readin' out of?" Emma snapped.

"Why, I'm reading from the Gospel of St. Luke, Mrs. Bass. I thought you'd enjoy hearing the Christmas story."

"Not outa that book I wouldn't! That ain't no Bible. That's that 'Piscopal Prayer book for heathens. How many times do I hafta tell ya me an' P. D. got saved in a revival meetin' up north?"

Anson started to reason with her, changed his mind, and apologized. "I know better than to read even Scriptures to you from the Book of Common Prayer, Mrs. Bass, but I left the house so quickly, I picked it up from habit."

"Jist goes to show." She snorted.

Anson went to hunt a Bible, and Emma sat up in bed.

"Don't bother to read none to me today. Looks like that's all you know how to do anyhow."

He stood in the doorway of her room, the Bass family Bible in his hand. "What would you suggest I do, then?"

Emma snuggled down in the covers, suddenly demure. "Well, it looks like you an' me could jist have a heart-to-heart talk once. Pull your chair up here closer to the bed. Seems like my hearin's gone bad lately, too."

"Look, I've brought your own Bible, now, and I'll find the same words to read to you. You'll enjoy them if they come from your Bible, won't you?"

"Not if you sit way over there. I said my hearin's gone bad."

Anson moved his chair closer to the window and laughed. "Rossie Stevens says one could hear me on Jekyll Island, if I decided to try it. I'm sure you'll get every word."

Emma sank weakly back onto her pillows and pulled the frayed patch quilt up under her plump face, watching him slyly out of the corner of her eye as he hunted up the second chapter of the Gospel of St. Luke. "Now then, here we are. 'And it came to pass in those days, that there went out a decree from Caesar Augustus, that all the world should be taxed. (And this taxing was first made when Cyrenius was governor of Syria.) And all went to be taxed, everyone'—"

"Shut up!"

The woman sat up in bed, sucking her lower lip in and out, her eyes blazing with anger, her face splotched.

"But, Mrs. Bass, I—"

"I said shut up!"

Anson jumped to his feet and stood watching, horrified, as she ripped her quilt and screamed.

"Help! Help! Somebody come an' help me!"

Anson ran from the house and met Sibby hurrying across the Dodge back porch.

"Mist' Dodge, what in the worl'?"

"Mrs. Bass is having some sort of tantrum, Sibby. I was sitting there reading to her, and suddenly she began to scream."

"What for? Why she yellin'?"

"I don't know, Sibby. Do you think you could go over there?"

"Uh-uh. Not Sibby. Sibby's got better sense." She studied him a moment, while the screaming died down and then stopped. "You been outside widout yo' hat an' coat again?"

"No, but when she started to scream I ran. I'm no good with hysterical women, Sibby. I left my coat and hat there. I'll go back for them if you'll go with me."

"You stayin' right here, Mist' Dodge. Dat woman's got a debbil. Listen. You don' hear no mo' hollerin' now yo' done lef'."

"But we can't leave her alone, her husband's gone to the Mills."

"Sibby'll handle dis. I'll go git Miz Taylor or Miz Stevens an' we'll go git yo' coat an' hat togedder. Can't leave 'em dere. You gotta' preach twice tomorrow."

Anson preached to a bigger congregation than usual the next day—twenty-six people, counting children—and, as always during Advent, he enjoyed preaching. This year he used St. John 1:14, "And the Word was made flesh, and dwelt among us." God Himself had broken into human history that first Christmas, and the wonder of it overwhelmed him as it did each time he preached on the coming of God to the earth to live among the people He created. People like Will and Belle Taylor, the Stevenses, the Postells, Deborah Gould, Maimie and her James, Anna, Horace, Procter and Sibby, himself . . . and Emma and P. D. Bass. He knew Rossie and John Stevens thought he preached too long, "got in" too much of the service, but today even the Taylor boys, Douglas, Archibald and little Reginald, stopped teasing their sisters and were as quiet as church mice. Anson's heart soared, and he centered himself in what he had to say to his people, unmindful of their unusual silence. Even when he shook hands with them at the door of the church after the service was over, he misjudged their solemn faces, believing them to have been sobered by the real meaning of Advent.

But when Horace Gould lagged behind and asked

to ride with him to his afternoon service at the Mills, Anson knew something was wrong.

Horace told him the whole ugly story as they rode toward the Mills: Emma Bass was accusing Anson of taking advantage of P. D.'s absence—she had declared to Rossie and Belle that he had "made up to her" in such a way that she had to shout for help; in fact, she had told everyone who stopped by to see how she was. "P. D.'s threatenin' to beat you up, Anson, if he can catch you by yourself."

"But, Horace, the people can't believe Emma Bass! They all know her."

Horace was silent.

"Some of them will have doubts about me from now on, is that what you mean?"

"Even the best folks on earth tend to let a story like that take root, Anson. You know that as well as I do."

By the time they reached the Mills, Anson was formulating a plan. "I'll tell you the details after the service, Horace. Meet me here at the buggy."

"Anson, I hope this won't make it too hard to preach down here this afternoon."

"Thanks, Horace. I'll be fine. I won't be going to the Kings' today. I can take you home. We'll need to discuss some details, make some definite plans. My mother arrives on Wednesday to spend the Christmas holidays. I want this mess settled one way or another before she gets here."

"I declare, I think I got more out of that sermon just now than I did this mornin', Anson," Horace said.

They were riding up Frederica Road toward Black Banks, and Anson sat beside his friend in silence for a long time. Then he said, "I guess I believed it more than I did this morning, Horace. The only thing that matters is that God did come down to earth to be part of all human life, including trouble. Horace, He'll be at the trial tomorrow night."

"I wish you wouldn't call it a trial, Anson. You're not on trial."

"Oh, yes, I am. My work at Christ Church and every mission church in my charge will be destroyed if the people don't decide for themselves about my guilt or innocence. It will be a trial, Horace, make no mistake about it."

They turned onto the Black Banks road, and Anson thought of his first ride up that road on Horace's mare, almost ten years ago. His dreams had weathered Horace Bunch Gould's death, Ellen's death, and all the problems facing an outsider coming to live and work among provincial people, but the ugliness facing him now was different. There was only one way to handle it—head on, testing the value of his life among them by putting himself at their mercy.

"Do you want me to take the day off tomorrow and ride around the Island to tell folks about the— meetin' at your house tomorrow night, Anson?"

"No, thanks, Horace. I'll do it myself."

"P. D. and Emma too?"

"They'll be the most important people there."

Horace jumped down from the buggy when they reached the Black Banks yard.

"Be sure to bring Anna and your mother and Maimie," Anson said. "I'll need them."

"Don't worry, we'll all be there."

Anna had fully expected Emma to come, but even Anna was surprised at the way she looked; the picture of health, dressed to the hilt in her old purple Sunday silk. Anson wanted everybody in any way connected with the church, Horace had told her, and they were all there, including her brother, James, who had recently been made a vestryman of Christ Church. As Anna watched the others file in and take their places in the circle of chairs Anson had set around the mahogany table in the large dining room, she noticed that no one did more than nod at Emma and P. D. She had to admire Anson Dodge, standing at the door of the big room, shaking hands with each one. When they were all there, he said quietly to Will Taylor, the senior warden, that it was time to begin the hearing.

Anna couldn't help feeling sorry for Will Taylor,

who got reluctantly to his feet and began nervously: "We're here, friends, on a most unhappy occasion. One which I think many of us feel is unnecessary, but our rector, Mr. Dodge, insists that you all be allowed to make your own decisions about—" Will Taylor coughed and cleared his throat "—about his innocence or guilt in the face of the terrible accusation made against him by Mrs. Emma Bass and her husband, P. D., our neighbors at Frederica."

Anna didn't miss Emma twisting in her chair, arranging her skirts, her pudgy face as pious as you please.

"We want you to know right off, Mr. Dodge, that the members of your vestry and their families have the utmost confidence in you."

Anson held up his hand to stop this kind of partial talk, and Anna felt sorrier than ever for Will Taylor when he struggled on, trying to word things, she supposed, the way he thought a regular judge would do it.

"We'll hear from the first witness now. Emma Bass."

Emma grabbed at her heart, tucked her fat lower lip in and out as though she were about to cry, and wailed, "Oh, it was awful, awful! Ain't nobody got to tell any of you I was too weak to defend myself, an' what decent woman would ever think she needed to defend herself agin the—*immoral* advances of a preacher of the Gospel? I ask ya, what woman? What decent, moral, law-abidin' woman'd think she'd have to do that?"

"Don't preach us a sermon, Emma." Will Taylor's usually gentle voice was harsh. "Just tell us what happened—according to you."

"Well, I was just layin' there by myself—P. D. had to ride in to the Mills. He didn't wanta leave me all by myself, but the pore man had to go or we'd'a starved. I been sick so long, ya know, an' he's stayed right by my side. Well, I was just layin' there sufferin', an' in come—in come that man!" Emma pointed her finger at Anson. "Said he'd seen P. D. drive off, an' when he said that, I commenced to shake all over. I tried to cry out to the Lord for help, but it was too late. He—he come over by my bed, just as holy actin' as you please, an'—an'. . . ."

Will Taylor cleared his throat again. "An' what, Emma? If you've got any more to say, say it."

Emma covered her face with her fat fingers and blubbered, "—an' with me too scared to yell, the first thing I knowed, he was lookin' at me, peerin' down at me—in such a way as to commit adultery in his heart!"

Some of the women gasped. P. D.'s face turned red, and Anna could hear him click his false teeth, nervous and angry. Anson looked steadily at Emma, waiting.

Will Taylor couldn't think of a thing to say, and Belle came to his rescue. "Emma Bass, you haven't said a thing that's helpful. You're just accusing—judging!"

"If I'm accusin', Belle Taylor, I'm doin' it with the full backin' of the Scriptures!"

Will rapped on the table for silence, but Emma rushed on. "Matthew 5:28 says ' . . . whosoever looketh on a woman to lust after her hath committed adultery with her already in his heart.' " Emma was no longer hiding behind her hands but stamping now on what she felt was righteous ground. "I reckon I was there. I reckon I know the way he looked at me, an' backin' it up with Scripture makes it true. If there's a Christian in this room, they know it's the truth. I been tryin' to warn you all ever since he come down here, me an' P. D. both, butcha wouldn't listen to us. The Lord Hisself tol' me long ago that this man brought nothin' but trouble to us here. What kind of a man stands up in a pulpit of a Sunday preachin' over his dead wife's grave? It ain't human to do a thing like that! An'—an' now, he's proved it. Actin' with me the way he did, with me sufferin' an' alone on my bed, my husband gone—"

Anna was sitting where she could see P. D.'s angry, red face across the table, and, involuntarily, she jumped to her feet even before P. D. lunged at Anson, shouting, "I've held onto m'self long enough! If you didn't have that collar on backwards, I'd—I'd. . . ." The old man shook with rage, his fist cocked.

Anson ripped off his collar and stood facing P. D. Some of the women screamed, and the men rushed to pull P. D. away, but his bony fist had shot out, and Anna saw blood beginning to trickle down over Anson's mouth. Without a word, she ran to him and wiped it away as best she could with her handkerchief.

Sibby, who was there to tell what she knew, hurried from the room and right back with a cold cloth for Anson to hold against his nose. Regaining his poise with an obvious effort, Will Taylor went on with the hearing.

"We will now hear from Rossie Stevens."

Rossie and then Belle and then Sibby told the same story: how they had gone, at Anson's request, to make sure Emma was all right. They said they had found her sprawled across her bed, the covers ripped, her hair standing on end, but all three women vowed and offered to swear on a Bible that when they slipped in Emma's front door, they heard her talking to herself about "fixin' that Yankee preacher!"

P. D. stared at his wife. "Emma, you didn't say that, didja?"

"Hush, P. D."

"But, Emma—"

"I said *hush*."

When Will Taylor got order again, he asked Anson to tell his side of the story. Anna watched him get to his feet and look steadily at each person in the room. Last of all, he looked at P.D. and Emma.

"I fully understand why you struck me, Mr. Bass. Quite naturally, you believe your wife. It is most unfortunate that I went alone. I had been warned not to do this, but I felt Mrs. Bass was a harmless, confused, embittered woman. I recognize this. I sympathize with it. In fact, I am greatly impressed that I have seen so *little* bitterness. I understand why Mrs. Bass and her husband do not like me, do not want me here, feel I am an intruder from enemy country. But God has instructed us to love our enemies, and I was attempting to do that— foolishly, imprudently. Before God, I made no attempt to do anything but read, first from the Book of Common Prayer, then from the Bible, to Mrs. Bass. When she began to scream and tear her bed clothing, I hurried from her house."

"You see?" Emma shrieked. "He admits he was there! He admits it!"

"Yes, Mrs. Bass, I was there. I even left my hat and coat in my haste to get away."

"That's the only reason he sent them women back, too," P. D. sputtered. "Don'tcha b'lieve a word of it when this nigger tells ya he sent 'em back to look after Emma!"

"Me an' Rossie said it, too," Belle snapped. "Wasn't only Sibby."

Will Taylor banged on the table and turned to Anson. "Is that all you have to say, Mr. Dodge?"

"That's all."

Anna felt for Will Taylor more than ever, now that this much was over. He seemed not to have thought ahead to how he'd end the hearing.

Just then, her brother James pushed back his chair noisily and stood up.

"I guess this is the first time I've taken an active part in the church, but I am on the vestry now, and somethin' in me can't keep still any longer. I think we all know P. D. and Emma, and I think we all know Mr. Dodge by now. There'll be some who will secretly hope there's a little truth in all this, but it seems to me we're wastin' time, Mr. Chairman. Why don't you just ask all those who believe Mr. Dodge is guilty to say 'aye'?"

"Aye!" Emma snapped, but P. D. hung his head and rubbed his knuckles.

Will waited a minute. "P. D.?"

"I ain't votin'."

Anna saw Anson studying P. D.'s face, as Will Taylor said, "All those who believe Mr. Dodge is totally innocent of any wrong doing, signify by saying 'aye.' "

As though on a prearranged signal, everyone but the Basses stood, and the chorus of ayes rang through the big room, some of the people repeating it over and over. "Aye . . . aye . . . aye."

Chapter Twenty-Six

All through the week before Christmas, every kitchen on St. Simons Island was noisy and fragrant with Christmas fixings. The woman in the white homes worked side by side with their cooks, filling jar after jar with spicy ginger and oatmeal and fancy-shaped iced cookies which slid hot and pungent from the ovens, tormenting the children, who tormented the cooks for "just one little ol' sample" from each new batch. By Christmas Eve, the night of the big Island party, held each year in a different home, the cookie jars would be filled, the lemon and chocolate and coconut cakes would be iced, the pumpkin and mince pies lined up on the sideboards, the hams and turkeys baked and ready.

In every kitchen this week, there would be whispering about the "trial" at the Dodge home. It was no surprise to Anson, as he rode from house to house in a drizzling rain the day after the hearing, to find the warm, usually talkative parishioners embarrassed, almost shy. Only Maimie Gould made no effort to hide her feelings. "I prayed for you, Mr. Dodge. This first visit around the Island is bound to be hard. Just give the folks time to put it out of their minds. Most of us are heartbroken for your sake. The others, who just like to talk, will forget it over Christmas."

He thanked Maimie and said he wasn't bothered by the strained conversations, but when he swung onto his horse to ride from the Goulds to Kelvin Grove, to call on the Postells, he felt a heaviness as gloomy as the rainy day. He longed to talk with Horace Bunch Gould. He missed Ellen more than he had missed her for months.

Purposely, he reminded himself that he must not forget to compliment Mack Postell for finding the right kind of cedar boughs for Maimie Gould's wreaths for the church—heavy and full of frosty blueberries. Maimie would make them into garlands, dip them in lime, to look like snow, and Mackbeth would help her put them up on Christmas Eve; then he would light the candles. Nothing made Mack smile more broadly than when Anson needed him to help out at the church.

He concentrated on Mack Postell's simple goodness and Maimie Gould's loyalty: the church would be fragrant at the Christmas Eve service, fragrant with cedar and pine and the warmth of their caring. His mother looked forward every Christmas to seeing the church adorned in its Island greenery for the Holy Season. Dear, courageous Queen Victoria. Perhaps her coming had stirred his grief again. Did his Uncle Stuart miss Ellen as he and his mother still missed her? Anson had seen him only since Ellen's death, just before Stuart returned to Syria, and it had been a mistake. "God is punishing you for what you did, Anson! It was wrong for you and Ellen to marry. I take comfort—cold comfort, but comfort—from the very fact that God is acting in an orderly fashion. God had no choice but to punish you in this severest way."

Anson's anger flared again as he cantered down Frederica Road, anger as hot and cleansing and energizing as during the first moment of shock at his uncle's words. It was safer to be angry; resentment would have been a waste. His anger was not directed toward Ellen's father but toward the man's twisted concept of God.

On their way to the Christmas party, Anson and Rebecca rode around the curve in Frederica Road, above the churchyard, as the moon climbed toward the tops of the tall pines that edged the woods. The church was silent now, and dark, Mackbeth's candles snuffed out, the early service over, the people gone.

"Your sermon was beautiful, Anson."

He laughed a little. "I'm sure some of my parishioners thought I shouldn't have preached a sermon, with the big party coming up at Retreat tonight."

"Nonsense. I'm glad the party will be at Retreat this year. The Kings are the best family on the Island, aren't they?"

He frowned and then smiled to himself. Naturally, his mother felt most at home with the Mallery Kings. They had lost all their wealth in the War, too, so that now Mallery King found it as difficult to make ends meet as anyone else on St. Simons; but the Kings had traveled, and so, of course, Rebecca would find it easier to be with them.

Had he begun to look forward for the same reason to his Sundays at Retreat after he preached at the Mills church? He did not want to think that was true, and he found himself emphasizing to his mother that the Mallery Kings, too, were poor now, like the Goulds and the Postells, the Taylors, and the Stevenses.

"Actually, one of the things that charmed Ellen so much," he said, "was the fact that the three King daughters still rattle around the Island from one social event to another in an old cart hitched to two oxen. It seems they get a modicum of speed by twisting the big beasts' tails. That amused Ellen."

He knew his mother was glad when they could laugh about her, and Anson felt a warm rush of gratitude toward the Kings.

"Oh, yes, Ellen was quite taken with the King girls, in the brief time she knew them." And yet, he thought, Anna Gould was her favorite.

"I think the King girls are very pretty, Anson. Especially the oldest one, Miss Frances Buford."

"She's more like Ellen than anyone I've met."

His mother said nothing, and suddenly he knew this was the right time to tell her about Emma Bass and the ugly hearing. Some tactless remark would reveal it before the evening was over, and she deserved to hear the story from him.

"Oh, dear, oh, dear," was all she said, and when he finished, she asked, "Are you sure the people are all with you?"

"I suppose there are a few who will hold reservations for a while. But the ones who matter will do everything possible to put an end to the whole thing."

"Those dreadful Basses won't be at the party, will they?"

"It's unlikely. Forget it, now, Victoria. This will be a good evening."

"But after all you've done for these people, Anson, it just isn't fair!"

He laughed quietly. "If I've learned anything these last five years, Mother, I've learned that life isn't fair. Has it been fair to you? Was it fair even to Christ when He was on earth? Why should I expect it to be fair to me?"

"You're doing much better without her than I am, Anson."

He thought about that for a long moment; thought about the awkwardness of his life as a country rector without a wife beside him: not only awkward and inconvenient when he entertained, but Emma Bass had driven him to look squarely at his vulnerability. He could not even hire a housekeeper to live on the place, because people would gossip. For years his heart had rebelled at the thought of merely *needing* a wife. Now he faced it, feeling lonelier than ever, more helpless. Finally he said, "Sometimes I don't do well at all, Mother. I just go on."

When the Christmas party at Retreat was at its noisiest, right after the children had been given their small packets of gifts from the big tree in the dining room, Anson asked Buford King to go for a walk with him. Realizing she went only because he asked so urgently, he felt awkward as they strolled through the remains of the old formal gardens beside the "cedar pleasaunce" that formed a windbreak between the house and the beach. Now that they were outside, alone under the full, sailing moon, there seemed nothing to say.

"I mustn't stay out here long. I am a hostess, you know." She laughed. It was a low, contagious laugh, with a music that belonged distinctly to Buford King.

"You seem so serious. Is anything wrong, Anson? I mean, anything new?"

He realized she wasn't going to mention the hearing unless he needed to talk about it. "No, but I would like to know if the Basses were invited to the party tonight. Is that an improper question?"

"Not at all, and they were invited, but you know they almost never attend an Island social function, not since they dropped out of Christ Church. They're too spiritual to have fun with the rest of us heathens."

He was always stimulated by Buford King. He found it almost easy to be natural with her, to be himself. With the others, he was always the rector, taken too seriously, he felt, most of the time. Except during his mother's visits, Anson had no one with whom he could talk about the things that mattered to him as a man. He wanted to talk to Buford King now, but he hadn't learned how to make the conversational bridges from outward things to inward. Ellen had always done that, had maneuvered him into honest, revealing talk so simply, so painlessly, he had never bothered to learn for himself. Now, he struggled to talk to the girl walking erect and graceful beside him, her long, full skirt throwing a rhythmic, circular shadow on the moon-whitened path.

"We all know how difficult it is for you, being alone, Anson. Most of the time we don't let you know, hoping it's best for you not to talk about it, but we do realize."

He could have kissed her hand with gratitude. She had made the bridge for him. And without another word, he took her arm, turned her toward him, and blurted out, "Miss Buford, I need a wife. Will you marry me?"

She made no effort to disengage his hand, and, for what seemed a long time, she didn't smile. Then, in the moonlight, he saw the smile begin, slowly, compassionately.

"I—I know this is abrupt, Miss Buford, but I'm not good at small talk, pretty speeches. And something you said made me certain you—"

"Made you certain I wanted to be your wife?"

"Yes. There really is no reason why not, is there?"

She was still smiling. "If I didn't know you so well, I'd declare you to be the most conceited man in Glynn County, but I do know you rather well. And there are two excellent reasons why I couldn't marry you. One, I don't love you, and two, you don't love me."

"Oh, but—"

"We could learn?" She laughed, not unkindly. "Perhaps we could learn to love each other enough to live rather well together. But I mean never to marry, Anson, until my heart forces me to it."

He dropped her arm.

"And anyway, Anson Dodge, I could never cope with the competition any woman would have in your life."

"The church?"

"No, not the church. You may marry some day, but you will never be able to love anyone the way you still love Ellen. My heart aches for you, but at a time like this one must face facts."

They both heard the sudden snap of dry branches and turned toward the thick cedar hedge.

"Anson, do you think someone has been eavesdropping?"

He pulled back the branches and stepped through to the other side of the row of cedars, looking up and down the empty beach, then went back to Buford, who stood staring into the shadows that cloaked the bed of massed azalea bushes separating their path from the garden. The bushes moved jerkily, as they watched, too stunned to call out. Then the movement stopped and there was only the slap of the water on the beach.

"Anson," she whispered, "I hope that wasn't Emma Bass!"

"How could it be? They didn't come to the party."

"But it *was* someone."

"It could have been a dog."

"No, Anson, a dog wouldn't be hiding up there in those azaleas standing stock still at this minute. Whoever it was is still there." She touched his arm. "I don't mind that we were overheard, except for you. I promise you I'll tell no one about our talk. No one."

"Thank you. But I'm not accustomed to giving up easily."

"Please do give up, right now. You'll only hurt and confuse yourself. I want to be your friend. I admire you, I respect you, but don't ask me again. It would be useless."

A week later, by New Year's Day, 1889, the whole Island knew that Anson had proposed to Frances Buford King and had been turned down. Anna had planned to spend New Year's with Rossie Stevens at Frederica, but long before noon she was riding toward Retreat on Horace's mare, Bessie. It was surely none of her business if Anson Dodge proposed to Buford King, but she would make it her business if Emma Bass had made the whole thing up. Anna hadn't stopped to analyze her desire to protect him, but protect him she would, if it was within her power. If Buford says it's a lie, then she'll help me hush the talk somehow, Anna figured, as she rode through the chill January morning. If she tells me it's true—Anna's heart tightened, and she left the thought dangling, feeling suddenly foolish. But somebody had to do something.

Buford King took Anna to her white-walled bedroom. "It's chilly up here, Anna, but at least we can be sure we won't be interrupted. I know you didn't ride down alone today just to visit." She plumped the velvet cushion on the rocker by the window for Anna and sat down on her narrow bed, her smile making everything easier, as Buford always managed to do.

"It's about the story Emma Bass is telling, isn't it? Anson and I knew someone was eavesdropping on our conversation Christmas Eve. I suspected Emma right off. When she and P. D. appeared at the very end of the party, I knew."

So it was true. He had proposed to Buford King. I feel sillier than ever now, Anna thought. What else is there to say? It's true, that's all. Emma had no business telling it around, but it's still true.

"Poor Anson." Buford sighed.

"Why do you say that?"

"I know you feel sorry for him too, Anna, or you wouldn't have come down here to find out if it's true."

Anna didn't mind Buford reading her mind. It helped her. Things like this were hard for her to talk about; she wished she could just get up and go without having to say another word.

"What can he do against the enmity of a woman like Emma?"

"That's what I'm wondering, Buford. What can anybody do?"

Buford walked to the window and stood looking out toward the big four-storied Retreat cotton house which had served as a landmark for ships in the years before Anna's grandfather built his lighthouse. For a long time she said nothing. Then she turned back to Anna.

"I'll do anything to help Anson Dodge. He's a good man, maybe a great man. He's done so much for all of us—why, do you know he tried to give us a new buggy for Christmas this year? I refused it, of course. People would only talk more, but he wanted to give us that fine, silver-trimmed one he and his mother rode down in Christmas Eve. Said we'd ridden our old oxcart long enough." Anna was silent, and Buford said lamely, "Maybe Emma's talk will just blow over."

Anna got up to leave. "I've got the ride back to think about it, Buford. Somebody's got to do something. I'm as scared of Emma Bass as you are, but somebody's got to do something."

Anna had ridden past the Black Banks turnoff and was on her way to Frederica when she heard a horse galloping up the shell road behind her, and Anson Dodge, calling, "Miss Anna! Wait, Miss Anna!"

For a moment, Anna wanted to escape him. Then she knew how crazy that was, slowed the mare instead, and waited for him to ride alongside.

"Good afternoon." He removed his hat and smiled at her.

"Afternoon, Mr. Dodge."

"I've been at your house looking for you, Miss Anna."

"Looking for me?" She gentled Bessie, who shied a little at Anson's horse, John Wesley, rearing and snorting beside her.

"Yes. I've something important to ask you."

"Well, I'm going to Frederica. You may ride along, if you like."

"Thank you."

For a few moments they trotted side by side up the sunlit road, Anna waiting for him to speak first.

"Your mother tells me you've been to Retreat this morning. Fine party we had there Christmas Eve."

"It certainly was."

"Miss Anna . . . ?"

"Yes, Mr. Dodge?"

"I'm sure you, being a woman, understand how difficult it is for me, alone in that big house, with no one to entertain for me, no one to plan meals, lay in supplies, take charge generally. I'd thought perhaps my mother would stay down this winter, but she had pressing business up north, she serves on several charity committees, and—well, this isn't a sudden thought with me. I've been thinking about it all week. You're a capable woman; you've helped me, you and Maimie, time without number, just for friendship's sake. So, I was wondering, Miss Anna, if—if you'd consider my needs on a permanent basis?"

Bessie seemed twenty feet high. Anna jerked the reins involuntarily, and the mare slowed suddenly; trying to cover her nervousness, she slackened the reins, and Bessie shot forward, so that it was a minute or so before they were once more trotting side by side.

"How does my offer strike you, Miss Anna? My mother thinks it's an excellent idea. I talked it over with her before she left."

His mother! *What* did he talk over with his mother? Was she supposed to read his mind? If he was asking her to marry him just one week after Buford King turned him down, she'd give him the surprise of his life.

"I'll pay you well, Miss Anna, and give you the

new buggy I just bought to make the trips from Black Banks to Frederica every day. It would be impossible, of course, for you to live in. I'm sure you know that. People would talk, and rightly so. But I do need you. I do need a housekeeper, and there's no one I'd rather have than you."

It was the best joke on her she'd ever heard, but she wanted to cry.

"Your mother and Maimie think it's an excellent idea, *if* it appeals to you, of course."

The chill breeze off the winter marsh felt good to Anna's hot face.

"Well, Miss Anna?"

Did he expect an answer just like that? Of course he did. He was Anson Dodge, wasn't he? Wasn't he used to having everyone jump when he spoke? Everyone but Buford King, she thought, and felt ashamed, wondering how deeply he had been hurt.

"Perhaps you'd like to think about it until tomorrow."

Tomorrow! A big thing like that, and he thought he was giving her plenty of time to wait until tomorrow.

"I've already talked it over with Sibby and Procter. They're both ecstatic at the idea of having you there all day every day."

Sibby and Procter and his mother and her mother and Maimie—why, half the Island knew already! Everyone also knew how badly they needed the money. They were passing the lower end of the churchyard where the big oaks stood, and Anna tried to concentrate on the clear winter sun glistening off their narrow, leather-green leaves. Then she turned to him, feeling herself suddenly dizzy and too free, falling, but still on her feet, the way she had felt running down the little hill behind their shanty in Burneyville—fast, faster, unable to stop.

"No, Mr. Dodge. I don't need to wait till tomorrow. I can give you my answer right now. If Mama says she can get along without me at home, I'll be your housekeeper."

Chapter Twenty-Seven

"Procter Green, if you weren't so big, I'd turn you over my knee. What's happened to all that ambition you had when Mr. Dodge first offered to educate you? Do you want to keep on currying horses for the rest of your life?"

Proctor was past twenty-one, but to Anna he was still a little boy who needed prodding. They were having one of their talks on the back porch of the Dodge house while Anna shelled peas and Procter rubbed and polished the silver trimmed harness.

"I'm gettin' edgecated right now, Miss Anna. Mist' Dodge an' me—Mist' Dodge an' I studies together every day he's not travelin'. We're studyin' Colonial history now. Want me to tell you what Patrick Henry said in the House of Burgesses when—"

"No, I don't. I want you to tell me why you don't agree to let him send you to a regular school. It's the chance of a lifetime."

"I aim to some day."

"Some day!"

"When I don't figure you need me so much here."

Anna stared at the young man. "Procter Green, explain that statement."

He blew on one silver ring and rubbed away an imaginary spot. "All I know is that Miz Bass set fire to this house once, an' she could do it agin. Or worse."

Anna set down the bowl of shelled peas and moved from her chair to the top step beside him. "Procter Green," she said, shaking her head. "Procter Green, I declare."

He grinned at her. "I think he needs me here, too. 'Course he don't say much, but sometimes me an' him talk. 'Bout somepin' besides horses, I mean. Like yesterday, before he rode off to catch the boat for Satilla Bluff, he said, 'Procter, you've been a good friend to me.' An' I know what he mean. I don't ask him no questions, but every time he's come back from the church of a mornin', every day for all these years I've worked for him, I know when he's been missin' *her*. Those days I try to have somepin' special to tell him— somepin' good 'bout one of the horses, or the buggy shined up—somepin' to let him know I'm with him. Mist' Dodge is a great man, Miss Anna. A good, kind man. I'd die for Mist' Dodge if he needed me to."

"Remember when you used to call him Mr. Anson Greene Phelps Dodge, Jr.?"

They both laughed.

"Mist' Dodge finally broke me of that hisself. But I still call him that once in a while, to make him laugh. He needs to laugh more, Miss Anna. They ain't nothin' in that man's life to make him happy but startin' a new church somewhere or seein' a man or a woman find God. Every day, mornin' to night, he's doin' somepin' for somebody else. Looks like nobody but you tries to do for him."

"Don't you say that, Procter Green, when you and Sibby carry him around on a splinter the way you do!"

"You know what I mean, Miss Anna. Me an' Sibby's black. You're the only one of his kind that's good to him. Miz Maimie Gould, she helps him fine with the church work, but you know what I mean."

Anna knew, and she was relieved that Procter knew, too.

"Things sure has been better since you started to work here. I think he likes havin' you around same as I do."

There had not been one morning during the eight months just passed when she had failed to jump out of bed, eager, not only for the ride up Frederica Road but for the work she could find to do for him that day.

Anna was thirty-four, now; her life was filled with serving the man who paid her well and was kind, the same man who almost ten years ago had stood, beardless and young and charming beside Bessie that first day at Black Banks and changed her world. She sighed.

"Procter Green, I declare, I'm wasting time sitting here talking to you."

"Miss Anna, can I ask you somepin' before you go in the house?"

"Well, you may ask. Maybe I'll answer and maybe not."

"No, it ain't nothin' like that. It's somepin' I been wantin' to say since last week. When Mist' Dodge rode back from that last long trip to Waycross an' Valdosta, he sure did act funny."

"What do you mean, Procter?"

"He got so white, an' when I watched him walkin' up the buggy road to the house, he had to stop twice to lean up agin' the cedar trees. Do you reckon Mist' Dodge is sick?"

"Oh, Procter, don't say that! I know he's working himself half to death without enough sleep, and heaven only knows the way he eats when he's away from home. But he seems to get rested up in between trips."

"I sure hope you're right, Miss Anna. I reckon maybe he was just plum wore out that night."

Anna was still at the Dodge house when Anson rode in at eleven o'clock on a windy, moon-lit night in September, 1889. She had stayed because the Reverend D. Watson Winn, the priest-in-charge of two of the mission churches, had arrived that day. Anna, unaware that he was even expected, had worked until after nine. And so she was waiting in the parlor by the front window when Anson rode up the road to the barn where Procter was waiting, too.

The shell road was silvery white under the high, windy moon as Anna watched Anson stride toward the house a few minutes later.

Suddenly, he dropped his valise, grabbed his chest with both hands, spun as though he had been struck with a rock, and fell to the ground. Shouting for Proc-

ter, Anna ran across the big yard. She was holding Anson's head in her arms when Procter reached them.

"Miss Anna, is he dead? Is Mist' Dodge dead?"

"No, but ride for the doctor—quick! Take John
Wesley, he'll be faster. Don't just stand there, Procter,
Reverend Winn can help me. Call him before you go.
He's upstairs."

Anna cradled Anson's head in her arms until she
saw Watson Winn cross the front porch on the run.
Then quickly, tenderly, because she had no right to
hold him, she lowered him to the sandy ground.

Rossie Stevens braced herself when she saw Emma
Bass waddling across her front yard. Might just as well
get it over with, she thought, dried her hands on the
kitchen towel, and met Emma at the front door.

Mr. Dodge was recovering from his heart attack, a
slight one, Dr. Massey had said, but Rossie knew the
excitement at Frederica had been like a tonic to Emma.

"Did you know that Reverend Winn is gonna stay,
Rossie?"

"Yes, Emma. Everybody at Christ Church knows
it. Mr. Dodge must have known he wasn't well. He
asked the vestry a month ago to select Mr. Winn to be
his assistant. It was agreed to unanimously."

Emma looked disappointed. "Well, don't know
how I missed hearin' it if that's the truth."

"If you still went to church, you'd know what's
going on."

"That Reverend Winn's a funny kind of feller."

"What do you mean by that, Emma Bass? He's
one of the kindest, gentlest, best-humored men God
ever made."

"Zat so? Make a nice change from them uppity,
high-an'-mighty ways Mr. Dodge puts on, then, won't
it?"

"Emma Bass, sometimes I think you're possessed!
After all Mr. Dodge has done for us on this Island, to
have you say—"

"Ain't done nothin' fer P. D. an' me but make trouble. But . . ."—Emma paced her words trium-

phantly— ". . . *now,* I reckon folks'll see I've been right all along."

Rossie knew Emma was waiting for her to grab the bait. She hated to do it, but she was too curious not to.

"What are you hintin' at, Emma?"

"I knowed long before he married his first wife that Anna Gould was sot on him. Now that I know he ain't gonna die, I kin tell what else I know."

"What else do you know?" Rossie snapped.

"Only what I seen with my own eyes the night he took sick in his side yard. Me an' P. D. both seen her run out an' grab his head in her arms and rock back an' forth like she was cryin' over him layin' there agin her."

"Emma Bass, if I hear that you've told that to another livin' soul, I'll—skin you alive!"

"Makin' a fool of herself right out there in front of her neighbors, smoothin' his face an' rockin' him like he belonged to her!"

"Emma, I meant what I said!"

"If she'd just gone out there to help the man, she'd a hollered for P. D. an' me. I ain't nobody's fool, Rossie Stevens, she jumped at that chance to git close to 'im. Anna Gould's gonna end up grabbin' him off for herself, or my name ain't Emma Bass!"

After the Watson Winns moved into the big Dodge house, Anna went there to live, too. Even Emma would have trouble finding something to gossip about, with a married man and woman living under the same roof.

"Frankly, Miss Anna, one of the reasons I've urged the Winns to come," Anson had said, "is because it's been an imposition on you, riding all the way from Black Banks every day."

It hadn't been. Oh, at first, Anna hated the shiny new buggy he had given her, the same one Buford King turned down, but she had learned to swallow her pride, as she learned more and more of what Anson Dodge was really like. "He's the most considerate man to be so *inconsiderate,*" she told Procter, and he understood what she meant. Anson was never cross, always courteous to the point of gallantry at home, but so engrossed in his work that Anna had lost count of how many specially prepared meals had grown cold while she and Sibby waited vainly to serve his dinner. In the same casual manner, he had given her the buggy, never thinking for a minute how she might feel about it; wouldn't have thought it mattered anyway, since Anna was his housekeeper, and he had wanted Buford to be his wife.

The fall of 1889 and the winter of '90 passed, but Anna knew Rossie Stevens worried every day because Emma *had* shut up about what she said she'd seen the night Anson had his heart attack. "It's just not normal for Emma to be quiet, Anna." Once Anna would have worried herself sick over it, but now she was able to accept her life as it was, with no hope of change. She loved Anson Dodge more than she loved her own life, and she would live out her life giving thanks for what she could do for him. After all, she told herself, I see him every day he's home, I sleep under the same roof at night, I serve his meals and take care of his clothes and make his bed.

From the moment she had cradled his head in her arms the night he was ill, she had known her heart. He needed her, and as long as he did, she would be glad and she would be there.

In a month he was laughing about his heart attack, and every morning that winter he was off with Mr. Winn, supervising the driving of every nail that went into the new chapel he was building on the south end of the Island on the beach for the tourists who spent the summers and holidays on St. Simons. He did everything with his whole heart, and in her heart Anna was proud of him. Afraid for his health, but proud. Outwardly, she could only show him respect as one of his parishioners, as his housekeeper; when he rode off for the day or a week or two weeks, she could only say, "Good-bye, Mr. Dodge, I hope you have a good trip." But in her heart she could hold him and ask God to bring him back to her safely. Only God could make him slow down, she thought, and God seemed to be having trouble.

"He knows he's not well, Miss Anna," Watson Winn told her. "I do the best I can when we're traveling together, but he's a difficult man to control. He lives for his work, and I don't think he'd want to live if he had to slow down. After all, you've known him much longer than I. I'm sure you know he has only his work to live for. His heart is buried under the altar at Christ Church."

Ellen.

Seven years she had been gone, and, in those seven years, Anson Dodge had mentioned at least three big churches he'd been offered on the mainland. When he told Anna, he smiled and said, "I merely informed them I'll never leave St. Simons Island. I couldn't," expecting her to know what he meant.

She did know. Ellen was on the Island.

He had told her about Ellen's death one night when he invited her to have coffee with him after she served his supper. "Some day, maybe not too far from now," he had said, "I'll be able to open that locked wooden box in my study. It's full of her writing. I mean to compile and publish it myself sometime, Miss Anna. A private printing, just to distribute among the family and her friends. One for you, of course. She would have been a fine writer."

"I know," Anna had answered. "I still have the letters she sent me."

"Splendid. Keep them. I may want to include them in the book."

Then he had drained his coffee cup, folded his napkin, said, "Good night, Miss Anna," and disappeared down the hall to his study. "To be with her," Procter said he had told him once. For seven years, every morning at the church and every night in his study, Anna knew he shut out the world to be with Ellen.

Chapter Twenty-Eight

On the first Sunday in May, 1890, the Right Reverend J. W. Beckwith, Bishop of Georgia, came to St. Simons for the consecration of the new chapel on the beach. The Bishop came often, Anna felt, mainly because the portly, dignified old gentleman loved and respected Anson Dodge. True, the Diocese was permanently indebted to him for his generosity: the number of mission churches across Georgia had grown to over thirty, and Anson had not only financed the building of many of them, he continued to pay the salaries of their priests and to visit them regularly to encourage and check on the work in each church. "He's the most apostolic man in the South," the Bishop had once told Watson Winn. "Not only has he given his fortune, he gives himself."

Anna was dog-tired when she climbed the stairs to her room. It had been a long day, with twenty-four people for dinner, but much of her weariness came from her growing fear that Anson would be ill again. Anna thought she had never seen him look so pale. For the past month he had ridden too hard, slept too little, eaten too fast, consumed too much coffee, and nothing anyone said could stop him.

The next morning Anson was going alone to take Communion to Mack Postell's invalid mother, and Anna promised herself she'd find a chance to talk to Mr. Winn while he was gone.

Comfortable Watson Winn made it easy by wan-

226

dering into the kitchen to sample Sibby's first batch of freshly baked cornsticks.

"Of course you're worried, Miss Anna. We all are. I wish I could tell you there is nothing to worry about, but I'm sure you want the truth. He has taken a rather unusual measure with the vestry, just last week."

Anna could feel her throat tighten.

"Mrs. Winn and I are leaving Frederica soon. Nothing will do Mr. Dodge but that I become the priest-in-charge at St. Mary's. Still, the vestry here at Christ Church has just chosen me, at his request, to be associate rector with the right of succession."

"Right of succession?"

"He wants to make sure the people at Frederica will not be one day without a rector. Should anything happen to him, I would automatically become the priest-in-charge here."

"Jesus," Sibby breathed.

"Thank you for telling me, Mr. Winn," Anna managed to say, and left the kitchen quickly. Knowing only that she had to be by herself, she ran up the wide stairs to the second floor, then stood in the big hall outside Anson's room, rejecting what she had just heard. She would not allow it to be true that Anson knew he might not live long. He was only thirty-one, four years younger than she. He had become her life, and somehow she would change things, would find a way to make him rest. A man with a bad heart should not have confusion around him, and from now on she would do even more to keep the atmosphere of his home peaceful.

In a moment the other news she had just heard from Mr. Winn crashed in upon her. The Winns were leaving! Right when it seemed Anson needed someone to help him, he was packing Mr. Winn off to St. Mary's. This meant she could no longer live in the big house at Frederica. . . .

Anna ran back down the stairs into the kitchen.

"When will you be leaving, Mr. Winn?"

"The last week in May. I begin preaching at St. Mary's in June."

Anna had a little over two weeks left. She was sure the Winns had expected to stay on. But no one should take anything for granted with Anson Dodge.

After Sibby had served the noon meal on May 24, three days before the Winns were to leave, Anson and Watson Winn went for a walk around the ruins of the old fort at Frederica. It had been obvious all through the meal that Anson's thoughts were far away. Something weighed on his mind, and Watson Winn waited for Anson to speak first.

"I just want you to know, Mr. Winn, that I have every confidence in the job you'll do at St. Mary's. I'm feeling well again, and with you to handle things there and at Woodbine, we should move ahead fast. It's good to be able to depend on someone as I depend on you."

Watson Winn smiled. "Is that what you came out here to tell me?"

"No, as a matter of fact, it isn't," Anson said, as though he were about to launch a new project. "I came out to ask you to perform a wedding ceremony before you leave—that is, if the details can be worked out."

"A wedding, eh? Whose?"

"Mine."

Watson Winn stopped walking. "Yours, man?"

"That's right."

"Well, if I'm not too inquisitive, could I ask—to whom?"

"Certainly, be glad to tell you. Anna Gould, if she'll have me."

"Uh—does she know about this?"

"No. No, Anna doesn't know yet."

"I see."

"But I plan to ask her this afternoon. I—I find I can't let her go back to Black Banks to live."

Chapter Twenty-Nine

On May 28, Rebecca Dodge sat comfortably in the sun on the window seat in her library and tore open a letter from Anson.

My Dearly Beloved Queen Victoria,
    For the first time in seven years my heart is making music! Unexpected for me, too, as I'm sure it will be for you—on May 29, I will marry Miss Anna Gould.

Rebecca half crumpled the page, closing her eyes against what she had read, as though she could shut it out. Anna Gould? His housekeeper? How had such a thing come about? Had she made a mistake not to move to the Island? Had she driven him to marry Anna Gould? Had he done it for convenience? Or merely out of compassion for this woman who had served him well?

She returned to the swift, hasty scrawl.

    Since we will be heading for New York the day after our marriage, it would be useless for you to come for the brief ceremony.
    Now, please meet us in New York on June 7. You will need to help Anna buy a new wardrobe. Perhaps Aunt Josie could go along on the shopping trip, too. At any rate, we will want to accomplish it all as quickly as possible since, at the middle of June, Anna and I will sail for Europe for a few months.

Rebecca folded the letter, stuffed it back in its envelope, and paced the big room. "Anna Gould, my son's wife. Anna Gould!" She corrected herself sharply. "Anna *Dodge* it will be after tomorrow. Anna Dodge."

In a moment, she faced the truth: for seven years she had refused to relinquish her own dream, centered first in her happiness over Anson and Ellen and then her pride in the way he had handled his grief. She must relinquish all that now. He would be married to another woman. Something like jealousy, and the choking resentment that accompanies it, swept toward her like a tidal wave. She walked faster around the big room to escape it, hating the destruction it would bring if it struck: the waste, the pain, not only to her, but to Anson.

"That plain, shy country woman will be my son's wife," she said firmly, aloud. "I *will* learn somehow to accept her as his wife, and"—she finished in a dry whisper—"I will also learn to accept him . . . as her husband."

Anna gathered up a pile of freshly ironed linens and hurried to the second floor. She had been hurrying through every waking minute since the afternoon a few days or years or minutes ago when he had asked her and she had answered, "Yes, Mr. Dodge, I'll marry you."

Climbing the wide stairs now, she laughed, remembering how she had always wanted a June wedding. Tomorrow, her wedding day, would be May 29, selected merely because it happened to be the first day she and Maimie could manage to finish her wedding dress. Dates, she knew, didn't exist for Anson, once he had made up his mind.

She had gone full steam ahead, not only with the wedding dress but with readying the house for their departure. Until tomorrow, she was still his housekeeper. Now, of all times, she could not neglect his house, or him. They had spent the morning, at his insistence, carrying her belongings down the narrow stairs from the third floor to the big master bedroom which she would share with him when they came back from their honeymoon abroad. None of it seemed real to her, and she was almost afraid to believe he was as happy and excited as he seemed to be. Over and over she wanted to caution him not to run up and down the steps, but she couldn't be herself with him. Not yet. Would she ever be able to act the way she felt with Anson Dodge, she wondered. And then laughed again, reminding herself that she'd no doubt act the way she felt when she got to New York with his mother—scared dumb.

Anna finished straightening the linen closet in the upstairs hall, covered the clean stacks of sheets and pillow cases with an old sheet, straightened her shoulders, and walked down the wide stairs, for a moment feeling almost as though some day she could believe herself to be the mistress. "Anyway, he didn't buy a pig in a poke," she said aloud in the downstairs hall. "He's had a chance to find out how much I've still got to learn."

"Anna! Anna, where are you?" His voice boomed from the back of the house, and he rushed in, rubbing his hands together in the way he always did when he was in the midst of a new project. The way he did that first day so long ago, when she had gone to Rose Cottage to help him get ready for Ellen to come. She smiled, and answered, "Here I am, Mr. Dodge."

They both laughed. She would have everything to learn—even to call him Anson.

In his study that night, the night before his wedding, after Anna had gone back to Black Banks for the last time, Anson sat alone at his big, roll-top desk, his journal opened before him—the thick, leather-cornered book he had begun on May 18, 1884, the Fifth Sunday after Easter. He remembered the night he first opened the stiff, new book and wrote: *St. Phillips, Atlanta, ordained diaconate: Sermon, Dr. Armstrong. In P.M. I conducted Evening Prayers at Redeemer, Atlanta. Ps. 19: "Creation Showing God's Glory."*

Creation. He looked up, as he had done each night for all these nearly seven years, and studied the big framed photograph of Ellen on the wall over his desk. She had been gone less than a year when the journal was begun. How far had he come since then? *You can begin now to build the second portion of your relation-ship with her,* Bishop Johnson had said. He had tried. Every night, sitting alone in his study, he had tried bet-ter to understand the Bishop's words; had searched for still one more way to allow God to make creative use of her leaving.

Now he looked at her almost perfect face—a haughty face to some, perhaps. He smiled. Ellen haughty? He had loved this paradox in her from the day he saw her at Grandfather Dodge's golden wedding an-niversary. He had adored her dramatic, almost remote beauty and had felt at home at once with her heart. El-len . . . full of mystery and light, gravity and humor . . . the kind of paradox that kept a man at her feet. He was still at her feet on the night before his wedding to Anna Gould, but his whole being was quiet. He knew he had tried to make Ellen proud of the way he had lived the strange second portion of their great adven-ture, and although Anna Gould deserved more, he was at peace with the thought that Ellen would like his shar-ing all that remained for him with her.

At peace? Yes, but almost happy, too. No other woman on earth would be able to make a life with him but Anna. He would enjoy showing her the world, teaching her to draw sustenance from great books, fill-ing her life with the things she had never known . . . filling her life, he hoped, with enough of himself.

He flipped the pages of his journal: . . . *made a priest at St. Mark's, Brunswick, 1885 . . . the church consecrated in January, 1886 . . .* he frowned to see how much time he had been forced to take out for sick leave. Frowned, also, that he had simply neglected to make entries for almost all of the past year. It had not been a lack of activity, more a lack of incentive. The empty pages were correct. He had been empty inside; but that was changed now, and he scrawled hastily across the blank page for May, 1890: *Time off to be married!*

In her room under the eaves at Black Banks, the last night she would ever spend there, Anna emptied her treasures into a pile on the bed. She had taken them to the Dodge house with her, tied in a piece of bright silk her sister Lizzie had given her one Christmas, but she had brought them back to Black Banks tonight, wanting to sort them all over once more. If Anson seemed interested, she might show him her perfect seashells, the chips of petrified wood from out west, the moon aggies from the days when she was a better marble shot than either James or Horace . . . but the small wooden box still tied with the white ribbon, which held the crystal gull, she would hide. Did he know the crystal gull? Had he ever seen it? If she kept it on the marble top of the bureau, as she longed to do, would it cause him pain? She had tried it there that afternoon, alone in the big bedroom, just for a minute, stepping back to admire it. The gull was a part of her, now, and she wanted it there on the gray and white marble where she could look at it every day. But she had put it back into the green-blue velvet of the little wooden box, tucking it and the bundle of Ellen's letters between the folds of the white silk brocade which Ellen had sent her. Tomorrow she would hide it all in the big bottom drawer at the Dodge house. She had resisted using the brocade for her wedding dress for his sake. There would come a time when she would need a white dress. Anna was well into her thirties; she was going to be married tomorrow in a light rose silk.

IV

Chapter Thirty

Anna thought she would never get it all told. Hour after hour she had tried to describe her wedding trip to her mother, to Horace and Maimie and James, to Belle and Rossie, both of whom kept giving teas and other trumped-up socials so they could hear still more about what she had seen in London, in Paris, in Milan, in Rome and Venice . . . it was all like a dream to them and it had all been like a dream to Anna: five months of a kind of joy she hadn't hoped for even in heaven.

Her new mother-in-law and Josie Dodge, Arthur's wife, had both been kind to her in New York—Rebecca, reserved but kind, and Aunt Josie enthusiastic, encouraging, and more than helpful in the selection of a wardrobe. "My dear, 1890 is definitely a yellow year," Josie declared, and Anna had sailed out of New York harbor wearing a white flannel suit trimmed in yellow, because "white flannel is catching on for the summer." They were on their way home before Anna began to feel her grand clothes belonged to her. But where in the world would she ever wear that gold-colored plush hat with the black ostrich plume back on the Island? For that matter, where would she wear those expensive bronze shoes with all that lacy open-work over the foot? On St. Simons they'd be full of sand in five steps, and if Emma Bass ever saw her in her new bronze-colored hose, she'd never shut her mouth.

Anson still seemed intent on making friends with the Basses, but here she could not follow him. Emma was hard to ignore, but Anna did her best, and when Emma managed to wangle an invitation to one of the socials where Anna talked about her trip, for Anson's sake she tried to tell only about the churches they had seen: Westminster Abbey in London, St. Paul's Basilica in Rome. This, she figured, would give Emma less to chew on, but what she didn't hear, she made up, so Anna mainly ignored her. When they met in their adjoining side yards, Anna nodded and Emma snorted, and that was as far as it went. Her joy had been too long coming, nothing would destroy it, Anna promised herself.

In most outward ways, her daily life returned to the routine of housekeeping. Anson was making his rounds of the mission churches, sometimes weeks at a time. Once more the meals she and Sibby planned waited and cooled, because back on the Island his work was first again. The times she liked best were their "reading nights." Under his guidance, a whole new world was opening to her, as she read up and down his crowded bookshelves. Some nights he didn't go to his study at all; other nights he did, and Anna waited, sitting alone on the porch under the big trees, for him to come back to her, wondering painfully on those nights, what she had been able to give him to compensate for his loss, even in part.

And then when the red gums were turning again along Frederica Road in the fall of 1890, she discovered the one gift which she alone could give him.

"Next summer—in July, Anson—we're going to have a baby."

Anson Greene Phelps Dodge, III, was born on July 23, 1891, and nothing was ever the same again for Anna. "It's little short of a miracle he's here, Anna," Dr. Massey had said. "You must never try it again. You could die the next time." The words hadn't frightened Anna; it was a miracle that she was Anson Dodge's wife. She had only smiled at Dr. Massey, forgetting the pure pain of the frightening, long hours, in the pure joy of the warm, wriggly miracle in her arms.

"I declare, he's almost too beautiful to be real," Deborah Gould had said, when she saw her grandson minutes after he was born. "It's too bad his Grandmother Dodge can't see him right now."

"He just couldn't wait for his Grandmother Dodge, though." Anna smiled down at the baby, then up at Anson. "He's too much like his daddy, always in a rush to get started."

Anson had stood speechless by the big bed with Anna's mother, then dropped to one knee to study the child's face, almost shyly. "Is he really like me, Anna?"

"I hope so, Anson."

"About when do you think he'll open his eyes, Mother Gould?"

"Oh, he's already opened them," Anna said.

"He has?" Anson peered more closely at the tightly squinted eyelids. "Anna, are you sure?"

"Of course I'm sure. Just for a second, just long enough for me to see that he's got your eyes, Anson."

Eyes like yours, my beloved Anson Dodge, she thought, and reached for his hand to hold it in hers against the baby's warm, soft back. She had always thought Anson had the most beautiful hands she'd ever seen on a man: slender, smooth, olive-skinned, strong. Hands that showed his sensitive heart to anyone who took the trouble to study them. Now, alongside the baby's tight little rosy fists, they looked stronger than ever.

"Did you really see his eyes, Anna? Enough to tell whether they're brown like mine or gray like yours?"

"They're your eyes, Anson. Dark, dark, dark."

"Mother Gould, look! Look at that hand. It's exactly like Horace Bunch Gould's hand."

Deborah patted Anson's shoulder and laughed. "Now, how in the world can you tell with his fist all doubled up?"

"Oh, I'd never mistake that, Mother Gould." He held up the little fist, and the baby fussed a bit. "Is it all right if I just—undouble it a minute, Anna?"

"I reckon he'll have to learn how to let go of that fist sooner or later. Go on, it won't hurt anything."

Slowly, tenderly, Anson opened the tiny fist with his fingers. "Look, my son's going to have a fine, broad, generous hand just like his Grandfather Gould." Anson stood up. "Oh, Anna, Anna . . . can you believe it?"

"I'm having a hard time believing it."

No, Anson Dodge, she thought, I may never really believe this could happen to me, but I aim to go right ahead loving this baby just the same as if he were real. I still don't believe his daddy's real sometimes, either, but for all the rest of my life, I will go on loving him as though he were.

"Anson, do you think you can carry him downstairs without dropping him?"

"So soon, Anna?"

"Yes. Mama, if Anson can't manage it, you do it. I don't want to keep Sibby and Procter waiting another minute to see him!"

Anna noticed that Anson spent a longer time than usual in his study at night, but she supposed he was leaving her alone to rest. After all, the birth had been bad for her, and Dr. Massey insisted that she stay in bed for at least two weeks.

One night, when the baby was ten days old, Anson came upstairs unusually late, his face pale again, his eyes dark circled. He walked toward her bed as though he were a stranger: remote, courteous, his voice tightly under control.

"Anna, I need those letters Ellen wrote to you. I've begun putting her writing together for the book I'm publishing. May I have the letters?"

For the past ten days, her mind had not once been invaded by the familiar, haunting thoughts of Ellen's beauty, Ellen's grace; never plaguing her, only keeping her humble, only keeping her heart bowed in gratitude that she had been permitted to share even a part of the man Ellen loved. Now, as he stood tall and weary beside her bed, looking at her almost as if he were her employer again, she felt the room fill with Ellen, felt her own heart shrivel and draw back.

"I'll get them right away, Anson."

"No, don't get up. Tell me where they are."

"I'll have to find them."

That was a lie. She had looked at her crystal gull just before the baby was born, had set it out on the marble-topped bureau to admire it, and when she heard Anson bounding up the stairs, had hastily tucked it, along with the bundle of letters, under a fold of the white brocade in the big bottom drawer without putting it back in its box.

"Just tell me where to look, Anna. I forbid you to get up. You're not well enough."

She sank back on her pillows. "All right, Anson. They're in a bundle, tied with a green ribbon, over there in the bottom drawer of the bureau."

He opened the drawer and bent over it, his back to Anna—rummaged a moment, then was silent. Anna saw him slip the bundle of letters under one arm, and, with the drawer still open, he stood up facing her, the gull in his hands.

The Westminster chime on the grandfather clock downstairs began to strike. For some reason Anna waited until it was silent again.

"She gave it to me—at Steamboat Landing, the day you left."

As if from a great distance, he said, "Thank you for telling me."

He held the gull near the lamp that burned on the bureau, turning it so that its wings and back caught the soft, amber light; and then he closed it once more inside the big drawer.

"I'll be late coming to bed. I plan to edit these letters tonight." In the doorway, he turned back, quite friendly now, more himself. "It's going to take longer than I expected. Everything she wrote is so beautiful, I feel miserably inadequate."

Anna lay awake until the first slants of dawn made the flame of the oil lamp look pale and useless. He still hadn't come, but for the first time since their marriage he had spoken almost freely to her of Ellen. Wearily, but deliberately, before she saw him again, she dropped her hurt pride that he had been working on Ellen's writing during the first ten days of their baby's life on earth.

Chapter Thirty-One

On the baby's first birthday, with their bedroom already piled with toys from his Grandmother Dodge, Anna watched Anson clatter around the turn in their private road, the buggy seat stacked with still more presents for his son.

Before the day was over, it seemed to her that everyone on the Island had either come, bringing gifts, or had sent stuffed animals, knitted bootees, hand-embroidered dresses, and homemade gourd rattles. Mack Postell had made a doll for him, its face carved from a walnut shell. Children were born often on St. Simons, but little Anson was everyone's pet. "He's too pretty to be on this earth," Rossie Stevens declared, when she and John came carrying the bed John had made for him. And Belle Taylor said over and over that he was just not like other children.

Anna herself had trouble imagining that her baby could grow up to be naughty and need to be spanked like other boys, but she would be able to spank him, she supposed, when the time came. Anson scoffed at the idea that all the attention would spoil his son. "My son will never be spoiled," he vowed . . . and Anna smiled, hoping she would be strong enough to see to it that he wasn't.

It had nothing to do with spoiling, to Anson's mind, that he bought the boy a pony before he was two . . . a pony and a pup named Puddy and a pony cart with red wheels and a baseball and bat and a tiny red wagon. Anson had the child walking long before the women thought it was time.

"He'll be bowlegged," Emma Bass shouted, hanging out her kitchen window as Anson led his laughing son up and down the big side porch, holding both his hands as he thumped along on his two chubby legs.

"I say, he'll be bowlegged if you keep that up!"

"I heard you, Mrs. Bass, and we thank you for your interest, but we're doing fine," Anson called back to her.

"At least Emma Bass has stopped gossiping," he said at dinner that noon. "I almost think our son is converting her."

"It does seem like Emma's not quite so hateful." Anna passed him the rice. "But sometimes I almost wish she'd go back to her old ways. At least she stayed away from our house then. This way she's over here half a dozen times a day when you're gone. She'll sit there in the parlor and just stare at him all the while he's taking his nap. Gives me a creepy feeling."

Anson leaned back in his chair and grinned at her. "Shame on you, Mother. You underestimate the power of your son's personality! He can make a new woman out of Emma."

Maybe Anson was right, she thought. Their child was a golden child with a disposition that could charm a hurricane into a summer breeze; a laughing child, surrounded with love, immersed in the joy he brought to everyone as he grew and learned and played under the changing Island sky. Not only had he made a tentative bridge for Anna with her mother-in-law, who now came often to visit them, the child had given his mother identity, so that at dinner one day Anson had quoted her father, with a tender smile, right before Rebecca: "That was a beautiful meal, my dear . . . but after all, you're our Anna." And Rebecca smiled a little, too.

On November 19, 1893, at dinner, shortly after little Anson had begun to eat his meals in the small dining room with them, Anson presented Anna with an inscribed copy of Ellen's book. The silence between them as Anna held the small, tan, cloth-bound volume disturbed the child. He wrinkled his face as though he were about to cry, thought better of it, and banged his spoon against his bowl, chattering. Anna reached over to quiet him, her eyes still on the book.

"Me . . . me . . . me!"

"No, Anson," she said firmly. "This book isn't for you. It's for Mother this time."

"'Tory book?"

"Yes," Anson said. "It's a kind of a story book."

This year she had forgotten November 19 for the first time. How like Anson to assume she had remembered. He occupied their son while she opened the book, waiting, she knew, for some reaction from her. She leafed through the poems, the short stories, Ellen's essay on Carlyle, and then page after page of the account of their honeymoon. Ellen's honeymoon with Anson . . . but he was playing with *her* son now, *their* son. Wanting desperately to think of something to say, she turned to the Preface he had written. It was less than a page, she could read it quickly, and perhaps then she could think. His opening paragraph mentioned the year 1883 and the city of Allahabad, India, and that this was mainly Ellen's record of their wanderings. In the second paragraph, written just last year, she read:

The never completed journey has left us these few letters which lack her revising touch, but which show such bright promise that her husband feels justified in giving them a permanent shape for those who shared with him the privilege of her acquaintance and her love. . . .

Her husband. . . .

"I'm sending copies to certain members of the family," Anson was saying quietly. "Uncle Stuart, of course. I know Uncle Arthur and Aunt Josie will want one. We'll take Mother's to her when we go up to visit next month. There's one for your mother, too. This one is yours. I want you to keep it always. She was your friend."

"Yes, Anson. Thank you. I'll keep it—always."

"In the safe in my study will be a dozen extra copies. These are never to be given to anyone who would not fully appreciate them."

"I'll remember that."

He was quietly giving her orders in his employer's voice, and she was accepting them, caught once more in the wilderness between her two privileges: serving him and belonging to him.

"Well, it's time for us to go, son. We'll just about make it when the Bishop's boat docks at the Mills." He lifted the child down from his high chair with a wide swoop, both of them laughing.

"Me go with Daddy! Me go with Daddy an' horsie."

The wilderness moment had passed. She was his wife again as she watched them ride off together through the woods. When they were out of sight, Anna returned to the family dining room, picked up Ellen's book, and took it straight to the big bottom drawer of her bureau. She would read it sometime, but not yet.

Chapter Thirty-Two

Anna couldn't remember a more beautiful Sunday morning than March 18, 1894. There had been a good crowd at church, almost forty people, and in his quiet, certain, pulpit manner Anson had preached well, intently sharing the deep things of God with the people he loved. He had asked old Reverend Phillips, who was visiting from a mission church, to assist in serving Holy Communion; and little Anson, all dressed up in his new blue coat and hat from Grandmother Dodge, wiggled beside Anna on the hard oak seat, pointing to his friend, Reverend Phillips, as the old man stumbled happily through the Second Lesson for the Third Sunday in Lent.

What Anson said that day was not new to Anna. Sometimes she felt that everything her husband believed was based on the simple fact that God will not waste anything if we give Him a chance to redeem it. She watched him lean toward the people, his penetrating eyes, his expressive hands entreating them to believe that "He is not only a Redeemer of our sin, but He is a Redeemer of our circumstances as well. He will not waste a single problem, a single heartache, a single tear. Our God is a Redeemer God, and He stands minute by minute before us, inviting us to let Him have the sorrow, to let Him have the pain, to let Him have the disappointment. To trust Him to make something useful, something creative of every tragedy that darkens our lives."

He had earned the right to preach that to his people. After all, he had preached every Sunday over the grave of the person he had loved more than anyone else in his world. Some of the people had taken up Emma's nasty remarks about "him standin' there preachin' over her grave, tryin' to act so holy as though nothin' could touch him." But almost everyone knew, as Anna knew, that he spoke out of his own knowledge of what God *could* do for anyone who would give Him the chance. He had seemed almost falsely strong to Anna, too, when he first became their priest. It just didn't seem natural for a man to be able to stand up there Sunday after Sunday and preach with his wife buried under the altar below him. Now that she knew him better, she knew it wasn't *natural:* he was able to do it because he was sustained every moment of his life by something outside himself, by the *supernatural.* He was not perfect, he still hurt her at times by his haste, his impulsiveness, his exhausting energy, but he was God's man and he believed what he preached to them.

When Anson finished his sermon, Mack Postell scurried, smiling, to the organ and began to pump the bellows as Annie Belle Taylor played and they all sang one of Anson's favorite hymns: "Take my life and let it be consecrated, Lord, to Thee. . . ." He had given his life, his fortune, his every energy into the hands of God as no other man she knew. Had she done the same with her life? Was he in a place with God which she could never enter?

Outside the church, when the service was over, she forgot her disturbing thoughts, proud as always at the sight of her husband, their little son beside him, both shaking hands with the parishioners. Small talk, Anna knew, had never grown easy for Anson, but he was still trying, and it seemed less difficult for him now that his son had begun to stand beside him every Sunday. The child had formed the habit himself, and Anson had boasted to everyone from Sibby to Bishop Beckwith that church attendance had increased since the boy had started greeting the people each Sunday with his bright smile, his gallant little handshake, and the inevitable speech he made to everyone: "G'morning. I wuv you today!"

"Why, I'd walk the whole six miles to church before I'd miss hearing that child tell me he 'wuvs' me," Maimie Gould declared. And she was not alone. People came all the way from the Mills to Christ Church, when the weather was good, and went home smiling over the child's greeting.

"Where did he get that, Anna?" Rossie asked. "Did you teach him to say it?"

"Nobody taught him. He's just so full of love, I reckon it's the most natural thing in the world for him to say. And he'd rather shake hands than eat. Shakes our hands every morning first thing!"

Even Emma Bass had no defense against their child.

"You couldn't get Emma inside an Episcopal Church with a rope," Anna would laugh. "But do you know, Anson, that baby gets her into her Sunday dress once a week? She's started to dress up every Sunday just so she can shake hands with him when you bring him home after church. Stands out there behind the bushes until your back is turned, waiting for him to march up to make his little speech to her!"

Anna always walked home with Rossie Stevens right after church, to help Sibby, leaving the two Ansons to finish their handshaking and come home together in the shiny black and silver-trimmed Dodge buggy. And on this sunny Sunday, she and Sibby hurried to set the table in the big dining room for company, with the china and the crystal and the silver Ellen had bought in England.

"I want to be at that front window, Sibby, when they ride up, because the sparks could fly. Reverend Phillips will be sitting right up there on the buggy seat with little Anson, and Emma's not going to like that one bit."

Sibby's high laugh rang out, and the two women were watching at the parlor window when the buggy rounded the curve in the road and clattered toward the front of the house.

"Dere she is, Miz Dodge. Dere Miz Bass peepin' roun' de bushes. She done seen de ol' preacher ridin' up dere big as life huggin' de baby." Sibby chuckled, savoring every minute of the little drama, as Anson reined in the horses and jumped down to give old Reverend Phillips a hand and to swing his son to the ground. Then Emma held out her arms to little Anson, who scampered toward her, ready for his speech and his handshake.

"Look at dat, Miz Dodge," Sibby whispered. "She's huggin' him."

Emma released the child, let him shake her hand, and, without a word to Anson or Reverend Phillips, marched, smiling to herself, into her own house and closed the door.

Anna sighed. "Only Emma Bass would shut her front door on a day like this, Sibby."

"Hm-hm. Dat a dark ol' woman, Miz Dodge." Sibby laughed. "Sibby don' min' bein' dark on de outside, but it sure mus' be cause for achin' to be dark on de inside."

Anson was collecting his Bible and sermon book from the buggy seat when little Anson ran back to the buggy, his chubby legs pumping so hard his hat fell off. Reverend Phillips had started for the porch but turned back to the child now, and Anna saw the expression of pure joy on the old man's face when her son tugged at him, instead of his daddy, to lift him back into the buggy for the ride to the barn with Procter. She caught her breath as the feeble old man barely managed to bounce the child onto the seat, then stooped to pick up the lost blue hat.

Anna knew Procter was running across the yard toward the buggy, but, although she relived that moment a thousand times, she could never remember where Anson was looking when the boy gleefully grabbed the reins, as he had seen his daddy do, sending the horses headlong down the road toward the barn.

She remembered Anson racing after the careening buggy, but she hid her eyes when she saw the little body hurtle from the seat and slam against the big catalpa tree.

"Jesus, help us!" Sibby cried.

For the first black instant, Anna couldn't make her feet move, then she pushed past Sibby into the front hall, commanding, "Give him to *me* . . . give him to *me*," as Anson walked rapidly up the front steps across the porch and laid their still, still child in her arms.

She bathed the crushed head with the water Sibby brought and held him on her lap, while Anson, kneeling beside her, begged God to let them keep their child.

Procter, riding hard for Dr. Massey, couldn't have been a mile down the road when Anna put her free hand over Anson's mouth almost roughly.

"Stop praying. He's dead!"

Anna was aware only of the grief that hung over the rainy churchyard when Reverend Watson Winn committed her child's body to the sandy ground in the center of the small plot Anson had selected just before they were married. In the measure her baby had brought joy to the Island, his death now brought grief. They had all come, she knew, from the Mills, from up and down Frederica Road, and of course, her neighbors from Frederica . . . but Anna couldn't have told you who was there, except, oddly enough, she saw Emma Bass for one moment, huddled shapeless and sobbing at the edge of the crowd. She reminded herself to be glad that Anson hadn't fallen ill again; that he stood beside her, gripping her hand.

She only half heard Watson Winn say, "Suffer the little children to come unto me . . ." and, a little later on, "Let not your heart be troubled. . . ."

Anna hated God.

Her baby was inside that small box John Stevens had built . . . her baby lying still and unsmiling on the soft white pillow Belle Taylor had made . . . that was her baby, and no one had a right to tell her not to let her heart be troubled! No one. Not even Anson. She would never again allow him to talk to her about giving God a chance to redeem one single thing. Not a thing.

The rain was coming down hard, and Anna could feel sobs shake Anson's body as Horace sprinkled a handful of wet sandy earth into the grave. And as Procter and his people, standing apart together at the back of the crowd, began to sing, the churchyard was filled with the sound of weeping.

She clung to Anson and felt his arm around her. Anson will need me to be strong, she thought desperately, and then lost hold even of that, when he pulled her suddenly to him in such pain she collapsed in his arms, sobbing out her protest for everybody to hear.

When Anson helped her down from the buggy, Emma Bass was huddled in the rain on their front steps, P. D. beside her.

"Anson, I can't talk to *them* now."

"I will," he said, supporting her as they walked toward P. D. and Emma. "Thank you for coming, but Mrs. Dodge is very tired."

"Me an' Emma's got somepin' to say."

"Tomorrow, P. D. Surely it can wait until tomorrow."

"Won't take a minute. Go ahead, Emma. Nothin' would do her but she had to be the one to say it.

Emma dropped her lower lip, pulled it up again, and said to Anson, "We're ready to sell ya the half acre."

Anson tightened his arm around Anna and replied quietly, "Thank you, Emma. But it may be some time now before I can see my lawyer, and—"

"Ain't no rush, Mr. Dodge. It's just that me an' P. D. knows now that God has punished you enough for marryin' yer first cousin."

Anna stepped toward Emma, but Anson held her.

"Ain't no use'n gittin' yer dander up, Anna Dodge. The Lord told us Hisself He was done punishin' him. Told us to sell him the half acre to prove it."

Anson pushed past them, hurried Anna inside the big, silent house, and closed the door.

Inside, for one good moment, her strength came back, and she gathered Anson into her arms and held him, smoothing the back of his head as though he were a child. He tried not to cry, she could feel his body struggling against it, and then he stopped struggling and wept all the tears he had not wept through the years he had forced himself to be strong for all of them.

"If God is punishing you, Anson, He's a devil."

He stopped weeping and looked at her. "God is not punishing me. Those poor twisted people have it all wrong. It's not like that at all, Anna—it is *not* like that."

Sibby brought them tea, and they sat together on the green sofa in the parlor until the long evening shadows darkened the room. They had never made a habit of sitting in the parlor, but this was a strange night. They would have to learn to live in a strange, silent world, empty of little thudding feet through the house, empty of laughter and chatter and the dear responsibility. Anson would have to learn to come home again in the silence, only to her. She would have to learn how not to be watchful through every minute of her days. There would never be another child in their home, but somehow she would have to learn how to make it a home again for Anson. She looked at him, slumped into the corner of the sofa, his head back, his eyes closed . . . his face pale, even in the half light.

"Anson—are you all right?"

"Yes. I don't understand it, but I haven't had a single twinge in my chest."

She reached for his hand. "Don't have any!"

"Hadn't you better go upstairs and lie down?"

"No, but if you want to go to your study, it's all right."

"I'm where I want to be, Anna—with you."

"Don't try to help me, Anson. Don't talk about an answer."

"I won't."

She studied his face. Had he discovered that God has no answer for grief? She felt her heart tighten against God because He had no answer even for a good, kind, faithful priest like her husband.

And then she suffered the painful loosening of her heart . . . she *wanted* an answer for Anson. His eyes were still closed, and she searched his pale, exhausted face: was it really peace she saw? Tears slipped down his cheeks, but there was no trace of fighting or rebellion. It's as though he's waiting, she thought, for the next thing to do. It's as though he knows that now he has to wait and not rush in, and he's willing. She was not. Her pain was too great, and all the days ahead, when the pain would grow greater, piled up before her, up and up until she jumped to her feet before they toppled in on her. "Anson—what are we going to do?"

He stood up, not touching her, but looking at her from the depths of his own soul. "Anna, we're going to go on. God does not punish by these methods. I settled that long ago. If He does, then Jesus Christ did not reveal Him rightly. He entered *into* human suffering, He did not remain aloof from it. I admit I once struggled with God for an answer to human grief. I pleaded for something to say to you when your father died. God gave me absolutely nothing to *say,* but He began to teach me how to cope with grief myself. I haven't learned much yet, but here—I have another chance. I love you now, Anna, and I wish with all my heart that I could bear this for you. I can't. Only God can do that. I won't be storming heaven for an answer this time, even for you . . . there are no words that form an answer anyway. But I'll be waiting for Him to show us how He is going to make use of—of this, too."

He had said it. She whirled to run from the room, then turned back to him. He had dared to say it to her—on the very day they buried her baby! Even Anson's God could make no *use* of anything so cruel and useless as her baby's death. And yet . . . something else Anson had said was pulling to be remembered. Whatever it was, it had kept her from running from him just now. It was nothing about God. What he had said about God had made her want to run. She pressed her forehead with both hands, straining to remember what he had said that he had never said to her before . . . straining to clear away the shock and the grief and the pain long enough to remember his words, and then he was saying them again.

"I love you, Anna, and that's going to help me wait for God to tell us how we can avoid *wasting* our grief. I know I'm not saying this well or clearly—but because I love you, I'll manage for us both, until you are able to believe Him too."

The room was dark by this time, but a slow, dim light edged some of the darkness aside in Anna's heart, as he reached for her hand.

Suddenly, she asked an irrelevant question. "Why didn't you wait for your mother to get here, Anson?"

"For your sake. It would have been cruel to you. Mother will understand."

Climbing the stairs was not the ordeal she had thought it would be, and although neither of them slept much that night, they lay quietly in each other's arms . . . only Anna weeping now and then when, in her half sleep, she thought she heard little Anson's cry.

Chapter Thirty-Three

Anna didn't want to go to Europe again, but Dr. Massey insisted that Anson needed a long rest, and knowing he would not slow down if they stayed on the Island, Anna went. She would have preferred the balm of her beloved trees and woods and the Island sky; would have preferred to stay close to the familiar places, inside the familiar rooms of the big house, near his toys, near enough to feed Puddy and comfort the dog when he went searching, as he had done every day since his playmate went away. She longed to stay close by the tiny grave, but Rossie Stevens promised to tend it, to keep fresh flowers or caladium leaves on it, and so she went abroad with Anson.

"Take good care of him, Anna," Rebecca Dodge said, as they boarded their ship in New York. "He's all we have left."

The two women had embraced, and Anna refused the thought that perhaps the baby's death had brought them together at last. Refused it, because it seemed small compensation.

For the next eight months, while they roamed Europe, Anson seemed to relax, knowing that his friend Watson Winn was making the trip weekly from St. Mary's, on the mainland, to serve the church at Frederica. Anna walked with him through the streets of London and along the shore of the south of France. She sat with him beside Lake Como in northern Italy; read with him hour after hour on hotel verandas in Florence and

Rome, watching his mind clear daily, his old energy return. She still longed to be at home, but they had never been so close, and although Anna would always wait for his moods, the last of her reserve melted away. She could talk with him now and not feel he was being forced to pull her along. He seemed to enjoy watching her shed her ignorance of so many things; he liked to teach her French phrases, to learn a little Spanish with her when they visited Spain, to be with her in a new kind of silence, with no barriers between them.

One evening in early October, in Madrid, he turned to her, his face solemn, and said, "Anna, the waiting is over. I know what we are to do." And then he talked about it for the first time since the night of little Anson's funeral. Anna found herself able to listen now, even to understand some of what he was saying. He had made his decision, had thought it all through before he spoke. This man who trusted God the way little Anson had trusted his father, who obeyed God as little Anson had obeyed him . . . this man whom she loved more than ever, was ready to move ahead in the way he believed God indicated.

Anna listened and felt his strength; strength like the wide branches of the guardian oaks which twisted and grew in another direction, when the storms battered them, but which kept right on growing. He spoke with great certainty, almost as though he were giving her a report. He did not exert pressure or try to persuade; this would never have occurred to Anson Dodge. He was simply ready to move ahead, and since she was his wife, she was expected to be ready too. And so she listened to his plan, killing off her inner struggles and conflicts one by one as he talked. They would go home now, back to St. Simons Island, back to their house at Frederica. But they were not to waste that big house any longer. In their son's memory, it would now become the *Anson Greene Phelps Dodge Home* for boys. He had known of the need for such a home in Georgia for over two years. Early the next year when he went to Atlanta for the Annual Diocesan Meeting, he would locate the first homeless boys, make arrangements for their travel, find someone to bring them safely to the Island, where they would never again be without a home. They would not be coming to an orphanage when they came to Frederica; they would be coming home. He and Anna would be their parents.

Anna's eyes brimmed with tears as he talked, and valiantly she fought back her fear that he would go too far, would let his generous heart rule his head, would agree to take more boys than they could handle. She tore at the last shred of self-pity, the last remnant of rebellion: that she take care of someone else's children when her heart and her arms would ache forever for her own baby.

"Anson," she ventured, when he finished, "maybe—maybe Dr. Massey was wrong. Maybe I can have one more child."

He was so gentle, he made her think of her father.

"I've thought of that, Anna. God knows I've thought of it a hundred times since we've been away. But I can't permit it. I can't lose you, too."

She closed the door on that hope and never opened it again.

And when the red gums and the butternut trees and the grapevines were turning color once more, they made the long trip home to begin their new life. To begin to give God a chance to make *use* of their broken hearts. She recognized her own willingness to give God a chance, as she rode beside Anson up Frederica Road in the Mill wagon. If she did it only on Anson's faith, it seemed, at least, to be working. It would be like losing the baby all over again, going back into the big empty house, but she found herself smiling as she always had at the whimsy of the yellow grapevines roping the trees with light, and that was a hopeful sign.

Chapter Thirty-Four

When it was time for the Annual Diocesan Meeting in Atlanta in January, Anson was too ill to go. All through the Christmas holidays, their first Christmas without the baby, he had forced himself to carry on with the program of the churches on the Island, in spite of a heavy cold. By the end of January, he was no longer able to make the weekly trip to the Mills church, the Beach Chapel, or St. Ignatius, even in the buggy, and Anna felt she should write to his mother.

> It is not his heart this time, at least Dr. Massey says it isn't. But he is so thin and pale, and can't seem to get rid of the cold he's had now almost ever since we came home from abroad. Dr. Massey says we should wait until next year for the children to come. Could you visit us, Mother Dodge? I know it would mean so much to Anson, and I would be ever so grateful to you. I admit I need help in trying to convince him to wait.

Rebecca Dodge came at once and stayed until spring. Mother Dodge would never love her as she had loved Ellen. Anna had never expected that. They had only Anson in common, but they did have him, and they could talk together on the front porch while Anson studied or walked alone by the river, working out his sermons or planning the changes they would make in the big house, even though he had agreed to wait another year for the first boys to come.

"You're a courageous woman, Anna, to be willing to go into this new dream of his."

"I trust him, Mother Dodge."

"Yes, I can see you do."

Rebecca looked older, Anna thought. The death of her grandchild had left its marks.

"I wonder where that boy is?" Rebecca looked out over the river in the direction Anson had walked an hour ago.

"He's making plans for something."

"You've learned about him, haven't you, my dear?"

"I try," Anna said.

"Have you found him so difficult?"

"He's taught me everything I know—about everything, Mother Dodge."

The older woman sat down again. "I'm understanding more and more why he married you, Anna Gould."

John and George Stevens worked every evening all summer and into the fall of the next year, knocking out walls on the second floor of the big house, enlarging the kitchen, building a seesaw and two sturdy lawn swings; Procter worked until it was time to leave for the fall term at trade school in Atlanta, clearing a thicket for playing horseshoes, securing heavy ropes in four tall oak trees to be used for swings, and even though Anna didn't think she could stand it, the last thing Procter did was to clean up the little red-wheeled pony cart. Anson said it would be all right once she saw the first little fellow ride in the pretty cart, and she tried to believe him.

Anna was so happy that Procter had at last agreed to go to school, tears came when she told him good-bye.

"Don't cry, Miss Anna, unless you're cryin' for joy like you said you did a long time ago. I've seen you cry too much the other way. I just plain won't go unless you stop."

She stopped, blew her nose, wiped her eyes, and

sent him off in the buggy beside Anson, with a big smile and a big wave and big expectations.

"I'll be back, Miss Anna—come spring," Procter called, as the buggy rounded the curve out of her sight.

"Dear God, take care of that boy and help him to learn fast," she prayed, as she walked slowly back into the empty house.

She called Sibby to tell her she'd be alone for supper. Anson had promised he wouldn't make the trip back to Frederica that night but would stay with his Uncle Norman at the Mills. Maybe I'll ride John Wesley down to Mama's, she thought. But passing the open door of Anson's study, she saw Ellen's picture hanging over his big roll-top desk, and stopped. No. I won't go to Mama's. This would be the right time to read Ellen's book.

Upstairs in the master bedroom, alone in the big bed, Anna was still reading when the grandfather clock struck midnight.

She had deliberately not read his Preface tonight, but the words were carved into her memory:

> . . . her husband feels justified in giving them a permanent shape for those who shared with him the privilege of her acquaintance and her love.

Tonight she did not feel shut out. *I love you, Anna* . . . he had said it at last. He was *her* husband too. She had borne him a child. And she was one of those who had shared with him Ellen's sensitivity, and for over an hour she read the account of their honeymoon trip to Japan, recognizing parts of the letters Ellen had written to her, woven into the narrative. The account ended abruptly at Agra, India, and Anna closed the book.

Would Ellen have liked living on St. Simons with him all these years? She loved him enough, Anna knew, but had there been a strange, inexplicable purpose in all that had happened? In *all* that had happened. No. There could have been no purpose in the death of her child! If there was no purpose in that, then there had been none in Ellen's death, either.

She lay motionless, holding the book. Had Anson ever said anything about God having a purpose? As though God caused their grief? Had he ever said he believed God took Ellen? Or their baby? All she could ever remember his saying was that in the haphazard of earthly life, God worked in and through the joys and the tragedies, always making redemptive *use* of everything: not causing either joy or pain, but *using* them. Slowly, she realized, this truth had come to belong to her, too. And lying there holding Ellen's book, she said aloud, as though to realize it more clearly, "I am no longer going on Anson's faith. I have my own."

The clock chimed half past midnight, and Anna opened the book again, this time at random, to a short separate piece called *A Dream*. Written, Anson had noted at the top of the page, in November, 1883, on the train from Agra to Allahabad, India. Maybe this was the last thing she wrote, Anna thought:

> *I have lain in the breast of a star, and danced on the lips of a ranbow; I have been caught in the laugh of the moon, and have tossed my limbs in the yellow hair of the sun and the white hair of the old, old moon. . . .*

She understood Ellen now, as she had wanted to understand her then; understood Anson's loss as she never had before.

> *. . . I have seen the morning hanging in the arms of the night; I have touched the verge of all eternity and found it one unending pleasure; and yet I have found something newer and sweeter than all. . . . I have found death.*

Anna dropped the book. "Is death—sweet, Ellen?" she asked aloud. "Is it as sweet for you who are there as it is bitter—for us here?"

Chapter Thirty-Five

March of 1898 came at last, but the children didn't come that spring either. Anson was again too ill. Procter came home from school and swore he wouldn't go back until Mr. Dodge was well.

Anson had insisted he felt well enough to make the rounds of his mission churches on the mainland late in March, and the first night he was home from that tiring trip, Anna awakened in the dark to find him gasping for breath. He remained in bed until the last Saturday in April, but when Procter's Aunt Rena lay dying, Anson took Holy Communion to her in her little shack in the woods at Harrington. Procter drove him, and Anna prayed until she heard the buggy return.

She knew he slept well that night, she had watched him through every hour, and when he dressed to preach at Christ Church on Sunday, April 24, she decided it was better to let him go without a word than to add to his weariness by begging him to stay at home. He preached four times that day on the Good Shepherd, and Anna was in the congregation all four times. She would not hear of his going to the Mills church without her, or to the Beach Chapel or to St. Ignatius. "The colored folk at St. Ignatius always give to me, Anna. If I miss the other two down the Island, I refuse to miss St. Ignatius."

He had missed none of them, and each time she watched for his pale, thin face to light up when he read: "I am the Good Shepherd. . . . My sheep know My voice, and they follow Me." Each time his face shone with a light of which the Island light was only a shadow.

On Easter Sunday a cloudburst kept everyone away from the church, but since Anson loved preaching his Easter sermon more than any other, he preached it on June 5. The sun poured over him through the stained glass window dedicated to Ellen, as he stood in his beloved pulpit at Christ Church Frederica. For a moment, he looked at the window, Ellen's window, larger than the others, depicting the Angel at the empty tomb of Jesus, speaking to the women who had come to anoint His body. The people turned to look at it too, and some of them read the inscription: *Ye seek Jesus of Nazareth. He is not here. He is risen as He said. Alleluia! Alleluia!*

They all knew Anson had chosen the inscription himself, and they listened as he preached to them of his own faith in the continuing life, in the life uninterrupted by death for those who believe . . . in the Great Going On.

And then Anson closed the Bible and his black book of sermon notes and stepped to one side of his pulpit. "My dear friends, I can tell you on this bright, beautiful Sunday morning on our Island that Jesus Christ is alive. He came out of His tomb. He could not have remained sealed inside because He *was* God. To us, in retrospect, it is ridiculous—laughable—for them to think they could seal Him in with a stone which He, Himself, had created! He is alive . . . and because He lives, our loved ones live also. Your loved ones, whose bodies lie outside in our dear, familiar churchyard, are not dead."

For an instant, Anna saw him look at her.

"My loved one, whose body lies here beneath this altar, is not dead. My little son, who loved all of you and whom you loved, is not dead. One day he will greet his mother again, and he will greet me. He will greet all of you, with the Father beside him, because whosoever liveth and believeth in Christ shall *never* die. We weep, our hearts break, our arms are empty and our homes are silent, but we do not grieve without hope. I could not follow a God who created within me such an insatiable love of life, and who would then snatch it away forever. If this life is all, if we must say a permanent good-bye beside those graves out there which will continue to open to us, one by one, then God is a fiend. But God, for us who know Him in Jesus Christ, is *Life*. Let it sound in your minds like a great bell, and let it keep sounding, that whosoever liveth and believeth in Him shall never die."

Anson was much better through the months of June and July, and Anna's heart sang as she worked with Sibby once more making ready for the boys to come. There would be three of them, one red-haired fellow of seven, one baby eight months old, and one almost three. "Much like our boy from his picture," Anson said over and over, the thought helping him as much as it frightened Anna. But she pushed away her fear. Anson was like himself again: up at six in the morning, his early prayer time in the churchyard, the brisk walk home, and, once more, he enjoyed the big breakfasts Sibby loved to fix for him. He took Holy Communion to the sick and aged, visited his families up and down the Island, telling about the new boys who would soon be his sons; and when they received word from the father of the two younger children that he was unable to bring them to St. Simons, they made plans to leave Monday, August 22, for Atlanta to bring the boys themselves.

"I'm glad, in a way, Anson. This will give us a chance to get acquainted with them before they get here. If you're sure you're up to the trip."

He laughed at her and hurried for no reason, except that he had never been able not to hurry, to his study.

Horace was standing in the hall when Anna came downstairs on Saturday afternoon.

"James is bringin' Mama and Maimie in the

buggy, sister. I rode ahead. Procter's after Doc Massey. How is he?"

She looked at her brother, then threw herself into his arms.

"Now, look here, Anna, Doc Massey says Anson'll have these attacks off and on. He's gonna be all right."

She clung to him, struggling against sobs, not wanting Anson to hear her weep.

"He'll come out of it in a few days, sister."

"Not this time, Horace. Not this time."

He led her into the parlor and closed the door. "Now, look here, Anna, you can't go all to pieces like this. Anson'll be wantin' you back upstairs with him in a minute—"

"Rossie and John are with him."

"Yes, but he'll want you back, and you've got to pretend you believe he's going to pull outa this."

She stepped back as though he had slapped her. "You don't think he's going to live either, do you?"

"Now, I didn't say that, I—"

"Stop trying, Horace." She spoke stiffly. "I'm all right now. You'd better ride down to the Mills and send his mother a telegram. I'm *all right* now. I won't say what I said again, but do you know *why* I won't? Because it can't be true. Anson can't die too! I won't let him die. Do you hear me, Horace? *I won't let him die.*"

After a moment, Horace said, "Yes, sister. I heard you."

"All right." Her voice sounded heavy, authoritative, unfamiliar. "If you meet Dr. Massey, tell him to hurry."

She straightened her shoulders.

"While you're in your office, send a wire to the father of those little boys in Atlanta, too." She walked briskly back to Anson's office, found the man's letter, then returned to the parlor where Horace waited. "Here's his name and address."

"I'll ride back up here just as soon as I take care of everything, Anna."

"Thanks, Horace. I'm ever so much obliged. I know it's a long ride."

"You know I don't mind that, sister."

As Horace turned to go, Rossie's scream from upstairs pierced the quiet:

"Anna! Anna, come quick—come quick!"

Chapter Thirty-Six

Walking the quiet, shaded streets of Charleston, South Carolina, helped some. They were strange streets. Anna had never gone there with Anson. She hurried past every church, turning her eyes from the ancient, well-tended cemeteries, concentrating on the elegance of the Charleston homes, the formal gardens, the parks.

Anna Dodge was a woman of means now; she owned half of St. Simons Island. Anson had bought every acre anyone would sell, and, although he hadn't thought it important enough to tell her before he went away, it comforted her somehow. Not because she cared about legal ownership—she had always felt she "owned" the whole Island—but because owning it must have made Anson feel less like an outsider. This comforted her, as much as she could be comforted. One had to *feel*, in order to know real comfort, and after three weeks of wandering alone from one city to another, by train and by boat, Anna was still feeling as little as possible. When it was meal time, she felt no hunger, and when her food was set before her in small tea shops or in ornate hotel dining rooms, she dreaded the thought of swallowing. She dreaded everything, especially waking up after whatever sleep she managed near dawn each day. Waking meant losing Anson all over again; meant struggling against another day. She found her happy memories the heaviest of all to carry from one place to another: Anson and their child in the buggy, laughing . . . Anson's face full of light when he

preached . . . Anson, standing with one foot on a
fallen log in the yard at Black Banks, eating a succulent
roasted oyster from the hot shell he held in a clump of
Spanish moss.

Walking the streets of Charleston and Birmingham
and Richmond had helped some. At least they were
strange streets. She hadn't dared go to Atlanta; she had
been there with him, and the children were there, still
waiting to make their home with her. Horace had post-
poned their arrival again, this time until November, a
month away, in time for Christmas.

She kept on walking. There was no definite time
today to be anywhere; no one was expecting her.

Anna had given her family the Charleston address,
and when she returned to her hotel, there was a letter
from Horace, urging her to come home.

> The children will arrive November 15, sis-
> ter, and you must be here to welcome them. We
> are all well and safe, but only by the grace of
> God. . . .

Anna's hands trembled. On October 2, the worst
tidal wave in the history of the Island had struck, and
page after page of Horace's orderly, even script described the terror and the destruction. Black Banks had
been hit severely, the front piazza torn off, and many of
their animals drowned as the giant waves chased back
and forth across the yard, floating away their food supplies and Ca's old cabin. Horace had just managed to
get Bessie out of the barn in time to save her life.

They needed Anna at home. She could mend their
houses for them. This is what Anson would have done,
with no thought for himself.

> Clifford Postell carried his invalid mother
> across the road to safety when the water hit Kel-
> vin Grove, and although Mackbeth tried valiantly
> to help save their furniture, when it came time
> for him to cross through the raging water, his
> courage failed, and he sank in a heap on the
> floor, sobbing like a little boy. Clifford had to
> wade back and carry Mack over too.

It had been sundown when she entered her room to read Horace's letter. When she bathed her eyes, the weeping ended, her room was in darkness. Now a deep struggle had been added to her grief. Those were her people, suffering . . . they were Anson's people. Nothing would keep him from helping, if he were alive.

She stood a long time by the window, looking out over the city, lighting up slowly for the night. A church bell tolled almost merrily somewhere, and she thought again of Mackbeth Postell grinning and tugging the bell rope every Sunday morning at Frederica, his whole soul glad with the chance to ring the bell for Mr. Dodge. Cautiously, one small bit at a time, she permitted herself to remember the day of Anson's funeral: the last time she had heard Mackbeth tug at the bell in the steeple of Christ Church. She had still been in the big bedroom at home when the slow, solemn tolling began. Her neighbors had swept the churchyard and cleared the fallen moss and branches from the roads for those who would come by boat from the mainland, and by carriage and buggy up Frederica Road from the Mills. That day in the big bedroom, she knew they were coming; was aware that Procter was driving the wagon bearing Anson's body around the curve in the road to the church; that Belle was helping her fasten her white dress, white to please Anson. In his will were explicit, detailed requests, and they were being carefully carried out, each one:

> Trusting the proven love of my wife, Anna Dodge, I instruct that I be allowed to keep a promise made to my first wife, Ellen Ada Phelps Dodge, before her death. Her body is to be removed from the church chancel in time to be buried in a joint grave with my own at the east boundary of the Dodge plot. Space is to be left between that grave and the grave of my son for my present wife, Anna Deborah Gould Dodge. At the far corner of the lot will be space for Rebecca Grew Dodge, my mother. I further request that my wife be dressed all in white to attend my funeral service.

Belle and Rossie had made the white silk brocade (which Ellen had sent, so long ago) into a dress for Anna, and Belle was helping her fasten the bodice hooks when Mackbeth Postell began tolling the church bell for Anson. . . .

Anna turned from her hotel window. She was not ready to go back yet. Not for Mack Postell or her family or any of the people whose homes were wrecked by the storm. She was not ready to go back—neither for the Island's sake nor for the children who had been waiting so long to live with her.

"Stay until you're rested, sister," Horace had written.

She remembered urging Anson to rest a dozen times a day for the past five years.

I can't rest, Anna, knowing my people are in need.

"And I can't go back," she cried aloud in the empty room. "Not yet, Anson. Not yet. I can't face it there without you. I've got to learn how to feel something first besides pain. I've got to be able to feel. I'm mostly dead, too—like you!"

In early November, she walked the streets of New Orlean's French Quarter, still moving through her empty days as though she were made of wood and string and pulleys. She slept a little better at night now, her conflict shut off. Horace had no address for her in New Orleans. No matter how much they needed her, she was free of knowing about it. Somehow, she kept telling herself, something would happen to help her. Any day now, it would surely happen, some one thing that would make it possible for her to do what she had to do. "The children will arive on November 15, sister." The children Anson wanted. She had worn the white silk for him at his funeral. Being conspicuous had always been painful for her, and widows dressed in black at funerals, but her pain was already complete, and if Anson wanted it, she had no choice anyway. For all the years she had loved him, making choices had been no problem for her. She did what he wanted because he wanted it. Was that changed too? Everything else in her world was changed, chopped off, silenced, gone. . . .

Was pleasing Anson lost, too? Mack Postell would be ringing the bell again on Sunday mornings because Anson had asked him to. . . . Watson Winn would go right on preaching the things Anson believed. . . . Procter was taking care of his horses, and Sibby his house. Life was going on back on the Island, as Anson would want it to go on—for everyone but Anna.

She hailed a hansom cab and instructed the snowy-haired colored man to drive "anywhere. . . . Just drive."

Mack Postell ringing that bell haunted her thoughts, and, out under the blue mid-afternoon sky, she remembered Anson standing beside his pulpit in Christ Church preaching his Easter sermon on June 5: *Let it sound in your minds like a great bell, and let it keep on sounding.* . . .

What else had he said that day that made even Rossie Stevens sit up and listen all the way to the end? Something about the Great Going On. . . . She pressed her fingers hard against her temples, trying desperately to remember. He had stepped to one side of his pulpit and had talked to them so quietly, but with such certainty, that Anna felt if she could only remember . . . could only lay hold of whatever it was that had made her able to smile back at him from her seat, she might begin to feel again without shrinking from what she felt. "Oh, God, help me remember," she said aloud, unmindful of the driver, or the people going past . . . unaware even that she had breathed her first prayer since her heart had hardened against God in the churchyard as Procter and his people had begun to sing while they buried Anson and Ellen together in the wide fresh grave. "Help me, God! Help me remember what he said."

The worn old hansom cab rattled over the bricks of Chartres Street and turned the corner into St. Ann at Jackson Square. Anna sat on the leather seat, waiting. He had said something that made her believe that she would see her child again, that he was still alive, that she would never again have to grieve without hope. It had seemed to be *her* faith that day, no longer Anson's. But when he went away, the door had slammed shut.

All these weeks of wandering alone had been days lived out against the blank face of that slammed door.

Suddenly, she was sitting tensed and erect, waiting for a word of some kind from somewhere, not even feeling foolish about it, just sitting erect and waiting. She would surely find it again, she told herself, if only she could remember what Anson had said. It would have to be hers, now, her own faith. Anson was gone. If she were ever to go back to the Island, it would have to be on her own faith.

The cab bumped along Chartres Street again; the driver had circled the Square. They were near the corner of Chartres and St. Phillip, or rounding it—she never could quite remember—when from somewhere came the pungent odor of steak and onions. It smelled good.

As though a danger had passed, she leaned back against the seat of the cab . . . and then it came, not in Anson's words, as she had expected, but in her own. And she said aloud, her voice clearing as she spoke: "My friend Ellen and my husband are not dead. My little son is not dead. Papa is not dead. They will all greet me again one day, because—whosoever liveth and believeth in Him shall *never* die."

The old driver turned slightly in his seat. "You talkin' to me, Ma'am?"

"No," Anna said. "I wasn't, but I am now."

She tucked in a stubborn wisp of hair and straightened her hat.

"I wonder if you'd take me to a restaurant where I can get some steak and onions? You see, I've just decided I'm catching a train tonight for Georgia, but I think I'd like a good meal first."

Epilogue

Anna Dodge went back to St. Simons Island that November, 1898, and for the rest of her life—until June, 1927, when she died in the big bedroom at the Dodge house—she lived out her husband's dream for the children who needed to grow up in the beauty of the Island and the security of a home where they were loved. The Anson Dodge Home did not close until 1958.

If you visit St. Simons Island, Georgia, and walk around to the side of the little Episcopal church at Frederica, you will find the Dodge plot, its low stone wall sprouting resurrection ferns. Beside the plain granite slab covering the joint grave of Anson and Ellen, you will find—not the grave of Anna Dodge, as Anson requested in his will; rather, a monument to her unselfishness—the grave of her mother-in-law, Rebecca Dodge, who became her close friend. Then, beside his grandmother, little Anson, his grave marked with a small stone cross, and at the far corner, Anna, who understood love as few women understand it.

Anson Dodge was only thirty-eight when he died, but in Valdosta, Georgia, in Waycross, in St. Mary's, at Woodbine, and on the Island at St. Ignatius and at Christ Church Frederica his work still goes on. Even in Allahabad, India, stands All Saints Cathedral, which he built in memory of Ellen . . . one more reminder, to those of us who live too near the surface of life, that there once lived a young man who refused to be knocked down by the years' steady succession of blows;

a young man who dared to allow God to make redemptive use of his entire life—of the tragedies as well as the triumphs.

The descendants of the Goulds, the Postells, the Taylors, the Stevenses, the Kings are still there, still worshipping in the little church he built, still burying their dead in the churchyard. They are still there, gracious and grateful that his story has at last been set down, even though by an outsider, who, with a friend, once having seen Anson Dodge's brave little church among the guardian oaks, the red gums, and the yellow grapevines in November, could never forget.

This outsider's deep and everlasting thanks to Mrs. Lorah Plemmons, Anna's devoted friend and helper at the Dodge Home in her later life, and to her daughters, Sarah and Mary; to Anna's nieces, Fé Powell, Mrs. L. W. Everett, Mrs. Douglas Taylor, and their husbands—all my dear friends now; to Dr. Junius J. Martin, rector of Christ Church Frederica, who gave me access to Anson Dodge's own journal, and to Mr. Watson Glissom, sexton of Christ Church, who gave me access, according to my needs, to the church itself; and to Mr. and Mrs. Billy Backus for the loan of one of the few remaining copies of Ellen's little book.

I shall be forever grateful for unusual help from Burnette Vanstory, author of Georgia's Land of the Golden Isles, from Mrs. Abbie Fuller Graham, Captain and Mrs. N. C. Young, Mr. and Mrs. Claude Crider, Mrs. May Wright Parker, Mrs. Ann Stevens Parker, Mr. and Mrs. Allen Burns, Mr. T. Q. Fleming, Mr. Mansfield Jackson, the late Mr. Willis Procter, and for cooperation far beyond the call of duty from Mrs. Fraser Ledbetter and Mrs. Lillian Knight of the St. Simons Library. And to all the interested people in Waycross, Valdosta, Woodbine and Brunswick whose doors were knocked upon without notice and whose shared memories enabled me to write an authentic story.

My gratitude also to Mr. and Mrs. Cleveland E. Dodge of New York for their enthusiastic help and encouragement; to Dr. Anna B. Mow, Frances Pitts and Easter Straker for line-by-line caring and criticism; to

Addison Pelletier and Marjorie Hoagland for special research; to Mrs. Lucie L. Bargamin of Alexander, Virginia, who was Rebecca Dodge's neighbor; and to Herbert D. Thomas, Secretary for Alumni Affairs at General Theological Seminary in New York.

Singular gratitude must go to my fellow researcher, Joyce Blackburn, who lived the story with me for over three years; and to my mother, whose unselfish love makes all things possible. And if I have made the transition from non-fiction to fiction, it is because Miss Tay Hohoff was my patient and wise editor. Last, but far from least, for superb handling of the typescript, I thank Elsie Goodwillie—another come-lately "outsider" to the Island—who, like me, could neither leave nor forget what she found there.

Eugenia Price
St. Simons Island, Georgia
February, 1965

ABOUT THE AUTHOR

When EUGENIA PRICE, whose nonfiction books have sold in the millions, discovered St. Simons Island, Georgia, in 1960, she "fell hopelessly in love with the Island." And, when she discovered the island, she also discovered a true story that could be the basis for a novel: the story of Anson Dodge, which she tells movingly in *The Beloved Invader*. In her research into the history of St. Simons, she found other true stories that moved her to plan a trilogy about the people living there during the nineteenth century. *New Moon Rising* is the second in that trilogy. Of her love for the island, Miss Price writes that she has now built her home "here in the woods, less than a mile from Christ Church and almost completely surrounded by the Marshes of Glynn. I pass the graves of all my characters every time I drive to the village. In a way difficult to explain, this is now *my* place to be."

BRING ROMANCE INTO YOUR LIFE

With these bestsellers from your favorite Bantam authors

Barbara Cartland

☐	11372	LOVE AND THE LOATHSOME LEOPARD	$1.50
☐	10712	LOVE LOCKED IN	$1.50
☐	11270	THE LOVE PIRATE	$1.50
☐	11271	THE TEMPTATION OF TORILLA	$1.50

Catherine Cookson

☐	10355	THE DWELLING PLACE	$1.50
☐	10358	THE GLASS VIRGIN	$1.50
☐	10516	THE TIDE OF LIFE	$1.75

Georgette Heyer

☐	02263	THE BLACK MOTH	$1.50
☐	10322	BLACK SHEEP	$1.50
☐	02210	FARO'S DAUGHTER	$1.50

Emilie Loring

☐	02382	FORSAKING ALL OTHERS	$1.25
☐	02237	LOVE WITH HONOR	$1.25
☐	11228	IN TIMES LIKE THESE	$1.50
☐	10846	STARS IN YOUR EYES	$1.50

Eugenia Price

☐	12712	BELOVED INVADER	$1.95
☐	11180	LIGHTHOUSE	$1.75
☐	11189	NEW MOON RISING	$1.75

Buy them at your local bookstore or use this handy coupon for ordering:

Bantam Books, Inc., Dept. RO, 414 East Golf Road, Des Plaines, Ill. 60016

Please send me the books I have checked above. I am enclosing $_____
(please add 75¢ to cover postage and handling). Send check or money order
—no cash or C.O.D.'s please.

Mr/Mrs/Miss_____

Address_____

City_____State/Zip_____

RO—11/78

Please allow four weeks for delivery. This offer expires 5/79.

Heartwarming Books
of
Faith and Inspiration

☐	11710	**THE GOSPEL ACCORDING TO PEANUTS** Robert L. Short	$1.50
☐	2576	**HOW CAN I FIND YOU, GOD?** Marjorie Holmes	$1.75
☐	10947	**THE FINDING OF JASPER HOLT** Grace Livingston Hill	$1.50
☐	10176	**THE BIBLE AS HISTORY** Werner Keller	$2.50
☐	12218	**THE GREATEST MIRACLE IN THE WORLD** Og Mandino	$1.95
☐	2866	**THE WOMAN AT THE WELL** Dale Evans Rogers	$1.50
☐	12009	**THE GREATEST SALESMAN IN THE WORLD** Og Mandino	$1.95
☐	12330	**I'VE GOT TO TALK TO SOMEBODY, GOD** Marjorie Holmes	$1.95
☐	10291	**THE GIFT OF INNER HEALING** Ruth Carter Stapleton	$1.75
☐	10405	**BORN AGAIN** Charles Colson	$2.25
☐	11012	**FASCINATING WOMANHOOD** Helen Andelin	$1.95
☐	12066	**TWO FROM GALILEE** Marjorie Holmes	$1.95
☐	11180	**LIGHTHOUSE** Eugenia Price	$1.75
☐	11189	**NEW MOON RISING** Eugenia Price	$1.75
☐	11291	**THE LATE GREAT PLANET EARTH** Hal Lindsey	$1.95
☐	11140	**REFLECTIONS ON LIFE AFTER LIFE** Dr. Raymond Moody	$1.95

Buy them at your local bookstore or use this handy coupon for ordering:

Novels of Enduring Romance and Inspiration by

GRACE
LIVINGSTON
HILL

☐ 11762	TOMORROW ABOUT THIS TIME	$1.50
☐ 11506	THROUGH THESE FIRES	$1.50
☐ 10859	BEAUTY FOR ASHES	$1.50
☐ 10891	THE ENCHANTED BARN	$1.50
☐ 10947	THE FINDING OF JASPER HOLT	$1.50
☐ 2916	AMORELLE	$1.50
☐ 2985	THE STREET OF THE CITY	$1.50
☐ 10766	THE BELOVED STRANGER	$1.50
☐ 10792	WHERE TWO WAYS MET	$1.50
☐ 10826	THE BEST MAN	$1.50
☐ 10909	DAPHNE DEANE	$1.50
☐ 11005	STRANGER WITHIN THE GATES	$1.50
☐ 11020	SPICE BOX	$1.50
☐ 11028	A NEW NAME	$1.50
☐ 11329	DAWN OF THE MORNING	$1.50
☐ 11167	THE RED SIGNAL	$1.50

Buy them at your local bookstore or use this handy coupon for ordering: